A BIRD STUCK ON THE SKY

GW00801675

A Psychological Tale

Gerald Alan Fox

A BIRD STUCK ON THE SKY

Gerald Alan Fox has asserted his rights under the Copyright, Designs and Patents Act 1988 to be identified as the author of this work.

ISBN-13: 9781 499375695
BISAC: Fiction / Psychological

First published in Great Britain in 2014 by Gerald Alan Fox.

This edition published by CreateSpace in 2015.

Copyright © Gerald Alan Fox 2014

A CIP catalogue record for this book is available from the British Library.

Grateful acknowledgement is made for kind permission to use lines from songs;

Where or when by RICHARD RODGERS & LORENZ HART
Published by Lyrics © Warner/Chappell Music, Inc., IMAGEM U.S. LLC

I wish you love by CHARLES TRENET &, ALBERT BEACH.
Published by Lyrics © Universal Music Publishing Group, EMI Music Publishing

Send in the clowns by STEPHEN SONDHEIM.
Published by Lyrics © Warner/Chappell Music, Inc.

For Hilary, Jax, David, Anna and Lauren.

A NOTE FROM THE AUTHOR

As a practising psychotherapist for over 30 years, my desire to write about my patients conflicted with the need to protect their privacy – a dilemma. Factual reports even with disguised identities carried some risk of exposure, so why not go the whole hog and fictionalise all the material?

I have done precisely that by incorporating disguised items from case histories with life in general to produce *A Bird Stuck on the Sky*.

The core elements of actual cases, woven into this narrative, do not lose their intrinsic impact. All the characters are fictional including Mike, a cognitive behavioural therapist – the central figure – although many scenarios that confront him are drawn from my own experiences. He and his wife are burdened with psychological problems and obsessive personalities – again based on real cases I've seen in psychotherapy. Testing situations, augmented by Mike's patients' trials, set him on a journey of self-discovery. To those patients – not fictional to me – I owe my eternal gratitude for teaching me so much over the years.

This book can be read simply as a novel or as a related collection of short stories. More covert themes will intrigue practitioner, student or patient – or anyone interested in psychology.

Set in three parts, the narrative can be treated as a challenge to examine, identify and connect areas into place before the last pieces are revealed and complete the picture.

The Author

He first embarked on a career in pharmacy on a P&O liner, followed by running a small group of pharmacies. That with the rare combination of a psychology degree engaged him in work with pharmaceutical manufacturers in the UK and Europe on psychotropic medicine and registration files. Concerned by the illegal drug scene, and the cavalier but legal use of tranquillisers and anti-depressants and sleeping tablets, he helped set up a drug helpline, a benzodiazepine dependency group, and gave a series of talks, on prescribing those drugs, to doctors in general practice (GPs) and psychiatric units, and practised psychotherapy.

Acknowledgements

I am greatly indebted to everyone who encouraged and helped me over the past few years in the writing of this book. With too many to name I make particular mention of Sally Page and Sylvia Berkovitz for their critical input and advice for the first draft, Professor Gary Kupshik for bringing me up to speed on behavioural therapies, Dr Dennis Friedman (in memoriam) and Rosemary Friedman for their enthusiasm for this project with guidance into their literary world, Neil Macarthur for his technical help, David Willis for the final edit, Jeremy Tatham for proof-reading – and of course my patients.

G.A.F.

A BIRD STUCK ON THE SKY

This story is set as a three-part jigsaw puzzle.

PART

ONE

Opening the box......

A BIRD STUCK ON THE SKY

CHAPTER ONE

The promise given was a necessity of the past: the word broken is a necessity of the present. MACHIAVELLI

He looked down. Unlike some people terrified by heights – unlike most people, naturally cautious and partially scared – he was unfazed by the sheer drop from his roost over the five-story building. Standing upright he lowered his head to gaze straight down the vertical red brickwork to the stone paved forecourt. At ease, rock-solid, not wavering an inch, he suffered no wooziness in his head or tension in his stomach. He was one of a tiny percentage of people. It was in his genes. The images below were compressed into upturned faces set on shoes. Fearless, in control, he was oblivious to the terror that gripped the crowd below. Their concerned calls amused him.

'Please go in,' a frantic woman begged.

'Get down – you could fall,' the man with one arm shouted up to him.

He held so much power. People were literally looking up to him. He ignored their pleas and gazed beyond them taking in the panorama of the city. He wished he had been born half a century earlier in America. He could have been in that photo, on his bedroom wall, alongside those construction workers sitting, eating sandwiches, at the end of a girder protruding high over New York.

His eyes were drawn to the trees that lined the driveway. They had shrunken into bushes. A bird flew to the top of one of them. It perched momentarily then took off again rising high into the sky above him. His spirit joined it as he watched it soar and glide away. A strange euphoria overcame him. The intoxicating chemistry of pleasurable endorphins produced a strong urge to fly – to be free to go anywhere – become a bird. He stretched his arms out and closed his eyes, imagining how it must feel.

'Stop being so stupid,' the caretaker's wife called.

'It's dangerous. Get down. Go inside,' another neighbour pleaded.

The drama was exhilarating. He was centre stage.

'Is it possible,' he pondered, 'I could fly?'

For a moment he believed it feasible.

'Do it! Jump, you fucking coward!'

The shout came from a yob. He stood apart from the crowd; apart from society, the type who'd steal any respite from his impoverished existence, however brief. He enjoyed this sort of situation as entertainment – whatever the cost to others – even death.

Two women broke from the crowd and set upon him. The yob hopped away backwards with a ghoulish laugh. Behind him a black carrion crow marked his retreat with a squawk and a single flap of its wings.

On the ledge above, Michael's ears absorbed the isolated command to jump. He thought he'd proved himself sufficiently brave. Did they need to see more heroics? Had the call been 'Go on – you can do it!' – an encouragement – it might have spurred his avian notion into action. But the yob had sworn at him. He heard swearing every day in Stoke Newington, but this was different. This venom was directed at him. Aggressive, critical and filled with bile, the injunction punctured his fantasy. All the desperate pleas from others concerned for his welfare had gone unheeded. This one, miserable, obnoxious outcast had brought him out of his stupor and possibly saved his life – with a single expletive.

He contemplated his next move, but continued to tantalise the crowd below by swaying to and fro, arms stretched out in front of him. Although his dream of supernatural powers had vanished he remained in a shrunken world of his own. Focussed on his central role, he failed to notice the approaching *triangular* figure – her shopping at its heaviest.

Head down, she turned into the entrance to the council estate. Then, alerted by the shouts of the throng before her, she lifted her eyes to the roof, dropped her bags of groceries and all but collapsed. She drew one deep breath and hurled it skywards.

'Michael,' she screamed. 'Get inside at once!'

The small figure of the eight-year-old boy carefully retreated from the ledge, terrified for the first time that morning.

'How long has he been up there?' his mother asked of a neighbour.

'About a quarter of an hour – mucking about on the ledge.'

'You need to keep an eye on that boy, Mrs. Daniels,' the caretaker's wife said.

'It was worse five minutes ago,' the one-armed man added.

'Worse? What do you mean worse?' the mother asked.

'It was scarier. He was as motionless as a statue with his toes over the ledge.'

'His arms were outstretched – as if he was going to jump,' another voice said.

'Jump! Wait 'til I get inside.'

'He needs a good belting, that one,' a stranger told the others, just in earshot of Mrs. Daniels as she left.

She rushed into the building, vibrating head to toe: furious – so it appeared to the spectators. Michael had no idea how badly he had shaken her. She seemed angrier than he had ever seen anyone – yet it wasn't rage. Her eyes were brimming.

'You could have killed yourself – one slip – one gust of wind.'

Gasping for air, she grabbed his shirt.

'They would have scraped you off the pavement,' she shouted nose to nose.

'Didn't you think of that?' she yelled through an asthmatic wheeze.

He sobbed deeply, cringing and covering his ears with his hands. He could not utter a word.

'What do you think you were doing?'

She paused to regain her breath.

'How did you get out on the roof?'

Michael gave a shudder but no reply.

'I demand an answer,' she screamed.

But, paralysed by fear seeing his mother so uncharacteristically out of control, he ran to his bedroom, slamming the door.

'You wait,' she continued, breathless, helpless, ''til your father gets in.'

Her staccato went on between demands for air.

'You stay in your room!' 'No lunch for you today.'

Eventually, her screaming evaporated.

The quiet hours that followed were disturbed by intermittent, low sounds that escaped Michael's suppressed crying, further muffled by the steamy, salty warmth of his pillow. He listened to his mother return to her usual task of preparing the chopped liver and chicken soup for their traditional, if not religious, Friday evening meal.

Michael awoke from a fitful doze to hear his father at the front door. His arrival set the storm raging once more. His deep, calm, authoritative voice quelled the onslaught.

'I'll talk to him while you get dinner.'

'Drink your tea first.'

She sounded her normal self again. He heard his father's footsteps along the passage and then a gentle tapping at the door.

'Michael,' he murmured twice, to no reply. He opened the door. His eyes rested upon the still feebly convulsive figure lying face down. He sat himself on the edge of the bed and gently placed his broad hand on the damp-shirted little shoulder.

'Can we talk?' he asked, in a kindly tone.

Michael lifted himself then put both arms around his father's neck, bursting into another torrent of tears. They held each other wordlessly for some minutes. Encouraged by his father's comforting embrace, Michael began to talk.

'Mum was *so* angry,' he sobbed.

'Yes, of course your Mum was angry,' responded his father. 'You frightened her.'

'I'm sorry,' triggered another flood.

'Why were you out on that roof?'

'It was because of Ginger.'

'Ginger dared you to do it?'

'No. It was because of him.'

'What do you mean? How because?'

'It's what happened to him yesterday.'

'Tell me, what happened.'

'Well, he had to run an errand for his Mum but the Everest House gang captured him.'

'Captured him? Why? How did they *capture* him?'

Michael started crying again.

'What exactly did they do?'

'It was horrible. I heard him calling out. They'd tied him upside-down to a tree trunk.'

'Did they injure him?'

'No. It was worse than that. His face and hair was all covered in green and yellow yucky slime,' Michael said, re-living the cosmetic insult to the curly red hair and pale freckled skin of his friend.

'Slime? What slime?' his father asked.

'They forced him to eat caterpillars and squashed them in his mouth.'

'The filthy sods.'

His father blinked and shook his head in disgust – but equally to excuse his language.

'But what's all this roof business got to do with Ginger?' he asked.

'We wanted to join the gang in our flats because one of them said they could protect us. First the leader said we were too young to join, but then they said they would let us if we could prove we were brave enough.'

'So you had to stand on the roof?'

'No,' Michael paused, 'I had to walk on the roof wall – all the way around.'

The gang had taken them up to the vast airing room where everyone dried their washing. It was the attic of the flats, ventilated by mock Georgian sash windows. Easy to get out to, the surrounding guttering and the low wall made a safe balcony for fine views over London. Kids regularly used it. The wall was topped with a flat, eighteen-inch wide coping that went around the entire building.

Initially as anxious as any parent, his father had proudly watched Michael clamber up park climbing-frames, graduating to small, then tall trees, as he witnessed his passage from toddler to boyhood. He could not help but feel admiration for his son's feat today: of course, he couldn't show it.

'It was stupid and dangerous. You could have slipped and killed yourself.'

'Sorry. I was worried about Ginger.' He paused then offered another 'Sorry.'

'And what about pretending to jump?'

'That was *really* stupid. I wondered if I could fly.'

His father detected the sheepish, fleeting smile Michael tried to hide under his mop of dark hair. The senior, despite himself, relaxed his tense expression. Michael raised his head. Their eyes met. They burst out laughing. His father's solemn countenance quickly returned.

'This is serious,' he said, but involuntarily joined Michael in another spasm of giggles. 'Promise me never to do anything like that again?'

'Promise,' Michael said.

'Right. Go straight inside and apologise to Mum.'

Noon, next day, Michael brought home a large bunch of wild flowers he had taken all morning picking for her. She melted, unable to resist his charms, and hugged him: his longed-for redemption.

'Promise me you'll never go on that roof again.'

He promised.

In the Daniels family, promises were kept.

A BIRD STUCK ON THE SKY

PART

TWO

Assorted stories in the main narrative serve as jigsaw pieces that will test the reader's observational skills. Clues and a covert repetitive motif hint at connections and thread together a diverse pastiche.

A BIRD STUCK ON THE SKY

CHAPTER TWO

Hue and Cry. In medieval times the law required all citizens to give chase to a fleeing criminal on hearing screams to do so.

Mike had just arrived at the hospital when the phone rang. Kate, a local GP, outlined an urgent problem regarding one of her patients.

Mike checked with his colleagues what extra hours were free for him at the surgery then called Kate back. She briefly went over her dilemma with a distraught wife and an inconsolable husband who had uncharacteristically attacked her. He had, however, a sprinkled history of bizarre behaviour. Psychiatrists at two London hospitals had seen him and prescribed medication – unsuccessfully.

'I can see them both privately, tomorrow evening,' Mike said.

'Thanks Mike, I'm most grateful. I'll send you over the notes.' Kate said.

'How bad is it?'

'Pretty bad; any more violence and I'll be obliged to inform the authorities.'

*   *   *

Phyllis, fortunately, was on duty for one of Mike's partner's assessment afternoons. 'Yes, of course,' she answered on the phone, agreeing to stay and hold the fort in case he was held up at the hospital.

Mike arrived early, well ahead of the appointment. Typically Phyllis immediately put the kettle on and made a most welcome cup of Darjeeling. She insisted on awaiting the arrival of his patient. What a gem she was!

It was the first chance Mike had to peruse Kate's papers. Sure enough two psychiatrists had seen her patient. Both labelled him with a personality disorder – a condition often deemed untreatable. They had hit a brick wall. So had Kate. If matters got any worse the police would be involved. That was the last thing this man needed.

Kate's patient was in deep trouble.

Liam shuffled into the room, head drooping and filled with shame. His red-eyed wife accompanied him, tearful, fearful and angry. They had been married for some ten years. Mike gently probed and quietly listened. Liam believed it *had been* a happy marriage but agreed lately he felt insecure and under stress. His wife concurred, declaring she loved him and that generally he *had been* a good husband.

Mike broached the nitty-gritty of their recent arguments. Immediately Liam's wife cut loose and between sobs screamed she could no longer tolerate his weird outbursts. His recent physical violence set the seal. She was terrified of him and demanded a separation.

'I bought myself a new dress. When I put it on for a party he ripped it off me.'

'Why?' Mike asked Liam.

He refused to give any explanation for his behaviour. Pressed – he lost his temper. It was weird. No wonder his wife was distraught.

Liam's previous episodes of *madness*, as his wife called them, were directed away from her but caused her great anxiety. They had occurred during the marriage in a random manner with no pattern of time or place. Nor were they a response to any crisis in their relationship. On one occasion, in an uncontrollable tantrum he stormed out of their holiday hotel shortly after arrival. Another time he refused to enter a theatre for a show they had booked for ages and were eager to see. Mike was as baffled as everyone else who had been involved in the case.

Apart from this outline history, Mike had gleaned some non-verbal clues from Liam. His mixed demeanour – fearful and anxious below the surface – turned to anger and aggression when pressed. Before Mike could attempt to address his current predicament he needed a brief account of Liam's life starting with his childhood recollections. He arranged to see Liam alone the following Monday.

Liam's mother died when he was three years old. His Irish family was poor with most relatives living in England. He had a brother eight years his senior. His father was unable to cope with work and the boys. The family decided that his brother would stay in Ireland with an aunt. Liam was sent to England to another aunt who brought him up as her own. His subsequent upbringing was in a stable family and poverty-free. Nonetheless, he recalled feeling lonely and sometimes edgy for no good reason. Free-floating anxiety in those circumstances was no surprise. He developed quietly, doing reasonably well at school, leaving at sixteen to become a carpenter.

Today, his manner was shy and friendly. Mike saw few signs of the aggression and madness seen and reported the previous week. Having established that Liam's marriage was, to quote him, 'the best thing' in his life, Mike moved to recent events. Liam had no control over his outbursts. They terrified him. He was full of remorse for the torment he had caused his wife – messing up things they should have enjoyed together.
'Do you ever accompany your wife shopping?'
'Not if I can help it.'
Mike had that much in common and genuinely empathised
'So you had no say in buying the dress? Is it money? Was the dress expensive?' Mike asked. More empathy.
'I've no idea how much it cost.'
'Why were you angry she bought it?'

'I weren't angry.'

'She and others said you were and scared them. Didn't you like the dress on her?'

'No! It was 'orrible.'

And Liam had told her so. She got upset and a big row ensued. Mike suggested if he disliked the dress he might have been a tad more diplomatic. He said he couldn't help it. He panicked.

'It was 'orrible,' he repeated.

'What was horrible? How did it not suit her? Was it a poor fit? Perhaps too sexy?'

'No. No. No. It wasn't to do with her,' Liam replied – aggressively.

'It was just the dress? So why did you attack her?'

Whatever the reason, any mention of the dress put Liam in a blind panic.

'She had to take it off – she wouldn't – that's how it got ripped.'

Mike asked him once more to describe the dress. The same word – 'orrible – ended the session.

The next appointment, aside from the extraordinary incident with the dress, Mike brought up the theatre and the holiday hotel episodes. None of them had a logical cause. Both were dominated by Liam's irrational anger and outrageous demands. Even more odd: all events should have been a source of happiness. Apart from the theatre trip and the holiday, long anticipated with pleasure, the wife's new dress should have elicited some positive behaviour, if only a modicum of tact. All these occasions were ruined by Liam's wild and unfathomable responses.

Liam insisted that he wasn't initially angry, but anxious, fearful, and frustrated. People saw him *their* way. *That* made him angry and out of control. On all three occasions, the dominant feature was his response to other people's attitudes. *What are the triggers? Could they be common or related?*

'Why did you change your mind about the hotel and the theatre?'

'I didn't. I got in a state at both and *had* to leave,' Liam said through gritted teeth and a contorted expression. He recounted the sheer terror that pervaded the incidents. It stalked his features; his eyes, his quivering mouth.

'I felt physically sick with fear,' Liam said.

He tried to explain the inexplicable. His wife's and others' attempts to placate him had made him even worse.

'What frightens you – why does their help upset you?'

'They make me angry. No-one gets it – how bad I feel.'

'Try and describe it. You must have some idea what's behind your reaction.'

'I can't. It's confusing.'

Liam was unable to describe his feelings. His most recent outburst caused shame and bewilderment. *What terrifies him?* Mike had him control his breathing. He became calmer.

'Sit quietly and try to think what was so horrible about that dress.'

'I were frightened. I couldn't bear to see 'er in it. It were a threat – dangerous.'

'The dress – dangerous?' Mike asked, genuinely surprised.

'Yeah – I felt I were going to throw up. I were paralysed.'

'Why? What specifically upset you?'

'I remember the fear. Trying to think what caused it makes me panic.'

Liam was irrational. He needed to re-live his experiences objectively to make any progress. Mike paused for him to calm down again.

'Can you remember any feature of the dress that especially terrified you?'

Many silent minutes passed as Mike patiently observed him search for an answer.

'It were the colour,' he whispered.

'The colour frightened you? What colour?' Mike asked.

'It were 'orrible, dark 'orrible purple.'

Now named, he acknowledged he hated purple. It frightened him. He quickly realised since childhood he'd had an abstract aversion to the colour. Mike had at last made some headway this session. Initially he put Liam's response down to an uncomplicated phobia, but this covert reaction to the colour perplexed him – phobias were usually out in the open.

Mike changed tack. He directed his attention to the other two episodes. Intrigued by the first breakthrough, he searched for the triggers behind Liam's unusual behaviour on those occasions.

The hotel incident occurred a year or two ago. Liam and his wife were on a week's holiday. On arrival they checked in and were shown to their room. Immediately they entered it, Liam shouted at the porter they must have a different one. They had no others to offer. He insisted they had to leave and go to another hotel. It seemed crazy. His wife implored him to be reasonable and stay the one night, then decide in the morning. He lost his temper, grabbed the cases, threw them in the car and drove off.

'Why? What was wrong with the hotel?' Mike asked.

'I were frightened.'

Liam found it impossible to say why. He described how he was nervous in the lobby. He remembered feeling intimidated signing in.

'You felt insecure?'

'Yes. It was posh. The porter was friendly he made me feel more comfortable.'

'So you were fine until you got to the room?'

'Yes. I couldn't go in. It were 'orrible.'

'What was horrible?'

A long silence dominated the surgery. Liam became agitated and sweaty and started to hyperventilate. Mike got him to breathe deeply and relax. The panic passed replaced by silent minutes of reasoning.

Liam eventually whispered, almost with relief, 'It were that colour again.'

'The same colour – deep dark purple?'
'Yes – the curtains and bedspread.'
'Did you ever connect that with your panics?'
'No.'

Two of the episodes indicated a strong aversion to the colour. A coincidence? Liam's behaviour was odd. Phobic sufferers actively direct anxiety to targeted fears – spiders, open spaces, or heights, etc – and are fully aware of them. Generally, phobias – overt, with well-defined reactions – are readily cured. Liam's aversion was suppressed. Mike had had to draw it out of him. He was unaware until pushed that his responses were in any way connected to purple.

Liam readily solved his tantrum in the theatre. He had monitored the tickets on the mantelpiece for months with keen anticipation. The day came.
'I froze in front of the curtains in the foyer. They terrified me. I tried but was unable to pass through them to the seats. They were purple.'

Liam's perception of purple, common to these events, had to be the catalyst for all three. He accepted his demon and at last actively named purple when recalling his past. Mike decided the original fear of the colour, unnamed, must be associated with a suppressed trauma. It was highly probable that Liam had suffered one in early childhood. Limited language and undeveloped memory processes would have left him incapable of dealing with a severe trauma adequately. Without proper naming and labelling it would have been well nigh impossible to even think about events, let alone rationalise them. Unresolved, disturbing memories would remain as destructive abstractions. Mike ended the session confident he could help Liam.
'During the coming week make a note of any more purple incidents and bring them to the next appointment.'
'I can see plenty – it even put me off eating beetroot.'

'Examine your childhood. See if you can identify more important connections to purple.'

Liam spent the week going over past events and noted other examples of his aversion. Even in childhood, he avoided the colour and reacted to its presence. He pored over many unresolved incidents and clarified his memories, using appropriate words for the first time. Purple was now tangible, a labelled entity, a well-defined colour – no longer an abstract stain on hidden emotions. He judged its past effects and reassessed his reactions as an informed adult. This new objectivity explained several minor foibles. One secret, however, remained withheld.

Liam had to discover the prime mover – the root of his problems. It had to be associated with purple – and dealt with. Mike's own youngsters misinterpreted what they saw and heard. Amy, as a naive toddler was convinced that a power plant with cooling towers was *a cloud factory*. Ben saw his first hovering kestrel as *a bird stuck on the sky*.

A child's unbridled imagination, left rampant to cope with a severe trauma, can leave profound lasting effects. Had that happened with Liam? Delving into his early childhood he cleared up a few mishaps – relatively minor ones. A major one was suppressed. Liam's brother could possibly unearth a vital clue. Despite not having seen each other on more than a handful of occasions since being separated, Mike suggested Liam make contact.

'His memory may be clearer than yours. It could be significant,' Mike said.

Secretly, Mike pinned his hopes on the older brother holding the key. He could possibly recollect some strange behaviour or incident when Liam was a toddler. It was a risk but Liam could make great strides if he found out first-hand for himself. Liam agreed to contact his brother.

Liam was out of contact for a fortnight. In those two weeks he found the solution to the once intractable. His brother was pleased to get his call. On hearing of Liam's difficulties he paid for a budget flight to Ireland, insisting he stay with him for a few days' break. He, too, was keen to catch up with the past.

He remembered Liam as the baby of the family and very much his mother's favourite. He spoke with a hint of jealousy. He had also suffered from the break-up of the family unit. The discourse progressed. The older sibling – back in the role of Liam's protector – told how he had been held responsible and taken the blame for some of his exploits. Apparently Liam was a lively, mischievous boy until his mother died. After that he became subdued. Liam asked about his mother's death.

At the house, prior to the funeral, her open coffin and room were covered in deep purple shrouding. Liam wept uncontrollably for several hours as he released himself from his terrible trauma. Naming the colour helped him rationalise his mother's death. The abstraction withered. His fear subsided.

CHAPTER THREE

I come from heights that no bird ever reached in its flight. I know abysses into which no foot ever strayed. NIETZSCHE.

He looked down. No longer impervious to heights as an eight-year-old, the now familiar mild vertigo niggled him again. Mike treated that as no more than a minor irritation. In his youth he'd had little trouble climbing trees with branches to hold or standing on high balconies. He was still basically OK with heights, reasonably happy in any vertical situation so long as it had a physical barrier – a window or a secure railing. But if exposed to an open fall and the possibility of impulsive flight he became giddy and nauseous. He had nightmares – clinging to the top of a vertical cliff, or stuck on a high ledge by a fallen ladder or a snapped rope, or falling from a height.

Since he had qualified as a psychologist and married, the vertigo had become more troublesome – particularly so since starting a family. He suppressed the motor behind what he deemed a petty annoyance. His feeble attempts to self-cure during his studies failed. With repetitive exposure, Mike assumed he would gradually accommodate to open heights. His self-diagnosis of a straightforward phobia went unquestioned. He was certain his self-administered treatment would succeed. But his reactions were getting worse with exposure – leaving him confused. As with most phobias his responses were as irrational as Liam's. So was his self-help.

He actively stored this trivial concern away from Helen even after they had settled down together. He kept it from everyone else without difficulty.

Since a boy, he sought challenges to prove himself physically and mentally. Confronted head-on they denied frailties. Outwardly he appeared assured. Inwardly he toiled, masking or trying to resolve *any* personal problem. No introvert – he was friendly and approachable – more, still waters.

Mike and Helen were on a week's holiday in the Lake District with their young children, Ben, Claire and Amy. In past visits here, before the children arrived, Mike had tested himself, over and over, scaling the fells with Helen. True, he did panic occasionally on the highest peaks – even at Castle Crag, a small but steep climb. He used the sterner challenges as therapy to accommodate to anxiety. He learned to cover fear. 'Wow! What a view,' distracted Helen's eyes from him on Striding Edge. 'Phew, I'm out of breath,' disguised another trial. He was hardly unfit, but it passed by Helen. He had no qualms over today's benign challenges with the kids in tow.

The family had enjoyed a pleasant morning walking up through woods, dense with deciduous trees and filled with birdsong, to reach the foot of Castle Head. They were soon on top of the small plateau overlooking Keswick town and Derwent Water. It was the children's first ascent. Below them a dinghy's white sail threaded through the treetops. Mirrored in the magnificent lake ahead, peppered with miniature boats, were the distant fells, with ant-sized walkers trudging towards the peaks. The children rested admiring the views – a well-earned reward for their effort. They were also happy they had pleased their father who, Helen told them, 'loved heights,' and so perpetuated the myth.

Helen glanced at Mike. He stood transfixed, gazing at the lake.

'Come on you three. Let's have a wander around and leave Daddy in peace to enjoy the view,' Helen said.

She had no clue that the reason Mike stayed so long at summits, far from enjoyment, was purely endurance: so many vain efforts to come to grips with unprotected heights.

Left alone, he stayed stationary a while longer. *Do it.* He slowly moved closer to the rim. *Force yourself.* Gradually the dreaded drawstring started to pull at his stomach – began to tie that unpleasant knot. *It's still as bad.* Relentlessly it drained the strength from his legs and the blood from his head, and mercilessly sucked the breath from his lungs. *This should be helping. Where's the improvement?* He struggled to stick with it. *It works for patients. Heal thyself.*

It was, once again, a losing battle and these exposures were making matters worse rather than better. Giddy with the risk of toppling over the edge he sat down on the ground a couple of paces away. Cowardice joined his sense of failure. What a wimp, they accused. *I ought to tell Helen.* He then retreated. *It might bother her.*

He remained sitting by the edge of Castle Head. Self-doubts gnawed at him. *I'm a pathetic conman. I can't resolve my minor problem: why should I be trusted with patients' major ones?* He reflected on his colleagues. *They'd be sympathetic – but let them treat me for something so trivial? They'd joke about it. I'd lose credibility.* He made no further attempt to cure himself.

His disappointment drifted away as he followed the leisurely progress of a ferry to the far side of the lake. He sought a positive side to his affliction. *It helps me empathise with distressed people. Don't I atone for deception with commitment?* Momentarily that lifted the gloom – he dismissed it as a rationalisation. Helen returned with the children and halted his self-criticism. 'Time for lunch,' she called up to him.

Helen was instinctual. Mike and his colleagues were different, introspective and analytical. Her carefree spirit kept his profounder approach to life in check. Their balanced partnership was sealed with mutual interests in the arts and sports. Helen, shorter at five foot six, and slimmer, was every bit as athletic as Mike. They were competitive at tennis and golf; keen on swimming, and enjoyed jogging and long country walks – a solid couple.

As any couple, though, they had their tiffs. Mike dressed casually – unconcerned over appearances or what impression he made. That was one source of friction between them.

'You wore that shirt yesterday,' Helen said.

'It's hardly dirty. Saves washing,' he said and retrieved it from the basket. He often wore the same shirt for two days.

Helen found that intolerable. Her attire was always pristine. She ignored fashion but complemented smart M&S basics with her own seal of a boutique accessory. She used makeup sparingly and kept her copper hair shoulder length, with minimal attention from hairdressers.

Neither was extravagant and they lived well within their means. They appreciated the free things in life, aware that some money helps. Helen's reduced income had scant effect on their lifestyle. She was as busy as ever with the children and her now part-time employment as a pharmacist. Originally she and Mike would play hard at the weekends and take strenuously active breaks. Nowadays they were more moderate.

Unease over heights apart he remained honest and open with Helen. He hadn't given Helen the slightest inkling of his frustration a few moments ago. He was relaxed and chatty on the stroll down towards Keswick, with the children in high spirits.

They stopped at a small café for a bite. Peckish, they had no option: it was that or a longer walk into town. The children chose soup of the day and a roll. Mike and Helen had the day's special, a rather mean portion of *chilli con carne* and rice.

31

'Can we do another climb?' Ben asked.

'Yeaah,' Claire said, enthusiastically.

'Yes,' Helen corrected her.

Mike accepted that and Amy's silence as unanimous. But knew he would have to carry her part of the way.

'Let's see...' he began.

'How about,' Helen interrupted and whispered in his ear, 'Surprise View?'

'Just the job,' Mike said.

'Are we all ready to go again?' Helen asked the children.

'Yeaah – sss,' said Claire, cheekily.

Ben silently puffed out his chest and pumped his boy biceps. The children were ready to undertake what they were warned would be a good two-hour haul. Mike went to the counter and added a bottle of water to the bill and – just in case – a cheese and tomato sandwich sealed in a convenient plastic pack.

They hiked up towards the gently forested Ashness Bridge trek. 'The Surprise' had been promised to the children as an inducement. As well it had. It was a test for their young legs, but they found it magical under the backlit canopy of trees and the flickering dappled shade. Mike and Helen were more sensitive to other aspects: the delicate scent of the cool green air; the less fragrant but evocative rust and decay in the soil under their feet; the sounds of overhead warblers, and a distant cuckoo.

The unfettered pleasure of the first hour passed. Amy began to wilt. The pace slackened. Helen and Mike were also tiring. The last mile became arduous, especially for Mike with his extra load.

'Let's take a little rest,' Helen said. She knew the precise moment to press buttons.

The children stopped immediately.

'Anyone thirsty, hungry?' Mike asked. He too was thankful for a break.

'I need a drink,' Claire said.

Mike handed her the water.

'I'm starving,' Ben said, eyeing the sandwich.

'Anyone else?' Mike asked, opening the pack.

'You three share it,' Helen said.

'No. I'm good,' said Claire.

'Half each then,' Mike said and doled out Ben's share.

He placed the empty package in his pocket where it bothered his fingers for the remainder of the climb.

Surprise View was a good choice. Even the most hardy Wainwrighters are enthralled by the view of Derwent Water and Catbells that arises from nowhere in a natural panoramic window framed by tall trees at the top of the walk. It was one of their favourite haunts. 'It gets better every time,' Helen said, as thrilled as the children with their first glimpse. 'It certainly does,' Mike said with one arm around her waist and one hand on Claire's shoulder. They remained immobile until Mike drew away and walked over to a waste bin he had seen by the adjacent car park. At last, he could get rid of the irritating empty plastic *triangle*. As he did so he heard Helen's piercing scream and turned in horror.

Excited, Ben was running towards the perilous edge of the sheer cliff that formed the base of the picture frame. Mike witnessed it all in slow motion. His head throbbed. He stopped breathing. From this set back position Ben appeared to be at the very rim. Uncontrollable panic grabbed Mike's throat and wrenched his stomach. His eyes bulged as he crouched, paralysed and voiceless, seared with terror. He watched helplessly. Ben and the precipice. A frozen inferno.

Helen's shriek abruptly stopped Ben many yards from any danger. It was barely a second or so later that she put her arms around Ben and hugged him with relief. She had run to him, her back to Mike. Mike stared at them.

'Mummy, why did you scream at me?' Ben protested.

'Didn't you see the drop?' Helen shouted.

'Of course I did. I wanted to get a closer look at the view.'

'But you were running. Why? Before we left I told *all of you* – it's *dangerous* on mountains,' she yelled, her voice now crackly. Amy whimpered. Ben was shocked.

'Why are you screaming at us?' Claire asked angrily. 'I haven't done anything and Ben was perfectly safe.'

The children peeked at each other, chastened and puzzled by her overreaction. All three of them remained standing in silence – until that noise.

It sounded like an animal at first. They turned towards Mike and saw him violently vomit again. Helen went over to him.

'It must have been the chilli,' Mike lied.

'You look ashen,' Helen said, recovering her regular poise.

'I'll be all right. Are you?'

'I'm fine, but I haven't brought any loperamide or anything,' Helen replied.

'Hmm. Cobblers.'

'Pardon me!'

'You know – cobblers and shoes,' Mike said, innocently.

'Oh that. Sorry. I'll get you something in town.'

'No – nothing needed – it's a tummy upset, that's all.'

That certainly was not all.

*   *   *

At the hotel that evening Helen was surprising how ravenously Mike ate. Unsurprisingly, the children had good appetites but the girls, particularly, were tired from the day's exertions.

'I want to go to bed,' Amy said, sleepily.

'Well, that's a first,' Mike said.

'Me too – is that a second?' Claire asked, aggressively. Upset at

Surprise View she had been stomping around and fractious since then. She was glad to leave and get to the bedroom.

'Well, I'm staying up,' Ben said.

'We could all do with an early night,' Mike said.

'You promised me a game of chess.' Ben said.

'Did I?'

Ben dropped his head to one side and raised an eyebrow in reply.

'Yes I did,' Mike said resignedly. 'It will have to be a quick one.'

'Mike, I'm exhausted. Try to come up soon,' Helen said.

She kissed Ben goodnight and ushered the girls up to their room.

Mike found it an effort to set out the pieces, let alone play. Although physically tired his mind was on other matters rather than fatigue.

'Dad, you let me win,' Ben protested.

'No I didn't,' Mike lied, uncomfortably. *Well at least I kept my word to play.*

'Can we play again tomorrow?'

'See how we feel,' Mike said. *No promises.*

They made their way upstairs and said goodnight.

Helen was in bed reading, waiting for Mike. After a quick goodnight kiss she doused the reading light and turned over. Mike lay with eyes open. Overtired, he was unable to get to sleep. This afternoon had brought matters to a head. He must stop his deception. *I'm a bloody coward.* He had to discuss it with Helen. *I'm going to broach the subject gently with her – now.*

'It was Lionel, wasn't it?' he asked.

'Where........ what? I'd just nodded off! What did you say?'

'Your scream – it was for Lionel, wasn't it?'

'What *are* you on about?'

'This afternoon – your screaming – upsetting the kids.'

Helen switched the light on and sat bolt upright. Mike felt her anger reverberate through the mattress.

'What's the matter with you? Of course I screamed. Ben was running towards the edge. What on earth has Lionel got to do with it?'

'Were you thinking of him when….'

'Off analysing me again – you can't stop can you? How many times do I have to tell you – save it for your patients.'

'Helen, I'm trying to help you.'

'I don't need help,' Helen replied through her teeth, stifling her temper.

'We all need help sometimes – even me.'

'For goodness sake, I don't wish to talk about it anymore Mike. I'm going to sleep.'

So much for Mike's gentle approach. And it was always Lionel who came between them. Funny really, because he was the one who had indirectly brought them together.

Mike first saw Helen coming out of the Head of Department's office at the hospital. It was the same office he had emerged from after his job interview some six months earlier. Her copper hair caught his eye. It danced and swayed to the bounce in her confident step. Her modest attire suggested a caring professional. Her manner hinted at a sociable and easy-going nature. Mike was immediately drawn to her. *Maybe she'll be working with me.* She came closer. *She's nice. Attractive eyes.* She was about to pass by his life. Their eyes met and locked. Mike smiled. *Her call.* Helen returned the smile.

'How did it go?' he asked.

Her pace slackened.

'Alright,' she replied, puzzled, as they strolled in step.

'Did you get it?'

'Get what?'

'The job.'

'What job? I wasn't here for an interview.'

Mike's heart sank. But her soft voice drew him in further.

'It was a private matter. He's a friend of my father,' Helen said sweetly.

They paused at the main walkway and talked – small talk – casually like old friends. A weird sense of *déjà vu* overcame Mike.

'Have we met somewhere before?' he asked.

'I might have remembered you if we had,' Helen replied with a smile – even that smile seemed familiar to him.

Mike's reluctance to reach the exit slowed their way down the corridor. He had to keep her from leaving. The hospital's café came into sight.

'Cup of tea before you go?'

'If you like.'

'I like.'

After the second cup Helen agreed to dinner the following night. And the following day, lunch. The veneers peeled off within days as they exchanged personal and childhood memories.

Mike found Helen comfortable to be with, easy to talk to – a genuine companion. With others he cautiously guarded his privacy – with her he was almost spontaneous. It was such a relief to feel so free – pure pleasure. In spite of opening up to her, his innermost secrets stayed within bounds.

'Did you ever do anything terribly naughty as a boy?'

'Armed robbery – would that count?' he asked.

'Go on then, tell me about it,' Helen replied, her chin jutting forward from shrugged shoulders – a quirky mannerism to some, but to Mike irresistibly magnetic. He paused and grinned, encouraging their rapidly growing bond. Helen smiled sharing its tangible warmth.

'I had a cowboy hat for my ninth birthday but no gun – my mother was against kids toting guns – but I fancied one. Woolworth's had some on open display. Next day I put on my hat and got on my horse.'

'Your horse?' Again that jutting chin pulled at Mike.

'Imaginary. I entered the store in a rocking canter, slapping my thigh, and grabbed a gun. I held it aloft and circled the shop and left unchallenged.'

'You crafty devil.'

'Under the glare of daylight I was overcome with guilt. I re-entered the store; replaced the gun, completed another circuit in a canter, and found myself outside, empty-handed and filled with shame.'

Helen stopped laughing. It was her turn to reveal a secret. She was confident with Mike and unlike him, set no limits.

'Remember the day we first met. I told you I saw your boss on a private matter? My father arranged it – he was worried – said I might need help.'

'No. I went to please him – about my brother, Lionel – ,' Helen paused mid-flow.

'And did you?' Mike asked.

Mike instantly sensed her deep emotion. Her eyes welled up – he kept silent – she drew her lips in between her teeth. Helen's chin gave a slight quiver. So did Mike's heart. He yearned to reach out, hold her hand, but that might bring her to tears. He quietly let her gain control.

'He was killed. Cycling. Hit by a drunk driver. Last week.'

'Last week?'

'Sorry. Last week, ten years ago – the driver was freed after two months – but my family have a life sentence.'

'And they're anxious about you? Were you close?'

'Very. I confided in him more than my parents. They say I've never got over it, but I manage.'

'Older brother then?'

'Yes, but only seventeen.'

'So how *do* you cope, Helen?'

'I get on with life. Mostly I'm fine. It's on that anniversary and his birthday that I get a bit depressed.'

'That's to be expected. Has it lessened over the years?'

'No. That's what everybody expects, but I don't want it to lessen.'

'It keeps his memory alive?'

'Exactly. You understand. No-one else has got that.'

'What did my boss say?'

'He was sympathetic. Perhaps he understood. He said very little.'

'Typical.'

He failed to reciprocate and tell Helen about his slight phobia. He sat feeling somewhat guilty, shamed and empty-handed – a boy outside Woolworth.

Within a week Mike knew he would marry Helen: a week perhaps in hindsight. In the early days of their marriage Mike was wary on 'Lionel days'. Helen could be quite tetchy. Her two bad days were almost six months apart. She coped better after the birthday visits to Lionel's grave. The anniversary of his death was different – tinged with suppressed anger – that is, until Mike's mother finally succumbed to her asthma and bronchitis. Helen followed Mike's Judaic custom and lit a memorial *yahrzeit* candle for her brother. She said it helped her get on with life – until Lionel's next birthday.

In her down moods Mike silently held her close – felt her tears dampen his chest. That was all she needed. If he was unsure: perhaps it was something else – he would ask 'Lionel?' If it was she would gently nod.

Helen's post-natal depression with Ben was no worse than many other first-time mothers suffered. Mike found it a strain to keep his conviction – that it was more to do with Lionel – to himself. But he did. And helped her through it; holding her close, spending as long as he could spare with her, helping with the chores, asking no questions, comforting her with unconditional love.

He had been clumsy tonight – it was a blessing – his phobia remained concealed. It had worsened despite his attempts to suppress and ignore it. He was shaken by his reaction at Surprise View. It played on his mind for several weeks.

CHAPTER FOUR

Wrinkles are hereditary. Parents get them from their children.
DORIS DAY

Helen strapped Amy into her car seat and drove off to collect Claire from school. She stopped off at the local shopping quadrant on the way to pick up Ben. It was exactly four o'clock with plenty of time to spare. She came out of the first shop.

'Where's Amy?' she asked Claire.

'She was with you Mummy.'

'No she wasn't. I left her with you. Where is she?'

'She can't be far.'

Helen scanned the pedestrian precinct – no sign of Amy.

'Amy!' she called. Her voice was drowned out by the traffic noise from the adjacent High Street.

'Claire you go that way. Check all the shops. I'll go the other way to search for her.'

Three minutes had passed. Helen had once read about young children getting momentarily lost. Ninety per cent of them are found within five minutes, the remainder within a quarter of an hour. She repeated Claire's words to herself – *she can't have gone far.*

In and out of the shops – past the five minutes mark – up and down her end of the precinct. No Amy. Claire returned – running.

'I've looked everywhere,' Claire said, breathlessly.

The quadrant clock showed 4.07 pm. Seven minutes gone! Unlucky seven. Amy had failed to make the first ninety per cent. Helen's heart began to pound. *Calm down. Most of the remainder are found within a quarter of an hour.* She noticed a security guard and ran to him.

'My little girl's gone missing.'

'It happens regularly here. Description?'

'She's four years old. She's wearing a red coat. She's got a pigtail today. Have you seen her?' Helen asked, her desperation starting to show.

'I haven't. How long has she been lost?' he asked.

'It's over five minutes,' Helen said, but glimpsing the clock noted it had sprinted to nearly nine.

'No need to panic – I'm sure she'll turn up in a minute. It's a small precinct. Have you tried the toyshop at the other end? They sometimes wander in there. I'll keep an eye out.'

Fifteen minutes. After that window more serious outcomes could arise – accidents or worse. Her watch raced to 4.10 pm. Total panic beckoned.

'Claire, I'm going up to the toyshop. You keep an eye out for her, around here.' A bundle of nerves, Helen set off in a jerky run. *Five more minutes left, please, please, Amy, where are you?*

The toyshop had not seen any child fitting her description. Helen rushed around, turning this way and that, her stomach churning, her head spinning. She passed the security man again.

'No luck yet,' he replied.

She saw Claire chasing about – alone. Frantic, she raced towards her. Claire's face was white. They grabbed hands as if to seek comfort from each other. Helen glanced at her watch – thirteen minutes past! Helen was shaking, her hand vibrating with fear. It transmitted to Claire. They turned about in autistic distress.

'I'll try again at the other end,' Claire said and pulled away before Helen could stop her. Raw panic left Helen helpless and desolate. Her quivering hand ferreted into her handbag for the mobile. She dialled 999.

*　　*　　*

No usual cup of tea awaited Mike on arrival that evening. He popped the kettle on and went to find Helen. She was home – her car was in the garage. He found her in the study facing the window.

'Hi, darling,' Mike said.

'Hello,' Helen replied without turning around.

Mike moved closer, side-on, and noticed her mascara had run and her eyes were red. He paused, stared long and hard at her, before draping his arms around her, his hands clasped over her tummy.

'What's up? Lionel?' he asked.

Helen's head motioned 'No'. She wiped her cheeks and regained her composure.

'It was Amy. I stopped off at the shops with the girls before going for Ben. I'd scarcely turned my back for a second. Amy went missing.'

'Missing?'

'Until we found her those few minutes were awful. An eternity with that gnawing hollow in the pit of my stomach.'

'So where was she?'

'Claire found her wandering around *The American Candy Store*.'

'Kids! Was she distressed? Tearful?'

'Distressed! Tearful!'

'She wasn't?'

'Guess what she replied,' Helen pushed forward two open palms in protest as Amy had. ' *I'm not lost. I know where I am!* "

'What a monkey – funny though,' Mike said.

'Yes I suppose it was. I tried to bite my cheek and be stern. But I was so relieved. My eyes gave me away – we both ended up laughing,' Helen said.

'So why the tears?'

'She insisted on keeping her coat on at home. I found her pockets filled with jelly babies and dolly mixture.'

'She'd nicked them?'

'Yes! And I'm afraid I lost my rag. I screamed at her and put all the sweets in the rubbish bin.'

'Helen! I love jelly babies.'

'For goodness sake Mike – grow up,' Helen snapped.

'Come on – it isn't that bad.'

'Yes it is,' Helen snapped again.

'She's a child: these things happen.'

'Is that all you have to say? Things happen!' Helen screamed.

'Why are you getting angry with me?' Mike pleaded quietly.

Helen's lip and chin quivered. She moved forward and draped her arms around him for a hug and a sob.

'I'm sorry Mike. Yes, things do happen. That scare with Amy has shaken me.'

'So where is she?'

'Upstairs in her room, still crying I expect. I was totally OTT.'

'It isn't the end of the world. She'll get over it. So will you.'

'I suppose. But it *is* serious. You were right, of course.'

'About what?'

'Lionel – last month – my scream.' Helen burst into tears again. Mike silently held her close.

'It's more than Lionel. I'm terrified it will happen again – that I will lose someone else: you, the children. It's silly but I can't help it.'

'Ben shook me up as well then – at least your scream did.' *You bastard Mike – blaming it all on her – tell her.*

Mike decided not to tell her. *That's all she needs – to have to contend with my insecurities as well!* He would have to keep a watchful eye out for Helen. Unable to open up to her added further guilt to the mix. He would have to address her concerns first – but how? Was it pragmatism or cowardice? Whichever, he let the matter rest and avoided tackling it at other opportune moments.

CHAPTER FIVE

The Lady Vanishes.

Mike welcomed the start to the new week. His automated routine on waking allowed him freedom to think and plan his days. Right on cue the radio greeted the morning announcing '7.25 – here's Garry and sport.' He had beaten his wake up call by some ten minutes listening to Helen's quiet breathing. She slept on. He slipped out of bed.

He drifted down the creaky old oak staircase, disturbing it from its sleep. The third stair issued the strongest protest with the usual low groan. He reached the bottom, opened the cupboard and unset the burglar alarm. He entered the warm kitchen and stepped barefoot onto the cold stone floor – he loved that life-affirming contrast – and put the kettle on.

If Alan C. is no better this morning I may have to discuss anti-depressants with his GP. He's trying. Is that fair or am I getting a bit down – making no headway with him?

With a grace and efficiency achieved by over twenty years of practise in this house, he plucked two mugs from the wooden tree stand, set Helen's dainty china one and his larger mug on a small tray after concealing its William Morris design with a paper towel, then removed the semi-skimmed milk carton from the fridge, poured half an inch into each mug, and returned the milk, retracing his footsteps.

This well-rehearsed ballet continued as he glided over to the larder, stacked several cereal packs along one arm and set them on the table, followed by bowls, plates and cutlery. *Flirty Valerie again this afternoon – she can be fun.* Mike grinned. He put a teaspoonful of Assam tea in the strainer. The kettle boiled

46

and cut out as he replaced the lid on the caddy. He poured the hot water quickly through the strainer for Helen's weak tea and left it in his filled mug to mature a deep orange brew. He made for the study, checked his e-mail and returned to take the tray up to the bedroom. Helen was sitting up bolstered by the pillows. 'Good morning,' Mike said, 'sleep well?' and leaned over for a kiss.

'No thanks to you,' she said. She returned a peck.

'And what precisely do you mean by that?'

'You were jumping in your sleep.'

Not Helen's intuition on this occasion – but Mike had done exactly that in a nightmare. They sat listening to the review of the morning papers, sipping their teas.

'Fancy going out tonight?' Mike asked.

'Anywhere in mind?'

'No. See what's on.'

Mike moved off into the recently refitted bathroom.

Re-set on autopilot he shaved jawbone, cheek, chin, neck and then upper lip in exactly the same sequence as he had done since he could remember. He noted the daily routines outside, at the birdfeeder down on the patio. *Tick- tock, Swiss clock.* The shy greater spotted woodpecker soon flew off, disturbed by his presence at the window, and was eagerly replaced by a chaffinch, then a posse of long-tailed tits followed by a range of small birds jostling for position and taking their turn in the pecking order – the *real politick* of the bird world. He watched two unperturbed green woodpeckers drilling the lawn and recalled the oil pumps he had seen pecking the sea by the Californian coast last year.

Mike's features were more wrinkled these days. It stamped his sense of humour at the sides of his deep-set brown eyes and the corners of his mouth. The salt and pepper of his still-full head of hair confirmed his age. His nakedness offered a kinder verdict. Sport had effortlessly kept him in trim without boring workouts in a gym.

He finished shaving and, with perfect timing, reached the shower as the unwelcome *Thought for the Day* started on the bathroom Sony. He shampooed and soaped himself under a hot shower, as ever singing. His favourite songs were tinged with melancholy – recognising life's risks. Today it was a sentimental love song *The Shadow of Your Smile*. Recent events had heightened his deep love for Helen and the children. It came at a price he had to accept. *The danger in those words: losing any of them. Why Helen reacts so badly. She's tasted life's perils.* He dowsed this moment of wistful emotion with an abrupt switch to freezing cold water to finish. It electrified him, fortifying his mind and body to take on the challenges of the day.

Once as a guest at friends' he forgetfully left the shower setting at cold, with an unpleasant surprise for its victim: unfortunately one of those people who wake up grouchy every morning. It could have turned sour.

'You must be into masochism,' the grumpy guest said.

'No, I love cold showers,' Mike said.

'A masochist, as I said.' His raised bushy eyebrow agreed.

'And I said I *love* cold showers. I'd take hot ones as a masochist.'

That defused the situation.

Mike's fixed ritual continued. His squeegee palms pressed his hair, neck, shoulders, chest, stomach, arms and legs until he was almost dry. This routine, set from boyhood with the smallest of towels to use after swimming, was efficient. He pulled the warm luxurious bath towel off the hot radiator and honed his slightly damp body until it glowed.

He returned to the bedroom, chose underpants from one drawer and pulled them on. From a lower drawer he picked out, at random, a pair of black socks. All were black: no decision required. *These are a bit daring – like ladies' sexy underwear.* He had picked out ones Helen had bought recently. They had shocking pink toes and heels. He dangled them head high disapprovingly.

'A hole?' Helen asked as she passed him.

'No. They're new – different colours.'

'Fusspot. They're still black but easier to match,' she called from the bathroom. 'You complain if they're paired wrongly.'

Mike made no reply. He pulled a sock onto the left foot, then the right, as always. He picked out a mid-blue shirt and threaded a maroon, fairly new, silk tie through the button-down collar. In harness, on autopilot, he tied a complicated knot learned years ago, with perfection. Occasionally he did it consciously with some difficulty in getting the sequence right. *Is that a risk for concert virtuosi, playing without a score?* He put on the chinos recovered from the bedroom chair and stepped into his comfortable, bruised leather Clarks: first the left then the right, as usual. He finished dressing, grabbed his lightweight tweed jacket, and made his way to the kitchen as Helen emerged from her shower.

She came down and joined him to follow her typical pattern at breakfast. No fixed routine – a repertoire that varied from day to day.

'Come on, you'll be late for school,' she called up to the children.

Mike's rote continued. He dropped one part of lightly rolled oats and two parts of water into a Pyrex bowl and placed it in the microwave, set for two and a half minutes. He poured himself, and offered Helen, a glass of cranberry juice from the fridge. He drank his intermittently as he reset the kettle, tipped a generous spoonful of the latest instant espresso coffee into a small fine china cup, and doused it with the boiling water. *Good. Nice creamy finish on top.* He preferred the genuine article but this satisfied weekday demands.

Setting the coffee on his place mat he poured a thin puddle of cold milk into his cereal bowl. He obeyed the microwave's demand for attention and poured the molten porridge directly onto the milk. He visualised the instant braking of the vibrant molecules. The effect – the resultant well-defined form – mirrored his freezing cold shower. He sprinkled the tiniest amount of sugar over the bowl then at last, morphed from automaton into Mike the person as he ate and sipped his espresso.

'So do you fancy going out tonight?' he asked.

'I'll see how I feel. I'm on all day, today.'

'I forgot. It's Monday, of course.'

Breakfast ended with a non-robotic goodbye kiss for Helen. As he left he grabbed a piece of fruit from the bowl: today a crispy Washington Red.

Mike's mornings were much the same. Mondays no longer felt different. It was nearly two years since they had. Helen noted the lightness of his step as he got into the Saab and his cheery wave to the kitchen window as he drove away. She accepted Mike as he was in the morning. She was far from her best then and slow to fully waken. His introspection suited her. She had good reason to label him compulsive and obsessive, but conceded he was well organised.

* * *

Mike arrived at the surgery. Predictably Phyllis was in early and had the kettle boiled ready for his first cup of Darjeeling tea. No milk, no sugar, but accompanied by a plain chocolate digestive.

'Morning, Philly.'

'Good morning, Dr. Daniels.'

He had been lucky to find Phyllis. She was, as they say, a handsome woman. She had lost her husband in his fifties, to cancer. Diligent and efficient, she had a quiet and pleasant personality that was ideally suited to her position. If first impressions were important, her understated tweed suit and simple hairstyle certainly gave the correct one. Her thin, light tortoiseshell-framed glasses added to the overall picture of a person of integrity. She fitted in perfectly as a part-time receptionist. Her duties, with generous gaps between patients, allowed her to pop out if she had to do any shopping. Her deputy in those brief morning periods was the answer-phone. It covered the afternoon sessions. Her absence went unnoticed by established patients.

Mike was insistent she stayed when a young divorcee proposed her imaginative cure for nymphomania. Phyllis treated it as an opportunity to organise and sort out bills and general correspondence. Mike was perfectly happy to let her bring in magazines and knitting to fill her quieter moments. She did so only after checking she had no other tasks to do. It made her feel guilty – even for her secret woollen scarf for Mike's Christmas present.

'I need to go out on one or two errands after your first patient has arrived. Is that alright, Dr. Daniels?'

'That's fine.'

He had invited Phyllis to address him as Mike, as he did for his patients. She did tentatively try – uncomfortable doing so. She preferred the formality. *Is it out of respect for me, or is it our old friend the ulterior motive? Perhaps she's gaining some secondary status?* He certainly couldn't begrudge her that. She was perfectly justified in creating a professional veneer over his deceptively casual attitude with patients. Here, he was in his element with one-to-one dialogues. Here, his relaxed manner, open mind and keen observation encouraged his counterpart to engage in honest debate. Here – it was *him,* un-programmed.

The doorbell sounded. Monday's first patient arrived – as so often at 9 a.m. – a new case. The slim, elegant lady entered in haste but, as Sherlock Holmes would have perceived, dressed at leisure. A substantial amount of effort and money had been invested in her hair, make-up, and co-ordinated cream and beige clothes. She gracefully sat down to blend in perfectly with the pale cinnamon walls and the taupe upholstered chairs. The tastefully crafted image of calm and control soon unravelled in Mike's presence.

'I need to jot down a few details,' he began.

She shuffled impatiently on her seat.

'It will take a moment or two. Date of birth?'

She became increasingly agitated. Mike calmly finished filling in her profile sheet.

'What can I do for you?'

'You must help me. Denise Green – your patient – my friend – says you're marvellous – I'm so nervous lately – do I look depressed to you?'

'I'm unable to...' Mike tried to answer.

'I feel so lonely – the children have all left home – nobody – I'm not needed,' she continued at machine gun speed.

'Can you....' Mike tried to interject.

'I want to be useful – I get so anxious – you must help me.'

He could barely get a word in after he had got the lady's basic details. Her body visibly vibrated. Sentence overlapped sentence, one idea cascaded down into two or three others at a time. The one-way conversations ranged from how nobody ever listened to her; the depressive interludes, her purpose in life, how much she missed her children, her anxiety being alone and most importantly that Mike must help her. All of it intelligent: all of it unintelligible.

Mike quietly assessed her body language. It was frenetically bent on wearing out her and anyone else in her vicinity. But it was an accurate reflection of her spoken word – her rapid gestures synchronised with the high-speed dialogue. She was charged with boundless energy with no constructive goal. Her attempts to sit with composure were met with the enthusiasm of a two-year-old for the task. Mike soon came to the conclusion that little was wrong with her. Apart from the astonishing speed of her conversation, mental processes and body movements, they were all in harmony. Her constant agitation could account for her mild symptoms of depression. She expressed herself well but at breakneck speed. He was *not* the one to treat her. She needed a few sessions with a behaviourist to slow her down and suggest ways to channel her abundant intelligence and inexhaustible energy.

'I'm not the right person to help you,' Mike said.

The verbal torrent switched to abrupt silence. The frantic childlike activity froze into a 'dead lion' at a stroke. *Icy showers: cold milk, hot porridge.*

'You are perfectly sane. I'm going to refer you to a colleague.'

With her energy levels restored during this pause of attentive listening, she resumed her madcap gallop to the end of the session.

Mike got to his feet to see her out. She jumped up, profusely thanking him for his help. Mike glanced down as he turned from his chair. She exited, facing him, with a goodbye. He turned to respond but found she had vanished into thin air. *Remarkable – how did she move so fast?*

He opened the door and saw nobody; no-one, no next patient in the waiting room, no Phyllis at her desk – she was out on her errands – and, through the far glazed door, no sign of anyone walking down the long exit passage beyond. *How on earth?* Confused, Mike returned to his room. *That's weird.* Her voice echoed in his ears. It was the strangest experience. *What on earth?* He heard the voice again. It really is her! 'Dr. Daniels, I can't get out,' she called.

In her rush to leave she had opened the wrong, adjacent door, entered and locked herself inside the surgical storeroom. Mike coolly opened it. She fluttered out, chattering away – a linnet released, and left by the exit he proffered.

His next patient was unaware, but if the cupboard caught his eye Mike had to stifle irrepressible smiles and even the danger of an uncontrolled giggle. For patient number three that morning he sat on the chair backing the hilarious door. To no avail – bad move.

Now what have I done? He usually had the window behind him and could clearly see his patients' reactions. His were less evident against the bright light. *Idiot, you've reversed things.* His patient could easily perceive the smile surging past his constricted throat, generated from the persistent images of the 9 a.m. encounter. It was a difficult situation. *Ludicrous – I'm supposed to be a seasoned professional.*

But it happens: often at funerals. Mike had an endogenous weakness for uncontrolled reactions to the absurd that prevented him ever again reading P.G. Wodehouse in public. He had done so twice. Once, as a student on a crowded commuter train surrounded by stuffy city gents, he was reduced to a quivering jelly. Instead of learning from it he repeated his mistake, as any fool might, some years ago at Heathrow Airport awaiting Helen's delayed arrival.

Browsing in W. H. Smith's he frivolously selected the lethal *Mr. Mulliner* to pass the extra hour. Once the plot and mishaps with Hooray Henrys had combined early in the prose, Mike fully surrendered any sign of outward normality. The people in Costa's may have concluded a suspicious substance was to blame. He stopped reading to avoid further embarrassment and saw wondrous faces, both young and old, fixedly staring at him. *What must they think? Here I am, a fully-fledged adult, chuckling aloud: cheeks flushed, eyes streaming.* He kept returning to the book, partly by way of explanation to his audience, partly to hide. The next page, sentence, phrase or even a perfectly chosen word, triggered a new spasm of painful laughter. Proper laughter. Stomach ache type.

I've got myself into 'another fine mess'. He eventually pulled himself together and managed to get through the rest of the morning. Apart from the retrospective smile that became a brief cough, and a novel use of a handkerchief, his patients had no clue as to the stoic battle he fought to maintain his professional demeanour on their behalf.

Next day he arrived at the hospital with his mood lightened by his non-professional reminiscences of the previous morning. Normally restrained, he related the 'cupboard' episode with abandon – identity, concealed of course. It lightened the management's obligatory, often impractical, and in Mike's eyes optional, tea-not-coffee break. Colleagues and nursing staff laughed at his uninhibited metamorphosis into a child rather than the incident.

CHAPTER SIX

The only truly serious questions are ones that even a child can formulate. Only the most naive of questions are truly serious. They are the questions with no answers. MILAN KUNDERA

It was a couple of years since he had set up his Monday practice. Mike remained pleasantly surprised. Tuesdays had *not* taken on the depressive mantle discarded with Mondays at the start of the hospital week. He tackled his NHS list with renewed vigour, refreshed by the in-depth private efforts of the preceding day. He scarcely did it for money – the morning fees covered his costs for the day – afternoon patients made up for the lost day's income at the hospital. He studiously ignored the theoretical dichotomy – it could whimsically blame morning patients for costs and create bias.

His surgeon colleagues who shared the premises made more from a ten minute assessment than he could in a fifty minute session and considerably more from a one hour minor operation than he charged for a full day's labour. But they let him use any free hours that remained before the end of their own allotted days without further contribution to overheads.

Prior to the Monday change he considered jacking it all in. Find a different job, perhaps abroad. Give up the NHS. Today he felt a freer man. Then, he was Gulliver in Lilliput, tied down by petty bureaucracy, unending form filling, best practise protocols, clipboards, performance evaluations, results and costs, and know-it-all managers. Those irritants – markedly diluted with new operating patterns – no longer itched. The clinical field had moved on a million miles since his first junior posting when psychologists and psychiatrists were the butt of jokes in and out of the medical world. How did he ever agree, then, to see patients for around half an hour, once a fortnight? It was a waste of his and patients' time and effort and taxpayers' money. Vast improvements over two decades helped raised his job satisfaction. It was somewhat eroded with major reforms and more administration. He yearned for autonomy to develop his interests. Two years ago he was unhappy employed in an NHS hospital. With well over twenty years of practise, Mike had polished his skills in communication, observation and problem solving. All he needed was modest self-counselling with the eventual minor change: both seen with difficulty.

One Monday, stressed-out, he had a full-blown row with Helen. They rarely let tiffs get overheated, having learned to compromise early on in their marriage. In those days their petty rows were perhaps sub-consciously engineered to test their love. The making up was deeply sincere despite Helen's conditioning from her mother over sunsets and anger. This major argument had deeper roots – an underlying frustration.

Until TomTom came to their aid Mike frequently raised his voice over Helen's weak point – her map reading. In truth he fared no better, as he often dozed off to her serene driving and failed to carry out his duties as navigator.

'Mike. I'm lost,' Helen said.

'Where are we?' he asked, opening his eyes.

The next road sign told him: Southampton 5 miles.

'How the hell did you get here?' he screamed.

'I followed the A34 as you said.'

'Didn't you see the sign for the A303 turn- off?'

'No. Wasn't one,' she snapped.

'Wasn't one? Of course there was. Are you blind?'

'Don't you get shirty with me. It's your fault. I wanted to take the M4.'

'My fault! You chose to miss both roads,' Mike shouted.

They were supposed to be having a romantic few days in the West Country for her birthday. He felt bad about that row. Next day he attempted to compensate. He handed Helen a new road atlas as an extra present.

'Thank you,' she said. But her faint smile was contemptuous. His inscription intentionally *upside down* inside the cover – a joke – had failed. *Why am I such an idiot?*

They soon forgot minor tiffs. But on that Monday – of all days – they were both upset by their appalling row. It was a wake-up call. Helen challenged him to explain his behaviour. He had no explanation. She had no idea what it was about, how it started, or why.

'It's you Mike – nobody else – you're overwrought. Perhaps it is work,' Helen said.

'Work? What's all this got to do with work?'

'Well, it's got nothing to do with me,' Helen insisted.

Mike left it at that realising it was indeed to do with Helen. He could make no headway with her. She resisted all his attempts to discuss Lionel. A certain friction had developed in their relationship since Surprise View and Helen's scare with Amy. *My fault.* She had somehow picked up his bad vibes. It had been bubbling below the surface for some while. He ought to address it – nip it in the bud – but how?

*   *   *

The topic of this month's hospital meeting was to do with economics rather than patient care. *Do we have to tolerate this nonsense?* An administrator set the agenda. As ever, she carried a bulging file as proof of her self-importance. *Did she say disincentivise – has she inventivised that?*

It irritated Mike how they were constantly being modernised, monitored, criticised, scrutinised, advised, directed, assessed, scored – and occasionally encouraged and applauded –

by a host of managers and outside consultants. *Why? Why the extra burden on taxpayers?* Mike accepted management was important but it angered him this morning – he had patients to attend. *Must they interfere in professional matters?*

Friends employed in education had expressed the same frustrations. Vocational, they claimed to work best unhindered – and within budgets.

The Chanel suit droned on and Mike turned off, distracted by the hovering crane constructing the new hospital wing at the window. It pointed high above to a jet trail scratched across the sky. Mike cogitated over the current dire warnings on carbon emissions and global warming. This morning's radio blamed airlines and cheap flights. Jet pollution was deposited high in the atmosphere – and into Mike's head on his way in. In the sterile air of the management meeting his mind wandered: and pondered. *Could jets, sucking in air be adapted to capture carbon – hi-tech vacuum cleaners – clean up instead of pollute?* He left that idea to synchronicity and boffins.

'We must take responsibility for costs,' the Chanel suit said, Thatcher-like. Her remark triggered a prescient paper from his student days. It applied stimulus-response theory, in vogue then but in essence basic economics, to fine a manufacturer double it saved when poisoning a river. *That was three decades ago – today countries trade pollution quotients.* Mike paid attention to the current discussion.

'The fundamental 20/80 golden truth of economics holds for the NHS. The first 20% of costs cover 80% of services,' the Chanel suit said.

Someone challenged her. *Good for him.*

'Hospitals aren't supermarkets,' he said.

'Accepted – but like them we must give value for money,' she replied.

'We're always making cuts,' he said.

'I also wish to see if restrictions on expensive remedies are necessary.'

Mike conceded she talked sense. During the past decade he had fought vehemently for more and longer sessions with his patients. In that period appointments had expanded from thirty to fifty minute sessions and increased, from monthly or fortnightly, to weekly intervals. Originally they were restricted to six sessions per patient. Mike had found devious means around that but was eventually brought to task. That was a watershed: he proved extra sessions were effective and management agreed to raise their limit to ten. But his list was scrutinised in detail from then on and he could get no extensions for patients he knew needed them.

That ceiling aggravated and led to his decision to see those patients privately at nominal fees to complete their treatment. His Monday absences gave him a stronger hand with his manager. He got the limit raised to twelve sessions per patient soon after starting his private practice.

Two years on he used his leverage to request the limit be raised again. He averaged twelve sessions per patient even in the private practice but it was insufficient for some patients. A sixteen limit at the hospital would encompass most patients who needed that extra bit of attention – with minimal cost. Far more expensive are patients who go elsewhere or return, after incomplete treatment.

One of the benefits of good management was evaluation of performance and feedback. In the last few years, cognitive behavioural therapy had proved to be an effective treatment and unquestionably value for money. It was sound economics, he had explained in his letter. It wasn't comparable to high strata expenditures where complex issues involving individual needs, human rights, enormous drug or procedural costs had to be finely balanced. Since he started his private Mondays, a mere handful of NHS patients had needed extra appointments. They would *consider* his proposal.

The management team set off for their long business lunch. Mike joined the remainder of the group for lunch in the refectory. He was rather partial to some of its institutional fare – particularly the over-cooked roast potatoes, but chose a light salad as a healthy option.

After lunch Mike set out a phobia desensitisation schedule for the new recruit to his clinic.

'It is strange how some people can be so scared of cats,' she said.

'Is it? Ask the ancient Egyptians,' Mike said, as he set out the chart.

'Do you think phobias have underlying causes?'

'I'm sure they have, but we don't necessarily have to find them,' Mike said.

'What do you think could have caused hers?'

'No idea. A cat may have scratched her or sat on her head as a baby. Who can tell?'

'Is it ever treatable without knowing?'

'Usually. We did have one last year we had to trace to source.'

'What happened?'

'The patient had to have some psychotherapy beforehand.'

'Why was that?' she asked, fully engaged with Mike's chart.

'Well, it turned out she had a bit of a complex. It had her carry a sense of guilt around with her. I can't recall exactly but she did 'a naughty' as a child – denied it – but was observed by the family cat.'

Mike glanced at his assistant with a feline grin.

'You aren't going to tell me the cat snitched on her,' she said with a nervous laugh.

'No. But it did watch her. Cats are inscrutable.'

'And that was the cause of her phobia?'

'Basically yes,' Mike said. He filled in the final conditions for his chart. 'Right. You'll use three levels of exposure over the next few weeks. Stick to level one today, even if her anxiety reduces down to a 2 or 3 on the pictures and cat chat. OK?'

'Yep. I'm used to the drill.'

'Good. I'll leave you to it and see how you've got on later.'

Mike had used precisely this form of treatment on himself, convinced his was a run of the mill phobia. He'd moved closer to sheer drops in stages. He'd begun with moderate heights, but the nausea and giddiness at a dangerous rim soon curtailed any further self-administered help. He resigned himself to the fact his problem was too trivial to warrant further attention. He would have to live with it. After all, how often could it affect him? As an adult he had reacted badly on no more than a handful of occasions. Nightmares apart, it remained dormant within him, more or less forgotten. True, the Lake District trauma came out of the blue and terrified him. That was exceptional and although it *did* disturb him he had managed to cover his tracks. Unlike a roofer or steeplejack, how often could he be exposed to such a situation-specific fear?

Feeling almost a cheat as a clinician, he searched for positives. Introspective, he was fully aware of his rigid personal behaviour and fixed routines. In a clinical setting they were often beneficial to his patients. Conversely, he was fixated – goose and gander – what helped them should help him.

An obsessive-compulsive patient arrived that afternoon. Her demons demanded, amongst other ideas, that she had to wear something green. Mike was the same with black socks – ah, but he had a reason – efficiency in his case. Maybe she had a similar reason. Perhaps a bizarre, illogical one neither she nor others recognised. Here he could empathise. If she didn't respond to behavioural treatment he might search for her reason, however strange it might be.

What about his rigid adherence to exactly two and a half minutes to microwave his porridge and precisely three minutes fifteen seconds for a boiled egg? Was that any different from the young man who insisted he had exactly forty-one, forty-three or forty-seven peas on his plate? Why these three prime numbers? Could that compare to perfection in cuisine? No. It was illogical – apart from some Kabbalistic type of explanation beyond Mike's imagination. Mike treated such behaviour clinically – as he had tried to cure his fear of heights. On the odd occasions that he did delve further, the answers were rather obscure and emotive.

His personal behaviour was a different matter. He once, often indeed, had an appalling round of golf. On those occasions he got angry with himself – not so much with his game – more with his compulsion to play. *How on Earth could I explain to a Martian why I expend so much time and energy to hit a ball into a hole?* Wasn't that obscure and emotive? He might well have added to his list his passionate love for his cars, his cold showers, and his unalterable weekday routines. Perhaps his daughter's school friends were right – he mused – and all psychologists were indeed nuts.

CHAPTER SEVEN

Under all speech that is good for anything there lies a silence that is better, Silence is deep as Eternity; speech is shallow as Time. Silence is more eloquent than words. THOMAS CARLYLE

Monday's new challenge at 9 a.m. was the reverse of the previous week. Cynthia arrived, spectral, slow in movement, expressionless and, as Mike was soon to learn, speechless. Brought by her husband, it was he who in desperation had insisted her doctor try something else – anything. Mike was the anything.

The doctor's covering letter outlined her past history and her current prescription for schizophrenia. Despite treatment, the illness had worsened over the past six months. Her husband was convinced that her medication was to blame. Since the diagnosis three years ago, her medicines had made her progressively worse.

Mike led Cynthia to a seat then quietly had a word with her husband outside.

'Is she usually this bad?'

'Not so much at home – more at the doctor's and in hospitals.'

'Has your doctor explained that if she is schizophrenic I probably cannot help her?'

'They're all wrong. They've got her into a right state,' pleaded her anxious husband.

'Relax. Come for her at ten. I'll see what I can do.'

Mike rarely attempted to treat patients with psychoses of any sort: limiting his role to confirming diagnoses like schizophrenia. Difficult for GP's to determine alone. Of those referred, most were plainly in the one per cent of the population suffering the disease. Could Cynthia be mimicking the illness with schizoid behaviour as a response to stress?

Cynthia sat motionless, staring ahead, as Mike had left her. He pulled a folder from his briefcase.

'Can we start with your full name?' he said, neutral as milk.

Silent: staring: rigidly motionless.

Mike slowly put the folder away and casually leaned into his chair.

He glanced at Cynthia, then again. Silence – the stare. That was all – no response. The entire session proceeded in this strange limbo abyss of her catatonia. She revealed nothing. He demanded nothing. A familiar abstraction came to mind. Mike could not identify it. This silence, this emptiness, filled him with intense awe. He had experienced it before. Not with patients. Where though?

Cynthia's eyes flickered slightly as her husband returned and the session ended. Mike lowered his hopes but, curious about the source of his own reaction, agreed to see her again the following week. She left with her husband. No goodbye: silence.

The following week Cynthia arrived for her second session. The same. Mike made no comment. The silence continued. He made no attempt to interrupt it but noticed small, almost imperceptible, facial movements. Most interesting were the nuances of change in her eye contact. He was following her eyes as neutrally as he could. It was difficult – they began to dominate the room – an overt reaction could upset her.

Cynthia's eyes expressed fear and anxiety. Mike analysed them as a boxer. But calmly, hoping that would emanate from his own eyes. He began to read her more clearly as the session continued. Shame, guilt, confusion, worthlessness, inadequacy and inferiority, danger, hate, rejection, anger: all presented and were met with empathy and Mike's naturally benign countenance.

The abstraction Mike experienced in the first session strengthened. It grew more tangible and vivid as the session progressed. It was to do with emptiness, space and danger. Then bingo! It was that same overwhelming sense of awe: the reaction he had on visiting Grand Canyon last year on the way to California.

Helen had insisted on going. He was wary – surprisingly panicky. The idea of standing by its sheer drop in front of Helen sent tremors through his body.

'How would you feel about Las Vegas instead? Mike asked her, feebly.

'What?' she said, 'You hate gambling – so do I. Why, in heaven's name, would I prefer it to the Canyon?'

And that was that. He was being unfair to Helen. He talked himself round. *Secure railings said the guidebook. It's the USA. Safe – Americans are litigious. It's another level of desensitisation. Positive thinking!*

The moment they arrived and drove alongside the Canyon, Mike started to get nervous and mildly nauseous. The size of it even distant from the road was beyond his imagination. Parked, they walked forward for their first close-up. Unfortunately it was one of the few viewpoints unprotected by any barrier: Mather Point.

'Incredible. The sheer size of it,' Helen said breathlessly.

Uncharacteristically, she marched several paces ahead of Mike's hesitant advance. His head was spinning. He searched for an excuse: food poisoning – perhaps a sudden migraine or an acute virus – any ploy. His body began to quiver involuntarily as he followed. His chest tightened. Fear skewered his stomach. Helen moved closer to the rim. He had to stop her. Panic gripped his throat. He could not call her away. He was fighting for breath when an enormous man, sporting Hawaiian shorts, triumphantly called to his wife.

'Say, honey, isn't this where that kid fell to his death last month?'

'Sure is – second one this year,' she said. The reply was jubilant.

'Boy, how far down is that? Some fall. You'd get your kicks on that one,' he said.

'Mind you don't,' she said.

They both chuckled chirpily.

'Darned terrible tragedy,' he said.

His loud sign-off fooled nobody as he turned away from the scene.

Mike was on the point of throwing up when Helen stopped and turned.

'Mike. Stay where you are. I know you. You'll insist on going to the edge,' she called and hurried towards him. He had seen Helen as an angel, especially with the children. She was the guardian sort on this occasion. His panic abated and he quickly pulled himself together.

'But you were keen a minute ago,' he said with feigned regret.

'Sorry, Mike, but that open drop – those sickening people.' Helen said.

It's Lionel again, he mused.

'That I might entertain them?' Mike asked.

'What! Fall off the edge? Of course not.'

Why did I react so badly? It was years since, but almost Surprise View all over again.

'So you're still happy to see the canyon?' Mike asked.

'Of course,' Helen replied, apologetically. 'Let's go further along and find a place with a barrier. Please.'

Helen seems in control in spite of her fears.

'If we must – I'm sure it will be quite as spectacular behind bars,' he said.

Helen shied away, implicated for caging him. Mike felt ashamed. *She doesn't deserve this.* He kissed her on the forehead. He was confused. *Should I tell her about me?* His mixed emotions had conveyed an expression of deep disappointment to Helen. *What a bastard, what a tangled web!* He had even got her to beg. *What a swine!* Guilt swept away any remnants of his fear. Worse, he had raised his profile another notch with his fake bravado.

At the viewing point half a mile along Mike utterly surprised himself.

'Sorry Helen – you're absolutely right – it's much safer here.'

He looked down.

Relaxed, protected by the safety rail, he was truly overjoyed to find himself free from fear and absorbed with the panorama. It was indescribable – impossible to share with anyone who had not experienced it first-hand. No photograph or video, however magnificent, could capture it. It was too vast.

Why did he react the same way to Cynthia? He connected it surprisingly to grandeur. He could not register why. Then *wham*. Grandeur: yes that was it. That *was* it. Grandeur. It was oddly his predominant thought.

Mike registered the sheer enormity of the task in front of him and the massive overload that burdened Cynthia. Her worries and anxieties were as broad as the Canyon, her emotions as deep and her suffering as long. Mike's reaction to the awesome space within that gigantic geological fault was reprised by Cynthia's silence and immobility. His abstraction had described the intense silence and the density of the emptiness, captured as far as the eye could see. And it had persisted along several hundred miles, spread across a width of many miles and trapped in its one-mile depth. It also perfectly symbolized the unbearable internal turmoil that enslaved Cynthia within her petrified fortress.

Mike was heartened by the tiniest non-verbal responses Cynthia made that session. They began to develop a dialogue of sorts between them. He was greatly encouraged at the end of the second session. Cynthia mouthed a silent 'Thank you'.

CHAPTER EIGHT

Believe nothing you hear and only half you see. JOSEPH FOX (1907-1987)

Bryan left his teens as his father departed this world. He related his discovery moist-eyed. Hot prickly tears of pure joy soon followed. At last he knew his father had loved and been proud of him. It had taken several sessions to unearth but it was worth the effort.

His late father, a disciplinarian cleric, was outwardly gentle and kind to his flock but harsh with his nearest and dearest. He was also an alcoholic. Bryan's mother bravely suffered the drunken brutality of his father's words and hands. Bryan suffered, all those years, from his own sense of helplessness. His father refused to seek treatment. How could he let down the Church by admitting his weakness: or risk losing his position and responsibility as breadwinner, however meagre the loaf? Unaffectionate, he had no cuddles or kisses or any physical sign of love for his wife and son. In his deepest, most self-pitying stages of inebriation he vaguely professed his regret, his love for both of them, and hatred for his wretched self. It was on one of those nights that he gave Bryan a slip of paper with the injunction to safely keep it. He had inked four lines of poetry that were meaningless without context. Bryan had stated a few weeks ago that was all he ever recalled his father giving him. He had kept his promise for the scrap of paper. Mike asked him to bring it to last week's session. Bryan considered it irrelevant. Mike disagreed. His father must have had a motive, even in *vino*, let alone *veritas*. 'Why write it out, give it, and insist it be kept?'

69

Bryan was to try and find the source of it in his father's poetry collection. He succeeded and found, underlined in pencil, the very four lines in a long poem. It was written by a father mourning the loss of his son in the First World War – a hymn of love and pride. Read in their full context, the four lines his father picked out referred specifically to the high regard he had held for his son.

'Weakest ink better than best memory.' After two and a half millennia Confucian wisdom remained relevant today – slightly differently for Mike. He frequently seized upon it to encourage stress-laden patients to keep a pad and pencil by their bedside to jot down worries for attention next day. Instead of adding debilitating insomnia by repeatedly rehearsing their problems, they could then forget them and get a better night's sleep.

'Do you need to see me next week?' Mike asked. He slowly shook his head as he made the polite and gentle enquiry.
'Could we leave it for a month or so and see how it goes?' Bryan replied.
'Sounds good to me,' Mike said, in conclusion.

The next patient was late. Mike reflected on Bryan's father – a man of the church. How little he had given his own son: how joyously Bryan had discovered he was in fact, loved by him. How different Mike's own father had been. He wasn't a religious man: Jewish, but not religious. Dad dutifully attended synagogue on the High Holidays – New Year, Yom Kippur – but even then he and his brother and friends talked more Spurs or politics or business than praying. That wasn't particularly odd. Such clusters could be found in most congregations in the East End or North London. Michael was bored with those obligatory long services apart from the singing. A melodious cantor eased the pain.

Michael came home from primary school eager to challenge his father to a daily game of chess. The elusive prize on offer was a pound if he won. It took several years before he won a penny. The money and the much greater trophy accompanying it proved elusive targets. Dad was a sound player, read no end on the game, and played out past matches from Masters as a form of solitaire on his old wooden board. It wasn't until his first term at grammar school that Michael gained his pound, his father's scalp, and a place in the school chess team. The money had become irrelevant. The honour at school was a great source of pride for father and son alike. But victory over Dad was mixed. The first excitement and joy of the conquest soon evaporated. He felt increasingly guilty and deeply sad for his father's additional loss of status whenever he won – an extra sorrow to the multiple sclerosis that was gradually destroying his father's active life. He should be the last person to inflict such cruelty. Only in his late teens did he discover that Dad had no such notions. The filial victories were a tonic for him.

In his teens, Michael excelled at boxing. It was strictly one-to-one – any failure or success was entirely his own. He felt exactly the same isolation entering the canvas ring as he did staring at the chequered board to begin a competitive chess match. No matter how many people at a boxing hall, he was oblivious to their presence once the bell sounded. Almost all he saw throughout a bout were his opponent's eyes. Those three short rounds in the ring stretched the minutes – especially the last one. He was at his fittest ever, training for boxing. Yet no matter how fit – no matter how hard he trained with skipping ropes, medicine balls and punch bags – apart from three fights easily won inside the distance, he was invariably drained both physically and mentally at the finish. If his boxing skills faltered he regretted the lost points. The hits were painless. It was akin to carelessly losing a piece or missing a pin or fork at chess.

The fight that did cause him real, but again not physical, pain was to be forever etched in his memory. He had won all of his competitive boxing matches. Dad had yet to see him box. Nor for that matter had he recently seen him play much cricket or football. It was difficult for him to make the awkward journeys and it was uncomfortable to sit for hours confined to his wheelchair by the worsening MS. That particular year Michael reached The Finals again. He was up against a strong opponent. It would be a good contest between two worthy contestants, but he was confident of a win. Those first chess wins over his father unexpectedly popped into his head the week preceding the fight. Their attendant guilt and remorse increased his desire to recompense his father by sharing his successes, so he insisted Dad attend.

The stewards placed his father's wheelchair ringside after removing two seats. The bell sounded and for once Michael didn't feel alone in the ring. Dad was alongside him. It was to have a profound effect on events that night. His taller opponent was a southpaw with a longer reach. Michael's tactics were to duck under his leads and get inside with some combination punches to the body and to counter with left crosses as he sidestepped those rights. He attempted to dictate fights from the centre of the ring and perversely make his quarry do the running around. The first round went exactly as planned until the last moments. He sent the briefest of glances towards his father at ringside. Fatal.

As his eyes returned to find their Magnetic North and re-lock onto his opponent's, he caught a heavy hit from a ramrod straight right, full in the face. He felt no pain but blood poured from his nose. He was acutely aware he was in trouble. He summoned all his wits to remain in the fight. By the end of the round he managed to avoid any further damage after his seconds had plugged the bloodied nose. They suggested he change tactics and circle his rival to protect his vulnerability from that long right. He must then take any openings to quickly reverse direction, and hit his target with left crosses and hooks. Doing as instructed in the next round, he soon got in two good points-laden punches. Both contestants were thinking out the fight at lightning speed. Then abruptly his adversary, no sloth, surprised Michael and started boxing with an orthodox left lead to change the shape of the contest.

What was he up to – Michael's tactics were succeeding – was he trying to make him reverse them again? His opponent's ploy failed.

Michael stuck with his plan and even more comfortably defended himself behind his right glove. He changed direction. His left leads to the head beat his opponent's feeble left to the punch. The dangerous right hardly threatened, dispatched from the more distant shoulder. He scored with several solid straight lefts and one peach of a left hook. But towards the end of this round, his nose took a second hit – the only one since the end of round one – from another right punch. The blow was less powerful than the previous one but opened the floodgates once more. Incredibly – through the bloody spray – he saw in his opponent's eyes a flicker of weakness. What did it mean? *Tiredness? Couldn't be.* Michael was doing most of the running around now. Was he embarrassed to shame this son in front of his invalid father – surely not?

The bout was interrupted for the seconds to attend Michael's nose and the round continued to the bell. Then panic. The referee threatened to stop the fight.

'No way,' Michael thundered through his gum shield, before it could be removed.

The corner frantically set to it and managed to staunch the flow of blood within the allotted minute. The attendant doctor gave the OK and the referee relented.

Seconds out. The bell. Last round. The tactics he had adopted weren't exactly making rings around his opponent; the eternal circles he described were sapping his strength. Not Michael's style of boxing but – damaged nose – it was his best defence against that telescopic right.

Both young men were drained. One from his efforts to maintain the lead on points he had gained from the dramatic endings to both previous rounds; the other from his attempts to make amends with a strong finish and perhaps a KO. Both boxers were set on winning and every atom of their being was invested in the effort. The clock seemed static – the minutes irrelevant. Mike was no longer calculating. He yearned to win for Dad. It was a supreme effort. Towards the end of this final round the red stream resumed its journey trickling down his mouth and chin. The referee ignored the injury. Neither boxer had enough energy left to do any further damage to the other. They remained fighting in ghostly slow motion. The long loud ringing of the final bell cracked the sealed world and the trance they had shared. It abruptly awakened them to the thunderous cacophony that had unrelentingly accompanied the fight, since the first round. The cheers grew louder. The crowd's highest accolade – a sanitised Nero's thumbs up – was their deluge of coins. They bounced onto the canvas from all directions. Michael slumped into his corner, head held down. His vest was so soaked in blood and sweat that he could scarcely distinguish the diagonal red sash across his chest. He knew deep down he had failed.

The Runyanesque MC came to the microphone and in the singsong growl of a market fruit vendor announced, to Michael's surprise, the judges' split decision. That was the solitary surprise. The melodic posh cockney roar issued the final stanza, 'Hend tha winnar, on points, hin tha blue cornar…' to herald his loss.

Michael sheepishly eyed his father, highlighted in the spotlights over the ring. He noted the welling tears and the pursed lips as he tried to control his emotions. Michael was familiar with that frozen rictus. But rather than Dad's labile MS – he had dealt him a further setback. He feebly waved goodbye as Uncle Bert, who had sat with him, steered Dad out of the hall home.

Over in his opponent's corner some frantic activity was taking place involving the seconds and the duty doctor. His team had trouble removing the right glove and were forced to cut the laces. On unwinding the boxing bandages they discovered a badly swollen hand. A fractured bone was diagnosed and he was immediately driven off to hospital to have his hand set in plaster. The thunderbolt right, unleashed at the end of the first round that gained the victory, carried his full body mass. But hurled from his left toes to Michael's nose, it had been delivered with a slightly cocked wrist.

It was *pain* his eyes had signalled with the blow at the end of round two. That was the reason he dumped his southpaw stance. He had bravely fought on to win with barely a threat for a right.

Michael had had no inkling about that. His team was too busy attending his nose to detect the brief grimace the trainer in the other corner received on pressing the right glove. He had been out-foxed as well as out-boxed by a fighter with only one good hand. He had exhausted himself by moving in the wrong direction all night. He had been fooled. If he had circled clockwise towards that imposter of a right he would have won the bout easily. And his father was unaware of that. It made the defeat even more unbearable.

After showering and changing, Michael bore few signs of injury. The inside of his nose was sore but without permanent damage. He re-entered the hall with its unique blend of boxing odours; of sweat and rubs, rosin and leather, and the unmistakeable sense of fear and excitement generated by adrenalin and testosterone. That concoction was potent. He met raw aggression in a group of so-called classmates – they jeered him.

'You klutz, he beat you single-handed.'

'Loser.'

'Daniels, you cost me five quid.'

Michael ignored them – they weren't worth the trouble – but the barbs found their mark. He moved past them to join his friends. Several had brought sisters and girlfriends. Stimulated and seduced by the atmosphere they gathered round him – groupies impressed by the fight. *Some hero* he mused.

One girl stood apart, stood out, from the crowd. He couldn't take his eyes off her. She had a curiously shaped, chiselled nose. It was at odds with her other features and her sleek natural blonde hair and smart dress. She returned Michael's long glances with a smile and came casually sideling up to him. 'You've scrubbed up well,' she said, and delicately adjusted his shirt collar.

Amazing. She was genuinely interested in him. Surprisingly well spoken, she confidently held him in conversation and rooted him to the spot with her eyes. In a second timeless zone that evening he engaged in the privacy of two people isolated from the rest of the world. Michael was fascinated. They chatted so easily that twenty minutes passed in a flash. The line of a song came into his head – tunes often did –'*It seems we stood and talked like this before.*' It was from his father's record collection: Peggy Lee's *Where or when – Dad's favourite!* He'd forgotten his upset father. He needed to get home.

'I must go,' he said reluctantly. Firmly rooted to the floor, hypnotised by her eyes, he waved a distant farewell to his pals.

'Promise you'll turn up,' she said.

'I said I would,' Michael replied.

'Promise.'

'I promise.'

'I may be late. Wait for me,' she insisted.

She let him go after he agreed to meet her outside the nearby tube station the next day.

Michael sat confused on the bus home, drained by the evening's events. He had badly let down Dad but his emotions were mixed – *that* girl dominated them. And *that* song welded them together. Dad had played it so often at home. 'Stoppit,' Mum said, giggling as Dad grabbed her, even recently on his good days, for a slow smoochie dance in front of anyone. *How many dances remained for them?* Michael heard it as a pleasant enough standard – then. Tonight the melody in his head had a distinct poignancy and pierced deep into his soul. And the words –he knew those by heart – by heart but not in his heart. Tonight it was different. He went through the lyrics and began to appreciate what a profound love song it was. For all the routine and mundane life they led, a deep love bonded his parents. Their song hadn't entered his head on a whim. Of course he would meet her tomorrow – wait all evening if necessary.

He returned home to minor pandemonium. Mum greeted him at the door, relieved to see him in one piece but aghast at the bloodied kit she seized from him to wash.

'Savagery – that's what it is,' she mumbled to herself. 'And your father watching.'

'You OK, son?' Dad asked. Michael nodded.

Uncle Bert shrieked 'What a fight,' as he entered the kitchen.

'Yeah, but I lost,'

'No-one lost. It was great,' Dad said, to his astonishment.

'Are you kidding, Dad? Ask the guys who lost money on me.'

'Lost money?'

'Yeah. 'Fats' Fisher was the one laughing.'

'Fisher the bookie's son?'

'Who else? He stopped taking bets on me at four o'clock – said he was up to his limit. He made a killing.'

'That will teach them to gamble,' Mum said, piously reviewing the evening.

'So they all bet on you to win?' Dad asked.

'I told them I would. And I conned you into going.'

'Conned me? I wouldn't have missed that for the world.'

'But you've got it wrong Dad. I should have won. He busted *his hand* in the first round.'

'*You're* the one kidding.'

'No I'm not,' Michael said angrily.

'Are you sure? He gave no sign of that.'

'Yes, I'm sure. He had to have it set.'

'Well I'm blowed.'

'I should have noticed and won. He beat me with one hand tied behind his back.'

'Unbelievable,' Uncle Bert said.

'It was a fabulous fight. We'll talk about it later,' Dad said.

'It certainly was, Michael. Your dad kept talking about it all the way home.'

'So did you.'

'Maybe I did – but *my* eyes were dry,' Bert said.

'OK, OK, so I'm proud of my son.'

Michael felt a fraud but was nevertheless relieved at his father's words. He had failed to decode his opponent's eyes in the ring, and he had also misread the embryonic tears and taut expression of a father *bursting with pride* at ringside.

'You went soppy over me?' Michael said and playfully held him in a headlock.

Dad laughed and struggled free, mussing up his hair.

'Your Uncle's exaggerating. I had something in my eye.'

''My eye' – *my eye*!' Michael said.

Their gaze – a moment of deep affection – was interrupted by Uncle Bert's goodnight as he left.

'You going to go to bed or will you have another cuppa first?' Dad asked.

Michael was too awake for sleep.

'I'll have some more tea if you're going to stay up.'

Dad nodded. Michael went to the kettle in the kitchen, filled it and switched it on.

'Anything with it?' Michael asked.

'A couple of biscuits with mine please.'

'Dad, I'm sorry.'

'Sorry for what?

'Losing – with you watching.'

'Not that again.'

'I could have made up for.......'

'Made up for what? What on earth's the matter now?'

'You know – things.'

'What things?'

Michael hovered over him by the kitchen door.

'Always beating you at chess,' Michael said teasingly with a grin.

'Not always,' Dad said. He wasn't amused.

'Let's be honest; you're as bad a loser as me. It must hurt you,' Michael said.

'You cheeky monkey – I'm no bad loser.'

On cue, the kettle whistled at the lie.

'But you always try to win,' Michael called from the small kitchen.

'Sure. Maybe I was a bit hard on you not letting you win.'

Michael poured out the teas and slipped two Garibaldis onto Dad's saucer.

'You *were*,' Michael agreed with mock anger.

'It was for your own good,' Dad called out.

'Really?' Michael said quietly, returning to the room.

'Yes. Really – in the end you had to beat me on merit.'

'*A Boy Named Sue?*' Michael asked with his 'funny clown' expression.

Dad smiled. They sipped their teas. Words deepened into an *I and Thou* conversation.

'How could I take that sucker punch and fail to notice his hand?' Michael waited for a response. None came.

Dad nibbled at his biscuit, listened and stared directly at him, expressionless.

'I failed to make the right moves – the fight was laid out on a plate for me.'

Dad grinned. He was full of smiles that night.

'You think that?' He took another nibble. 'Let me tell you this. I've seen some fights over the years. Remember that night at Wembley I told you about – the Cooper/Clay fight.'

'Yes, I remember, but....'

'Well your fight was on par with them as far as I'm concerned.'

'*His* fight maybe,' Michael said.

'It takes two people to make a great fight and tonight you were one of them.'

'Dad, I was far from great. I missed the signals.'

'I say both of you were great.'

'His hand was *kaput*, Dad.'

'No one watching knew that. He boxed brilliantly to cover it and so did you to protect your *shnozz*.'

'I should have won. He was there for the taking.'

'You were two men giving your very best.'

Men. Michael liked that.

'When you left I thought you were disappointed and upset.'

'Yeah, how many tears of joy do I get these days?' He finished his biscuits. 'I've often told you: believe nothing you hear and only half you see.' His smile radiated yet again.

Michael laughed, moist-eyed.

'But you say that as a cynic. Remember, when Uncle Bert splashed out on that Jag the year his business folded?'

'Michael, it's a rule of thumb. And I'm no cynic.'

'But you say believe nothing,' Michael persisted.

'Did I say disbelieve everything? Assume your senses are infallible and you may succumb to illusions. Don't let them bamboozle you.'

Michael warmed to this homespun philosophy.

'You're absolutely right Dad.'

'At last we agree on something.'

'Yes. I mistook bravery for weakness from three feet away.'

'We all make mistakes.'

All the trouble he had caused as a boy flashed fleetingly across his mind. He paused before he spoke again. He needed to control his feelings. *That* girl had loosened his defences tonight – peeled off layers of armour – let Dad get to him. He didn't want to be over-emotional about it, and set Dad off again, but had to respond.

'Nobody is closer to me than you and Mum and I have misread you for years,' he said in a much quieter, quavering voice.

His father maintained his eye contact and gently and slowly nodded twice to acknowledge the tacit apology.

That conversation went on until the early hours. Mike didn't know it then, but it was clearly a seminal point in his life. It helped set an irresistible path for his analytical mind, his compassion for others, and his chosen career. He reflected on it as the start of his adult life. Dad's comments had helped change him from a youth to a man in an instant. The doorbell heralded his next patient.

CHAPTER NINE

After silence, that which comes nearest to expressing the inexpressible is music. ALDOUS HUXLEY

It had been a long, tiring day. Mike arrived home late, but quickly showered and changed. Revitalised, he was soon driving Helen down to London to meet up with their best friends for a bite and a chance to catch up with their lives.

He slowed and flashed for a car to escape from a side street. The driver gratefully raised his hand. *You're welcome.* Mike was not merely being polite. *Can altruism exist without ulterior motives?* After a few hundred yards the driver exaggeratedly gestured to a large lorry to join the road. *Not the ideal prize!* Theoretically, cooperativeness should mushroom penalty-free. His goodwill *was* reciprocated – his target *had* played the game. Mike played it to increase the chances of someone giving way to him in future. *I'm dawdling in a convoy, and late!* 'Damn it!'

'It's your own fault. You let people in too easily,' Helen said, hardly helping.

'It should make no difference,' Mike replied, attempting to be philosophical and calm. Eventually, the lorry's indicator cheerfully signalled its turn into a transport café, and the car in front turned right.

'*Voilà* – you see.'

The road ahead was clear and he soon caught up with the original traffic in front. 'We're still running late,' Helen said, eager to see everyone again.

Win one – lose one.

They found their friends in the bar, already somewhat mellowed out. 'Hi.' 'Great to see you again.' 'How are you?' These were people Mike and Helen were genuinely delighted to see – kisses and big hugs all round.

'Try some of this. We've got a drop left,' John, their rotund architect friend, gestured.

'Not for me, thanks,' Helen replied.

'Nice bouquet – what is it? Mike asked.'

'A Carmenere – very reasonably priced.'

'It's excellent,' Mike said. 'Another bottle?'

'Absolutely. The night is young,' Liz, John's wife, replied with a giggle.

They were the lively ones. The other, shyer couple, Alice and Archie, were rather thin and anaemic-looking; like the customers you see leaving health food stores. They were music teachers and regularly played in various orchestras.

Mike ordered the wine along with two soft drinks – one for Helen – one for John, who brought the others and remained jovial in spite of his partiality for wine. They had agreed to their dry night, their turn to drive home: Helen less reluctantly than John.

'How long since we were all together last?' Helen asked.

'Must be nearly a year,' Liz replied. She remained pleasantly plump in spite of her regular attempts to slim.

'Nobody's changed,' Helen said.

'That's why it's so great seeing you, Helen. You – all of us – have not aged.'

'None of us seem to have changed since college days,' John said.

'How's your painting going?' Helen asked.

'Well. I've had one or two exhibitions and sold several this year,' Liz replied.

'Great,' said Helen.

'It's the smaller galleries, but I'm happy. One or two good prices.'

'Helen's have been coming on,' Mike said.

'Come off it Mike. I'm not in Liz's class. Nobody would buy mine.'

'I wouldn't wish them to,' Mike replied.

'I love your watercolours Helen,' Liz said.

Mike persisted proudly, 'Helen's latest are excellent.'

'We'll have to come up and see,' Liz said.

In other ways different people – Helen slim, athletic and more reserved – but art brought them close. Always had. True friends.

They ordered some bar food and found a table, chattering away non-stop throughout their meal. A family gathering.

'Mike, you've been rather quiet. How's your private venture?' John asked.

'Fine,' Mike replied.

'He's much happier. The practice is going well,' Helen said.

Mike raised his glass of wine, scrutinised its colour, and proclaimed a toast: 'To the vineyards of Chile,' he said, quietly. He lowered and twirled his glass, playing the connoisseur that he *wasn't*, and sipped from it again. Helen and John shared slightly envious glances.

Replete with the good food, their warm friendship and their extensive exchanges of recent news, they sauntered over to a snug settee and some comfortable armchairs, set by a window dressed with rather faded tartan curtains.

'Come on Mike. You're so reserved. Tell us what *you've* been up to,' Liz said.

Mike felt relaxed in their company and, encouraged by Liz's giggles, amused them with one or two incidents with patients. Liz always managed to bring him out of his shell. *It's strange: I'd probably be more like John if I'd married someone like Liz.* Unusual for him – it was perhaps Liz *and* the wine – he introduced the recent difficulties presented by the (unnamed) Cynthia.

'It reminds me of the Silent Symphony,' Alice said.

'Never heard it,' John boomed.

'No-one has,' Liz said and managed to painfully squeak, 'by the *sound* of it,' before surrendering to hysterics.

Alice and Archie glimpsed at each other, hurt and bewildered.

'Ignore them,' Mike said.

Mike had found a tenuous musical connection to Cynthia's plight – her abstraction echoed the finale of Sibelius's Fifth. The long silent rests that punctured the crescendo were so profound they made Mike's ears buzz. He had forgotten – dismissed John Cage's 4.33. Alice and Archie described how they had performed it many years ago.

'We tuned-up as normal,' Archie said.

'The conductor addressed us and raised his baton,' Alice said.

'We watched closely and awaited his signal to play,' Archie said.

'For unwritten notes,' Alice said.

'We 'played' the three movements – all written as rest bars in the score,' Archie said.

'It was strange – we had a genuine rapport with the audience,' Alice said.

'We did, and were playing as one, turning the pages of the score in unison,' Archie said, as if revealing a state secret.

'It's true. Our eyes were fixed on the conductor – as was the hall,' Alice said, in a similar whisper.

'Amazingly, exactly four minutes and thirty three seconds later we finished,' Alice said.

'Yes, we reached our destination as punctually as a Japanese Bullet train,' Archie confirmed. Gentle and mild-mannered, Archie's eyes were mystical. Mike was astounded.

It was uncanny. Their story was a perfect allegory of how he had gone about his task. *I've sat silently for two full fifty-minute sessions with Cynthia.* He had been the same as them.

Mike's friends agreed that the intensity he described was exactly what they experienced in their profound silence. Moreover, they too were involved in a dialogue – in their case, the 'music'. Everyone in the concert hall heard the sounds of that night, be it the magnified litter of suppressed coughs, or rustling of programmes, or creaks from uncomfortable seats that were integral to a live performance. Most of the musicians experienced more than that.

The 4.33 originally hit the scene in the '50s to responses that it was a gimmick, a joke: nonsense.

'I suppose someone had to write it,' Alice said. 'Nowadays it was generally regarded as inevitable.'

'It at least established a baseline for composing,' Archie said.

'That's odd. It reminds me of scanning a blank canvas,' Liz said.

'I often discover ideas for my pictures, gazing at a bare surface,' Helen said.

'It's the same with me,' Liz said. 'I just stare and stare at the texture.'

'Even the shape and size matters,' Helen said.

'That does get me going,' Liz said and wiggled suggestively.

Helen alloyed her amusement to Liz's raucous laughter with a polite smile. She was rather more reserved by nature.

The comparison of the Silent Symphony and Mike's patient intrigued them. They leaned forward to hear more about his cases.

'Some of it is boring,' Mike said.

'Not to me,' John boomed.

'If I can't see the wood, it is.'

'You see it in the end though, *Monsieur Poirot.*'

'It's not always that easy. Cognition can be a bit of a slog.'

'Cognition? What's Mike on about,' Liz asked Helen.

'It's difficult to say. Think he tells me what he does?'

'But you must have some idea.'

'It's to do with …' Helen began but was interrupted.

Their attention was directed to a car horn. Some minor fracas was going on outside their window.

'Someone had an accident?' John asked.

'No. Trying to park,' Archie said.

A red saloon, attempting to get into a space almost large enough for two cars, was holding up the traffic in both directions. They watched as the driver reversed straight for the pavement, then pulled out again and reversed to a position at least three feet from the kerb. He moved away again, blocking a new, longer line of cars. They were headed by a BMW eagerly coveting the space. Its left hand indicators signalled imminent disappointment. The red car's piercing reversing lights announced another futile attempt to park.

'The guy can't drive,' John said boisterously.

'No. It's parallel parking. I find it difficult, especially with a lot of traffic around,' Archie's more sympathetic, melodic voice protested.

'He's got no spatial awareness...' John amiably but insensitively added.

Mike raised a dismissive eyebrow.

'... or it's bad co-ordination – or both,' John said.

'He doesn't need either, John,' Mike said. 'Top footballers might.'

'Well *he* definitely ain't Premiership material,' John said.

They watched the car's next attempt.

'He needs help – someone to guide him,' Liz said in a motherly tone.

'Yes. He's no different from some of my patients,' Mike said, smiling at her.

'Is he – so how would you treat him?' Liz asked.

He paused – observed her with a furrowed brow. *Go on then, clever clogs.*

'Has he turned towards us?' Mike asked.

'No.....I don't think so,' Liz replied, falteringly.

All of them, Helen included, were perplexed.

'Why should he? So that we can signal how large a space he had?' John said. Puzzled, he parted his hands. A bragging angler.

'No. Not at us – but our way,' Mike said.

'Oh that – and park easily. I often do that,' John said dismissively.

'Exactly. Many people do.'

'Do what?' Archie asked in a whisper.

'His reflection,' John boomed.

'He needs a tiny tweak. That's all,' Mike said, sympathetically releasing Archie from John's unintended put-down.

Through the Looking Glass,' Alice murmured in a trance.

'So are you going to dash outside and tell him?' Liz asked, giggling in anticipation.

'What? And get a bloody nose for his trouble. Men get sensitive over their driving,' Helen said, and laughed accusingly towards them.

'Mike sees life so differently,' Liz said, admiringly.

'Yes, I suppose he does. He would call that one of his NanoMOs,' Helen said.

'A NanoMO?' John asked.

'Merely shorthand for a tiny change or moment that makes a big difference,' Mike replied, with a mumble.

'NanoMO – a NanoMO,' John repeated. 'You shrinks do use some strange names.'

The driver finally turned off his engine and locked the car – half a rear tyre and his incompetence left on the kerb. Helen turned to Mike with her familiar shrug of the shoulders and gently jutting chin. Mike added his full stop to the incident with his usual response of raised eyebrows and a clown-mask smile.

Somewhat enlightened, the group conversation broadened into lateral thinking.

'We know people who had a NanoMO,' John said, his memory triggered by the window.

'Who?' Liz asked.

'That bright couple who bought that house,' John replied.

'I remember. *That* one. They certainly did!'

A house near them had had no takers for over a year, in spite of a strong sellers' market. It was delightful with a magnificent secluded mature garden – and reasonably priced – but had one major flaw. Women lost all interest in the house on seeing the modern fully equipped kitchen.

'It was perfect – any housewife's dream, with every conceivable latest appliance included,' Liz said.

'The fly in the ointment was a window,' John said.

'It was,' Liz agreed.

'At home, women spend seventy per cent of their day in the kitchen,' John added.

'Do we need statisticians to tell us that?' Liz gave a wink to the other women.

'This kitchen had one large window that looked directly onto a high wooden boundary fence,' John said.

'No view of the delightful garden – no view at all,' Liz said dramatically.

'Could they have made another window and moved the sink in front?' Helen asked.

'No other outside wall – even so that would have been costly,' John said.

'They were stuck with a kitchen designed around this offending window,' Liz said, spreading her chubby arms.

'So? How did it sell? Did it go cheaply?' Helen asked.

'It *did* sell – a bit below the asking price. What happened was…'

Apparently the couple allowed the agent to think he had talked them into considering buying the house. They were actually keen. Citing the window, they feigned reluctance. Eventually they made their offer – the first and solitary one received. Firmly rejected initially, it was accepted a fortnight later.

'Huge surprise – the kitchen became the highlight of the house,' John said.

'The new magnificent outlook was utterly captivating,' Liz said.

'The original window surveyed the glorious garden,' John explained mysteriously.

'How did they manage that?' Helen asked.

'With one of Mike's NanoMOs,' John said with a raucous laugh.

'It was all very clever – planned prior to their offer,' Liz said.

'They set up an enormous angled mirror, disguised by a frame and creeping plants. It brought the garden to the kitchen. The *trompe l'oeil* even fooled a couple who'd rejected the house – they were adamant it was a different one,' John said.

'That must be to do with cognition,' Alice whispered to her husband.

'Pre-cognition,' Mike said, with a chuckle into Archie's other ear.

The chatter went on to other examples of lateral thinking, magical illusions, and distortions of perception, until they had talked the topic out and the evening came to an end. On the way home Mike resolved to continue treating Cynthia for the moment, unless he had proof positive that she was an incurable schizophrenic. That Silent Symphony was exactly the spur he needed.

CHAPTER TEN

The Devil is in the detail.

His receptionist, Phyllis, left a phone message from Cynthia's husband asking Mike to ring him. *That's a pity – I'll bet he's cancelling her appointment.* Disappointed, he returned the call but was pleasantly surprised. Cynthia had raised hopes after the last session and was impatient for her next consultation.

'Do you think you can get her better?' her husband asked.

'It's too early to say. But it is encouraging she's happy to see me again,' Mike replied.

Cynthia arrived, murmured a weak hallo that Mike returned. 'I'm very nervous,' she said, after a couple of minutes of silence.

'That's quite all right,' Mike said.

A long silence preceded her next words.

'I was rude not talking to you last week.'

'Rude? You were anxious. That's all.'

'I'm sorry.'

Mike silently nodded, as his father had done that night of the fight.

'Do you think you can help me?'

'I'm going to try my best. Let's concentrate on your history to start.'

Cynthia slowly opened up and began what was to become a marathon dialogue over the coming months. She'd had a desperately unhappy childhood. Mike sympathised and tried to explore her reactions to her past.

'You don't realise how bad a person I am,' Cynthia said.

91

The bare bones of her account pointed to the hard toil ahead. The strong possibility of psychosis remained. Her speech was inordinately slow. What if her husband was right? Perhaps her medication *had* made her worse.

The next day Mike checked with her doctor and went through his notes. Cynthia's symptoms were severe. On diverse referrals, she had been diagnosed as being endogenously depressed, and more recently as a catatonic schizophrenic. Her doctor had prescribed antidepressants in the past. Latterly the hospital had tried out a range of modern psychotropic drugs but Cynthia responded best to chlorpromazine. Although an old drug, it was effective as a basic treatment for schizophrenia but most importantly, it could prevent her getting worse. It had the unfortunate side effect of causing drowsiness and sedation in high doses and could interfere with normal sleep. Cynthia initially responded well to low doses of this medication. They had been upped by the hospital over the past year.

Mike pondered. *Is it the illness or the drug's side effects?* Her medicine could be behind her persistent poor nights. Sleep deficits, whether deprivation or poor quality, have negative consequences: in particular they can interfere with cognitive processes. Her medication might improve matters by lowering her high anxiety levels, but higher dosage could produce daytime drowsiness and worsen her depression.

Mike got home ahead of Helen. She was on a day's locum at a nearby pharmacy. The kids were doing their homework upstairs. He called out, 'Hello,' and merely got a muffled reply. As youngsters they had run to greet him – those days were long gone. He made a cup of strong tea and set one ready to pour for Helen.

She arrived as he sat himself down and received her equally feeble response from the kids. He filled her cup.
'Good timing – I'm dying for a cuppa,' she said and leaned over and kissed him.

They sipped tea, unwinding in each other's gaze.

'Had a hard day?' Mike asked.

'Very busy – one of the technicians was off sick. You?'

'Yes, busy as ever. I've got a dilemma you could possibly help me with. You're familiar with the 20/80 golden ratio that gets quoted by economists?'

'No. Do tell,' Helen said, bracing herself for one of Mike's deeper moments.

'You've heard of 80% supermarket sales generated by 20% of stock lines?'

'Actually no – but do go on,' Helen said, patiently.

'Well I was wondering if it could be applied to medicines.'

'I see what you mean,' Helen said, 'I suppose it might. A small range of cheap generics form the brunt of NHS supplies.'

'No, sorry Helen, I meant dose; efficacy against side effects,' Mike clarified, and offered Cynthia's medication as an example.

'They don't prescribe chlorpromazine much these days, particularly with new patients,' she said.

'It helps in this case but it may be causing side effects.'

'That's no surprise bearing in mind its history.'

'History?' Mike asked.

'Yes, it was found by chance.'

'Was it?'

'Yes, pure serendipity – like aspirin and penicillin – it became the Adam of anti-psychotic drugs.'

'How?' Mike asked. He was amused by the mysterious tone in Helen's voice.

'It was originally developed as an antihistamine. Prescribed as such to the elderly in care homes and patients in mental units, doctors noticed a remarkable improvement in their lucidity.'

'Fascinating. But you haven't answered my question.'

'You aren't the least bit interested are you?' Helen snapped. She was tired out from a frantic day's dispensing and feeling uncharacteristically ratty.

'Sorry, darling; it *is* interesting, but I'm rather concerned about my patient.' Mike's sense of duty prevailed upon her.

'You couldn't apply that sort of ratio to antibiotics, for example, but it could be a useful template for drugs like chlorpromazine,' Helen said.

'Starting from a low dose?' Mike asked.

'Possibly too few side effects to tell.'

'But on the higher regimes?'

'Side effects would certainly increase – possibly disproportionately as you're suggesting – and exacerbate depression,' Helen said.

'Perhaps I'll get her doctor to reduce the dose and see what happens.'

The next day Cynthia's doctor checked with the psychiatrist. They were happy to try out Mike's suggestion to gradually get her from 300mg a day down towards her original 75mg while he was seeing her. In the weeks that followed, Cynthia was less confused, definitely less drowsy, and said she slept better, but was also getting more anxious. Overall she communicated more freely and her husband was pleased that she was more her old self.

Mike spent many hours gathering Cynthia's history. During the weeks that followed, as her medication reduced, she became more alert and slowly the details of her distressing past emerged.

Her mother was an unemployed, inadequate single parent who regarded Cynthia as a burden. Later, when Cynthia was aged six or seven, she got married. The stepfather had sexually abused Cynthia almost from the beginning. Mike's attempts to commiserate and sympathise were dismissed – she blamed herself.

'You all pretend there's some good in me. You won't find any. I am a bad person,' Cynthia again insisted.

Mike put aside that remark to concentrate on getting more facts. It was difficult: she put up a barricade of defences and was reluctant to talk about the matter. Gradually he managed to coax further details out of her.

Cynthia's ordeals began left alone in the house with her stepfather and his so-called 'comfort'. Mike began to extract her anxiety, guilt, and self-disgust. Ignored and chastised by her mother, her stepfather was paying her the attention she craved. His perversion worsened her situation. Her ambivalent responses bonded together. Super-glued, they confused her loyalties – foiled explanations. Mike had found these defences the most difficult to resolve in cases of child abuse. Once she desperately tried to tell her mother. She was dismissed as a liar. Mike had no doubt that her mother had rationalised her own inadequacies. Her guilt put her in denial and projected her anger towards her daughter. She also needed the support of her husband – financially and otherwise – depraved or not.

Mike was genuinely involved and empathic with his patients. But of necessity he concentrated on the clinical nature of their condition. Periodically he may have appeared distant and uncaring as he sifted through their accounts of events, seeking out salient features. With Cynthia he made an extra effort to give perspective on her predicament aligned with kind words and encouragement.

'You can't accept it,' she said. 'It's me – in a way, I enjoyed it – I'm wicked.'

Maybe objectivity reduced his compassion as he probed. Maybe it showed. But he was fully committed to resolve her awful history and relieve her distress. 'You don't get it,' and 'I am a bad person,' were phrases she repeated again and again during sessions. At least she was more forthcoming about her past and her intimate secrets, as her trust in Mike grew.

'I was evil from infancy.'

'All children are naughty – heard of the terrible twos?' Mike replied.

'I mean *evil*.' My mother told me, 'You've got a wicked streak in you.' She said she'd knock it out of me.'

'How did she do that? Did she hit you?'

'Yes. Often. The worst was being locked in the cellar – it was pitch black.'

'For how long?'

'Hours at a time: all day if she was properly angry.'

'She must have treated you better on her good days,' Mike said.

'She didn't have any. She hated me.'

'Surely not – didn't she have a pet name for you?'

'If you can call it that – Cyn.'

Hmm. Freudian. He immediately dismissed that as academic and irrelevant. He concentrated on Cynthia, at the mercy of this inadequate and malicious woman.

Worse was to come. The encounters she initially described had also occurred with at least two or three other men. 'Uncles', her stepfather called them. She saw them hand over 'a tenner or so' and he left her to their dirty deeds. The abuse continued throughout her childhood until she was twelve. It left her convinced that she was a bad and worthless lot.

'How could they *all* have abused me by accident? I must have enticed them,' she said, trying to sort her mixed reactions.

Although she felt abused and feared the unsavoury episodes forced upon her, to some extent she encouraged the advances as they gave her some secondary gains. These men were interested in her and sometimes gave her presents. Since she was the common denominator – she was convinced – she *must* be to blame.

Mike examined how these events had caused such colossal damage. Cynthia's distress was magnified with each case of abuse. The mental confusion and ambivalence of her bonded responses added to her woes. Combined as a set, they created gross psychological distress. She repeated accounts of each episode with consistent details. She also expressed the same reactions and emotions that reinforced Mike's early impression that the recall was genuine rather than false memory. The repeated appalling abuse by these three or four people had to be *one* if not *the* cause of her present illness. No doubt. The resultant supercharged mixed emotions destroyed her self-image.

'You appreciate what astronomical luck you need to win the lottery?' Mike asked.

'Yes. What's that got to do with me? I've never won a penny.'

'Exactly. You're the opposite – you've had extremely bad luck, you've drawn the short straw in life – that's why you've suffered so much.'

Whatever resultant torment each perpetrator had caused, it weighed heavy on Mike's scales. Multiplied exponentially with the subsequent repeated episodes, severe damage had been done: impossible to measure, probably impossible to fully repair. So many people had identified her symptoms as schizophrenia. *They could all be wrong.* Throughout the previous sessions he had seen no definitive signs of psychosis. That all changed in the last minutes of this session.

'You don't get it. I *am* wicked,' Cynthia said. She was even more insistent than usual.

'I'm sure you feel you are, but that may not be true,' Mike said, in vain.

'I am – I'm evil.'

'That's part of your trouble – *thinking* that'

'You may be clever. Some secrets you don't know.'

'Tell me about them.'

'You'll be like all the others. You won't believe me.'

Mike accepted odd perceptions as a patient's truth no matter how far-fetched.

'I'm shock proof. I've dealt with many strange stories. Trust me.'

She drew in deep breaths but offered no response other than a tightly chained vibration of her head.

'It could help you get better.'

She stiffened her resolve but maintained her silence. Her eyes said it all.

'Don't be afraid,' he said.

Her minutes passed as hours. She fought against the long odds: calculated the risks over and over again. Finally she plunged into the abyss. In a hoarse whisper filled with fear, she growled out her secret.

'I've met the Devil,' she said, terrified, her body shaking.

A punch to the solar plexus – it caught Mike completely off guard. He showed no weakness or shock as he rode out the last minutes of the session, focusing on Cynthia's crazed eyes. He knew instinctively that this was a pivotal moment in his fight against her illness. Maintaining his composure, he strained to hold her trust. His father's words came to his aid. *Believe nothing you hear and only half you see.* Mike calmly wound down the session.

'I believe you.'

And he was being truthful. He accepted her perception as skewed cognition. Or psychosis.

'We'll talk about it next week.'

*   *   *

Cynthia was embarrassed by her revelation the previous week. Mike encouraged her to tell him more about her Devil. Its source could help solve her idea of being evil – or prove schizophrenia. She was reluctant to humiliate herself again. She wanted to avoid further exposure to the disbelief others had shown for her story. Mike accepted her account as her truth. He needed to examine the detail. She, once more as a full-grown adult, wife and mother, swore to him that she had seen the Devil. She was certain it had not been her imagination. She had no doubt.

It was that certainty that concerned Mike. Was she, as diagnosed by doctors and psychiatrists, psychotic? Her account returned to the many occasions she had been incarcerated in her mother's cellar. She was convinced that the Devil came to punish her.

'He was tall with penetrating, deep-set, red eyes that sent out a fiery glow,' she said. She waited for Mike to react. He silently studied her, expressionless, with no reaction.

'They coloured the cellar – turned it into his red hell.'

Mike continued to listen without a comment.

'I couldn't escape from him once he arrived.'

Cynthia went on to describe how she cowered in fear until released from her prison. Fantastic as they were, these perceptions were her reality. The description of the cellar events formed a mind-set that had permeated her life. Mike accepted her experience as authentic, fully aware of a fault in her cognition. It had to be addressed by 'the man on the Clapham omnibus,' free from fear, guilt and stress. *What would he make of her story?* Mike became coldly objective.

'Did anyone else ever go down into the cellar?' he asked.

'My mother.'

'No-one else?'

'Apart from the man who read the meter.'

'The Electricity?'

'Yes, him. And I feared he would awaken the Devil,' Cynthia said.

Mike leaned into his chair, lifting the front legs off the ground. He gently rocked to and fro on the rear ones as he weighed and balanced the facts.

'Do you think your tall Devil in the cellar could possibly be electrical?' he asked, with a furrowed brow.

'What do you mean?' Cynthia replied, her intonation a blend of hope and astonishment.

'Two red diodes.'

'Two what?'

'Two red warning lights set high on the wall. Part of the mains equipment,' Mike said.

'The Devil – just two red lights?' Cynthia said in a confused whisper.

Mike docked his face into his steepled fingers – oblivious to the *triangle* he had formed with mirrored fingertips and elbows. He monitored Cynthia's intense expression – and studiously watched the interpretation strike home. Her Devil slowly disintegrated in front of him. The supernatural slipped even further away as he casually collapsed the *triangle* and placed his hands in his lap. The steady motion on the heels of his chair resumed. Cynthia had the kick-start she needed. Mike silently observed her loosen her childhood chains.

She gradually accepted that the Devil didn't arrive shortly after she had been incarcerated. He was not a tall figure. Neither was the cellar turned into a red hell by his penetrating eyes. Her *own* eyes did that. Instantly cast from bright daylight to the blackened basement, they slowly sensitised to the high-set red warning lights. The pitch-black darkness vanished as she gradually detected the red glow filling the room.

'All those years! Ohmigod!' she said.

That was her turning point. Released from Satan she started on her long road to recovery.

Such minor breakthroughs were Mike's Holy Grail. Benjamin Franklin told a progressive tale of a horseshoe nail that lost a kingdom. Mike was obliged to take the opposite direction and wade through a forest of emotional damage to trace often tiny, causal components, from the wrong end of a telescope.

It was only recently that his papers achieved much recognition. His peers already knew crucial factors could produce great changes. To them it was a bit showbiz. Ginger Rogers' performances *backwards and in high heels,* mirrored Mike's speciality – both taken for granted. Latterly, however, his coined term NanoMO had become virtually synonymous with his name as he made his mark in academic circles.

CHAPTER ELEVEN

We are simple-minded enough to think that if we were saying something we would use words. We are rather doing something.
JOHN CAGE

Unusually, Helen had a free week with no locum bookings. Her other voluntary role with disabled children had a half-term break. It was a rare opportunity, so Mike grabbed it and joined her in a day off and some R&R.

They were fortunate. It was a perfect sunny morning, with light cloud and just a slight breeze. After the rush-hour traffic had subsided, they set off – roof down – in Helen's cherished Mazda. Helen adored driving it in these conditions and they both grinned as she negotiated the winding lanes towards the motorway. They planned a jam-packed day together in London.

'I've got to stop at Brent Cross on the way,' Helen said defensively.

'Let's not spoil our day. I hate shopping, especially in malls,' Mike said.

'I'll be done in a flash. I can't get much in my boot,' she said, using her female wiles and fibbing.

In truth she regularly got her golf clubs and trolley to fit into the space. But it was such a nice day: he did love her, and what the hell, as she so often told him, she was not a BMW – a Big Maintenance Wife. As usual she needed a number of items – mainly for other people – birthdays and such.

'Promise you'll be quick.'

'I'll *be* quick, you old grouch.'

The youngest in her family, Helen was used to being patronised as a child. She was constantly curbing Mike's paternal streak. Forty-five minutes later they returned to the car with her credit card a micron thinner. The seven carrier bags did comfortably fit into the deceptively spacious boot.

'Well, that's done. I won't spoil your day out any further,' Helen said. She twisted her head fully round with a strong hint of sarcasm in her smile. She enjoyed standing her ground with Mike.

They parked the car at the tube station. A month ago, after they had topped up their Oyster cards, they had made for the Docklands Light Railway around Canary Wharf and the new City buildings. Helen had said it should be on every tourist's list of freebies: at the top, with New York's Staten Island Ferry and the Vaporettas flowing through Venice.

Today, with its pleasant weather, they chose to get off the Northern Line at London Bridge and stroll up the Embankment, past The Globe and the Tate Modern and then down to the London Eye, where surprisingly few people were queuing.

'It's empty. Let's do it. We may never get a better chance,' Helen said.

'This very moment?'

'Sure. It's a lovely day. It will be fun.'

Mike hesitated. He had a nervous flutter of butterflies – a buzz in his ears. He thought he would be perfectly safe at Grand Canyon, didn't he? Well he was, more or less, thanks to Helen – she had insisted upon the secure rail – he became relaxed behind that. He even stared straight down into the abyss. After that visit he suffered one or two nightmares involving standing, without rails, at the edge of the Canyon. But that was all. He resolved to keep any full-blown panic away from Helen. It might easily set things off with her over Lionel. Since their big row Mike had avoided addressing her fears or revealing his own – but so far so good. Those sources of tension were well below the surface and they hadn't had any further bust-ups.

He searched for an excuse to avoid doing it. On the 'Eye' he would be trapped high up in a pod for thirty minutes. Yet it was another chance to help accommodate his fear. It was more than height – situation-specific – he had to be vulnerable to an impulse to fly. The secure wheel and the enclosed pod presented no such risk. It was a racing certainty. He gambled.

It paid off; it was a beautifully bright day, the views were exhilarating and none more so than to Mike. He peered directly down from the top, unperturbed.

'Was I right?' Helen asked.

Mike stroked her hand, happily relieved she was.

They reached the bottom and dismounted: Helen excited, Mike smiling – two kids leaving a fairground as they meandered away with arms swinging, hand in hand. The idyllic morning had transformed them into teenage sweethearts, or soon-to-be parted, illicit lovers.

'Love you,' Helen murmured as she nestled up to Mike's chest.

'Doesn't show.'

They kissed standing in the middle of Waterloo Bridge.

'Can you beat that view?' Mike said.

'Nowhere else in the world can match it – nowhere we've been.'

It was true. Regularly, after they had an enjoyable evening at the National Theatre or at a concert at the Festival Hall, they would make for that bridge on the way home and take a romantic stroll to end the evening.

After crossing the river, defending sharp appetites from the morning walk, they eagerly made for their favourite trattoria hidden in a side street off Covent Garden. It was a haunt of West End busy bees and appropriately buzzed with a mixture of raucous gossip and impressive business talk and the gentler courtesies of the Italian staff. Perfect *'al dente' pasta alla puttanesca* and a pleasing bottle of *Nero d'Avola,* followed by mint tea for Helen and espresso for Mike, set them up for the afternoon.

Typically English weather, the sky clouded over during lunch. Under even gloomier skies they picked up tickets in Shaftesbury Avenue for the evening's Arthur Miller play. 'It's pouring. We've got no raincoats or brolly,' Helen said, as they came out of the box office.

'We'll make a dash for it. A drop of water won't kill us.' Mike replied.

'Where to?' Helen asked.

'You said you fancied a visit to the National didn't you?'

'Yes, I'm keen, especially with this weather.'

'Well come on then – let's catch that bus.'

They hopped on and got off at Trafalgar Square and ran hand-in-hand into the gallery's refuge. Fortuitously – it again turned out so on this London trip – a talk on Caravaggio was about to start. A group of around two-dozen people assembled at the meeting point. Most were dry and had planned attending. Helen and Mike, and one or two others, were damp and slightly dishevelled.

The lecturer – a good-looking, courteous young man – led them through the galleries. He briefly stopped at religious paintings that pre-dated Caravaggio and set the contrast they were soon to see. He sketched out the artist's life, his rebellious nature and the fact that for years he was sought for murder – he had killed a man in a duel but was pardoned shortly before he died. The group were led to the stopping point for the talk in front of his masterpiece, *Supper at Emmaus*.

Caravaggio used deep shadows in his painting to contrast with illuminated and highly expressive figures. The guide pointed out that he had created what must have been a most disturbing scene for the Church in those days. The words heretic and blasphemy must surely have shared the same narratives as the artist's name.

Supper at Emmaus is set in a common inn. A youthful, robust and a clean-shaven risen Christ sits at the head of a

Spartan wooden table. To his left an astonished man, bearded, older, leans forward, his arms outstretched sideways. Opposite him another man, glances away, bends forward and grasps the table. These are the two disciples to whom Christ has revealed himself. Behind them lurks the innkeeper, unaware of the momentous event.

Mike and particularly Helen listened attentively as the lecturer drew attention to the detail in the still life on the table and the vitality of these figures and how the artist had dared to portray Jesus.

'Culture fatigued, are you?' Helen whispered, with a gentle elbow in Mike's ribs.

'Not at all,' Mike replied with a furrowed brow and a shake of his head to reinforce his muted response. He had found it a most interesting account of how this particular picture had led to a major change in religious paintings. The setting was no longer extraordinary or fanciful. It depicted a mundane scene familiar to anyone then. The inn was ordinary with a bowl of imperfect fruit carelessly set near the edge of the table by the rather uncouth-looking innkeeper.

The lecturer appeared to be an expert on the life and times of the artist. He explained how Caravaggio had cleverly integrated religion and art without overt offence to the Church. This Christ bore no resemblance to paintings preceding his and was identified indirectly by the astonished older man. The talk ended with a brief Q&A and the group's appreciative applause.

Mike had listened silently during the talk. He detected deliberate clues Caravaggio had placed in his painting. He was surprised and marginally disappointed with the lecturer – he made no reference to them. Or was he annoyed with Helen's attentiveness to him? He saved his observations for her.

'Cartier-Bresson would have pressed his shutter at that exact moment,' he said.

'Why do you say that?'

'The position of the fruit bowl.'

'It's on the edge of the table. So?'

'And note the man on the right. His napkin on his lap – a loincloth – his arms outstretched as if he was being crucified.'

'So?'

'In other words he is saying, 'Here is Christ'– it's symbolic! Our guide missed that.'

'But it's a gesture. A split second,' Helen said.

'Exactly – and in that brief moment the fruit bowl was pushed to the edge of the table, jolted by the surprised disciple rather than the carelessness of the innkeeper.'

'Well I think Caravaggio may have tried to represent the world going over the edge,' Helen said, intently studying the painting.

'As our guide suggested?'

'Yes. He's the expert. I agree with him.'

'I'm sure it mainly indicates surprise,' Mike said.

'Are you an authority on art, now?' Helen asked.

'No need to get stroppy,' Mike said. He was irritated, jealous even, by Helen's support for her 'good-looking' guide.

'Can you see any ripples on the water in that flask?'

Mike had missed that one.

'No. You're right.'

'Say sorry?'

'Shan't,' Mike replied and put on his best clown face.

Helen smiled. Mike should have left it at that and stopped digging, but he persisted. 'Perhaps it was more than a jolt. Maybe the disciple brushed the bowl aside, stretching out his arms, without disturbing other items,' Mike said, alerting himself to a weakening argument.

'Perhaps, perhaps, but I'm unconvinced. I think you're rationalising.'

Helen had a natural instinct for psychology.

'It takes much longer to paint than take a photo. Caravaggio must have spent ages painting all the detail in the tableware and food and may have forgotten the ripples,' Mike said, his stubborn persistence confirming her observation.

'Interesting thought – you could be right.'

Helen had no desire to argue and left it at that. With over two decades of marriage behind them she was accustomed to Mike's takes on life. Their relationship suffered few conflicts mainly because of her leniency with him. He appreciated how her gentle nature smoothed over their differences of opinion. Holding her placid hand he led her down to the basement café. The rain persisted. It played a continuous snare roll on the skylights. A pot of Darjeeling was all they needed to refresh their spirits.

'We might as well stay. Let's go next door. It's been ages since we were last in the Portrait Gallery,' Helen said.

'Good idea.'

'How well he's handled the light on that cheek,' Helen said.

'You could never trust that woman. He's caught her smile spot on – ice-cold eyes,' Mike said, as ever absorbed by the nuances artists discovered in famous people. They lingered the remainder of the afternoon absorbed by the galleries, staying until they closed: Helen extolling artists' talents and Mike engrossed analysing gestures, features and expressions.

The rain had ceased. They sidestepped puddles on the way to Gerrard Street and another favourite haunt for supper. After particularly aromatic, especially crisp, crispy duck they walked directly from Chinatown to the theatre and a riveting performance to end the day. Mike had no insights to offer here. Miller's so authentic portrayal of the human condition and the actors' impeccable interpretation said it all.

Outside the tube station, The Mazda dutifully awaited them, bejewelled by raindrops sparkling under the streetlights. Mike steadily headed home as Helen dozed off to the soporific tones of a Chopin nocturne and the comforting purr of the MX5's engine. Such days were priceless to Mike and Helen.

CHAPTER TWELVE

You know, somebody actually complimented me on my driving today. They left a little note on the windscreen. It said 'Parking Fine.' TOMMY COOPER

Mike's journey to the hospital was easier than to the surgery. The ring road led to its site on the border of town. A young black cat interrupted the usual uneventful run. It shot across his front wheels to emerge in his wing mirror – intact from its daredevil exploit. *Eight left*, Mike mused as he glanced in his rear-view mirror, relieved to see the cat safely reach the other side of the road. Behind him, through the morning haze he could barely detect the outline of the long stream of traffic. This was the very stretch that Helen and the kids referred to as *Cognition Road*. It acquired that soubriquet years ago in identical conditions.

Mike and Helen left home early that morning for an Easter break. They had packed the cases and bags and the three youngsters into their ancient Citroen CX Familiale. The children were in high spirits. Over breakfast Claire had confronted Mike over the teasing she had got at school – 'You're as nutty as your father,' they had said. Fortunately she was a confident young girl and parried the jibes with ease. But she had no idea what he did. Mike's generalised description failed to explain. In the car she projected her frustration onto him.

'Daddy, you are supposed to be a psychologist but nobody understands a word you say.'

He had heard it all before. He made no reply.

'Claire!' Helen warned her with a cold stare.

'Daddy, I think they may be right,' Claire said, undaunted.

'Who?' Mike asked.

'The girls in my class: they all think psychology is mumbo jumbo. You never explain – they're spot on.'

'Don't be rude – Daddy's driving,' Helen said.

'You try and tell me then, Mummy.'

Helen valiantly tried to explain, but for all her innate intelligence she was no wiser than her daughter over Mike and his psychology. Claire changed tack.

'Daddy, please, what *do* you do?' she asked.

'It's hard to put into words. I try and help people sort out their problems.'

'How?'

'Mainly by changing the way they view life.'

'Grandpa says you shouldn't believe half what you see,' Amy said.

'He's right, Amy,' Mike said.

'Is that what you do – tell them they're wrong?' Claire asked.

'Not exactly – that would help nobody.'

'What then? I'd like to know,' Claire said, vexed.

'Yeah, me too,' Amy said – keen to be included.

'Can it be that difficult, Dad?' Ben asked.

'Quite simple really – it's to do with – er, cognition,' Mike said, involuntarily mumbling the dreaded word.

The children, often the whole family, sang on long trips: generally pop songs with no other purpose than entertainment. During tedious periods towards journeys' end they would chant the usual 'Why are we waiting?' or 'Are we nearly there yet?' It was unusual for any discord at the *start* of a long journey. Early that morning it was a double surprise. They wove a strong thread of irritation into their aggressive conga rhythm.

'Daddy what's cog*nition*? Daddy what's cog*nition*? Aye, aye, aye.'

Mike glanced at his raucous offspring in the rear view mirror. His eye, caught by the traffic behind – as with today's cat – presented a clear example.

'The road ahead – what do you see?' he asked the reflected faces.

'Lots of cars,' Amy said.

'Yes. Anything unusual?'

'They've all got headlights on,' Ben said, with the trademark uncertainty of youth – ending statements on a rising voice – as if intending a question.

'Right,' Mike said.

'So – Mummy says you always use headlights,' Claire said.

It was true. Mike had researched drivers' reaction speeds. Apart from obvious influences such as alcohol, diverse factors included the visibility of other road users. His joint paper revealed fewer accidents if headlights are used – particularly with bikers. It led to the campaign for them to use headlights, even in the brightest sunshine. Since then Mike drove with dipped headlights, day or night.

'Do cars usually use headlights during the day?' Mike asked.

'Motorcycles do – few cars – apart from us,' Ben said.

'But why have they done so this morning?'

They tried to fathom it out in an uncharacteristic, long silence.

'Check behind you,' Mike said.

They turned round to gaze out of the large tailgate window.

Helen discretely pulled down her sun visor and sneaked a peek from her vanity mirror. She was as surprised as the children. The road was on an East to West axis. The early morning sun was directly behind them. It had burnt off the overnight dew to create a thick haze that obscured the road. Cars were indistinguishable through this miasma – faint shapes dissolving in the distance – driven without headlights on.

'No lights. Weird,' Amy said.

'Weird and dangerous,' Mike said. 'Oblivious to being almost invisible.'

'That's crazy – Daddy explain – I don't get it,' Claire said. She was getting tetchier.

'Claire,' Helen said and cautioned her with what the kids knew as her 'laser beam'.

'Well, how often do people question what they see?' Mike asked.

'Question – how do you mean?' Ben replied.

'Drivers, coming towards us, see the mist and automatically use lights.'

'What if they use *their* mirrors?' Amy asked. The youngest, she surprised Mike with her lateral observation.

'Clever girl – you're right.'

'How's she right?' Claire asked.

'They could see cars behind them in sunshine and *might realise*,' Mike said.

'*Very* clever girl,' Claire said and gave Amy a hug.

'Some people completely ignore their mirrors,' Mike said.

'They're stupid,' Amy said.

'Maybe – but even if they did use them, many would still *think* they needed lights.'

'Would they? Why?' Claire asked.

'It's their mind-set,' Mike said to a chorus of groans.

'Mind-set? *More* gobbledegook,' Ben said.

'Stop being cheeky,' Helen said. She had been intently listening, keen to learn for herself. Mike playing the wise old father was extra entertainment.

'Drivers see the fog – think they need lights – right?'

'Right.'

'If it stays foggy they will keep that mind-set,' Mike said.

'How?' Ben asked.

'They will continue to use lights without thinking.'

'It doesn't matter then. You always do. Mummy says it's a bee in your bonnet,' Claire said.

'In the engine?' Amy asked.

Claire was right. Driving a sunlit car with headlights blazing was a tad idiosyncratic. Mike held to his lecture mode. The children listened.

'The traffic behind us is a danger,' he said with theatrical solemnity.

'Danger – why?' the kids asked.

'They see traffic in bright sunshine. It fixes their mind-set to disregard using lights.'

Without gathering what he meant they nevertheless silently nodded.

'Do you get it – mind-set, sunlight, lights?' Mike was unconvinced they did – justifiably so.

'Not rea-a-a-lly,' they baa-ed in unison.

'They think it's sunny,' Mike shouted.

'So?' they bleated.

'Even seeing fog in their rear mirrors – right?'

Mike grew more impatient. He could never have been a schoolteacher.

'Right,' Ben said.

'But they're hidden in fog. Got it?'

'Okey dokey,' Amy said, and yawned mischievously to her siblings.

'It isn't funny. It can cause an accident,' Mike shouted again – all patience lost.

'No lights – fog – I see,' Claire said, and then patiently explained it to young Amy.

The children argued who was right, who was stupid, who understood.

'That's enough,' Helen said, ostensibly to her offspring but intended for Mike.

'People rarely see other people's point of view,' Mike said despairingly.

'Accept it dear – you're obsessed with driving,' Helen said.

He gave up, hoping that Helen, at least, gathered a bit about cognition.

'Believe nothing you hear...' Claire began, re-quoting her grandfather's mantra.

The others joined in, '...and only half you *see*.'

'Exactly,' Mike said.

Mike was far more tolerant dealing with patients. He would get them to describe their views and opinions and then, wading through a nexus of material, would try and identify what needed to be addressed and corrected. On Mondays, he was free to explore this form of treatment to its limits. His past efforts in the NHS had been difficult to cost empirically. It had been almost impossible to prove its efficacy and value to the closed minds of bureaucrats.

Today's bright start gave a zest to the early morning and increased Mike's good spirits. They remained high from his previous pleasant day off until, that is, he arrived at the hospital car park. As he turned the Saab towards his space, it stalled and cut out. He tried to restart. An acrid smell seeped into the cabin followed by smoke rising from the front grille. He turned off the ignition and opened the bonnet. It was filled with smouldering electrical fumes. *Perhaps it's the coil.* No sign of any coil. This modern engine and its components obstinately resided in a world otherwise insulated from the basic car mechanic skills he had acquired over many years. He disconnected the battery and the smoke relented. He left the Saab straddling two parking spaces.

The clinic was well underway as he entered, greasy-handed, going directly to the Gents to tidy up. He phoned the breakdown services. They would come within the hour. He felt unsettled at having to relate another breakdown to Helen. She insisted on having Japanese cars, like her runabout and her six-year-old Mazda. Both were frugal and bullet proof. All they ever needed was basic servicing. If he was honest with Helen he would admit he even enjoyed driving the MX5, rather than complain he had to rake the seat to accommodate his 5′10″ frame, in order to see through the low windscreen. Helen unreservedly trusted her cars, unlike the old Citroen and Mike's current choice.

Mike, concentrating on a tricky case, had no further qualms until the breakdown man arrived and inspected the car. 'It's too big a job for me,' he said.

'You can't help?'

'Sorry,' he said, then feebly suggested with considered wisdom, 'Four years old, 50K on the clock – it's a pity the car didn't catch fire. It's probably worth more as a write-off.'

Mike was shocked at this dismissive attitude so prevalent in a throwaway society. He braced himself for the potentially large bill. The breakdown man took the car away for Mike's garage to assess on arrival.

Mike concentrated on his patients, hampered by concerns over Helen: the anticipated repeat of her reaction the last time she had to collect him. Then, four months after he had bought the two-year-old car from a dealer, it was the belt-tensioner pulley that had disintegrated, leaving him high and dry in remote countryside. On that occasion it was covered by the residual guarantee, but the inconvenience it caused was way beyond any of the minor hiccups the aged Citroen suffered. Mike had rapidly learned to identify and cure those on the spot. He enjoyed what he called the car's character. He would triumphantly flaunt the dirty hands that removed and cleaned grimy timing sensors or reset and tightened the jubilee clips on loose air intake collars. Those were trivial breakdowns.

The Citroen did have *one* repetitive design fault – failing roller bearings on the trailing arm of the rear wheel suspension. These were way beyond Mike's limited skills and tools. They needed replacing every sixty to seventy thousand miles, but gave ample warning of their demise with a characteristic clickety-click over bumps. An expensive job at a main dealer but Mike found a bearing engineer who was delighted to keep the grand old girl going, for trifling sums.

In spite of Helen's hint each year for a newer, more reliable car, it carried them two hundred and fifty thousand miles until terminal rust intervened. That two and a half litre, four-cylinder engine continued running as good as new to the end. Here in a more modern car Mike was facing major repairs or a replacement engine after no more than fifty thousand miles.

Helen failed to come to terms with Mike's relationship with a coldly mechanical car. She could fully appreciate his affection for his old tennis racket and the impassioned crush he had on his new putter. She had similar feelings for her own sports equipment. She also empathised with the tragic account of how he lost his favourite, perfectly balanced, cricket bat at college. She was fond of her sports car but with Mike, cars, and that old CX in particular, were full-blown love affairs. Aside from her jealousy of that demanding mistress she also found the ride 'wishy-washy'. Mike loved the way it cornered, with hips sashaying. It was sensational. Helen harshly dismissed its unique hydraulic suspension as wallowing at sea. She had to sit in the front. She found the rear seats induced severe nausea. By contrast, Mike would go on about its 'sweet nature'.

It was organic and quirky by any standard – particularly on its introduction in the mid '70s. It was all soft touch. Mike caressed the steering wheel unimpeded by its single spoke. The brake pedal responded to his lightest foot pressure – the car instantly halting as his accomplished tango partner. Most of all, Mike was ever-captivated by the graceful start to each journey, as this sleek goddess attained her full majesty with the slow, deliberate rise of the suspension prior to moving off. Helen was convinced this was somehow priapic. She also behaved as if his fiddling around under the bonnet was some weird form of sexual foreplay. If this rival interrupted an evening out with her husband by commanding Mike to administer such TLC, she could get quite frosty. 'Why on earth can't you get a reliable car like mine? Japanese: a Toyota or Honda?'

'Boring, bland – no character,' Mike answered.

'Character! Faults, you mean.'

'I'll soon have her up and running,' he replied, unruffled, as he methodically adjusted a component.

'Haven't you enough to do with your patients? Do you have to *treat* cars as well?' Helen knew Mike for what he was. She tried hard to remain supportive and loyal, even to his wayward concubine.

'Patience. One more minute and she'll be as right as rain.'

'You're crazy. You love it more than me. It's your mistress,' she said dismissively.

'*I'm* crazy? He said. 'You're jealous. You must be even crazier!' That kind of banter usually ended in laughter once the mechanical fault was rectified.

*　　*　　*

A mother, a victim of the child support system, became the subject of the weekly group assessments. Mike soon forgot his personal spot of bother. It was agreed that social resources would be responsible for this patient's welfare. The psychology unit would be on hand as monitors. The psychiatrist was adamant she should be put on antidepressants, being in such a bad state with its attendant risk of suicide. They all concurred and the pharmacist agreed to keep a check on her progress and compliance. She was also to get support from one of the trained counsellors in social services.

Mike was saddened by this case but knew they were doing the best they could. CBT, as cognitive therapy became named – measured on a behavioural scale – had its limits. As the meeting ended, Mike was buzzed on his pager to take an outside phone call. In the blurred scenery of the rushed morning's traumas he had forgotten a promise to return the call of a desperate patient. *Damn it – how could I?*

But it was Harry from the garage. Mike braced himself for gloom and despondency in the anticipated verdict.

'It's all done Dr. Daniels,' Harry said, with a chirpy squeak. 'Can you collect or shall I have it dropped off at the hospital?'

Mike was stunned.

'It's ready?' he asked.

'Yes, it wasn't much. The coil pack was burnt out. We unbolted and replaced it.'

Joy of joys! Mike could sense the pleasure the jovial Harry felt and imagined how his more than adequate body wobbled with glee as he imparted the news. The large flat unit he had noted smoking on top of the engine was a modern electronic hybrid coil.

Harry's lad dropped the car off later that day and Mike pragmatically determined to keep today's saga from Helen. Deliciously guilty – he was a bit crazy exactly as Helen said. She was no fool. He was falling for the Saab as his new mistress.

CHAPTER THIRTEEN

When a father gives to his son, both laugh: when a son gives to his father, both cry. JEWISH PROVERB

Mike had married out or, as Helen put it, she had 'married in.' He was even less religiously observant than his parents. The children had been brought up as reform Jews. Six years after Amy, the youngest, was born, Ben turned thirteen. His bar-mitzvah was a low-key affair with a modest party for the immediate family and a few friends. But his big present was the 'backpacking adventure with Dad' he had asked for to celebrate the start of his manhood. Mike tried to assuage the girls' jealousy with a promise of a special trip when they were older.

'Older? I'm nearly *seven*,' Amy said.

'How can we be sure you'll keep your word?' Claire asked.

'Has Daddy ever forgotten a promise?' Helen replied.

Mike warmed to Ben's idea from the start. Helen and the kids were the most important things in his life. But he felt lately that his job, their homework, their growing up, had pulled him somewhat apart from his children. Ben had developed into a cool, pensive lad; studious, less interested in sports, but shared his father's sense of humour. The trip was a great chance for them to bond, away from Helen and the girls. They thoroughly enjoyed being in each other's company.

Ben was interested in the sciences and was set on physics at university after the hurdles of GCSEs and A-levels. However, he had a broad interest in all subjects at school. He was particularly fascinated by history and geography, with romantic

119

notions of other cultures and their past. An odd choice for Mike but Ben was insistent; he craved to explore Guatemala: the Mayans were one of the few ancient civilizations that remained intact today. It was his call. Brutality still threatened that country with rebels, robbers and political unrest. Helen overheard them discuss that.

'Mike this sounds dreadfully risky. You can't take him.' Helen said, ever nervous, ever sensing danger.

'I've checked it out with the Foreign Office and travel agents. We will follow guidelines and be perfectly safe,' he tried to assure her.

'Guidelines! What do those people care? I'm not letting him go.'

'Do you think *I* would put him in any danger?'

'He's a boy.'

'He's a young man.'

'So was Lionel.'

'Helen, I'm as concerned as you. But he's going to leave the nest one day – fend for himself – then what?'

'I can't help it. I'm really worried about you going.'

'He'll be with me. It'll be fine. I promise.'

'How can you promise safety?'

'I am going to keep my word to him. We'll take every precaution. I promise you that.'

Helen relented – her stomach and heart overruled by Mike's logic – knowing she would blame herself if anything happened to them.

So off they went: father and son, *both* on an adventure. On arrival they moved directly from the sprawling city to the countryside. They cheerily roughed it, using local buses full of farmers and peasants and livestock, rather than take taxis or tourist minibuses. It was safer. Buses were large and slow, weighed down by triple the passengers they were designed to carry. However, they were a much surer bet to reach their destination, even allowing for the odd breakdown. And their passengers would have more protection in a crash than most of the tearaways on the road. The latter placed their lives on the line each journey. Flowers marked the losses every few hundred yards. Apart from accidents the country harboured bandits. They saw tourists as soft targets. It was sensible to keep a low profile and good fun to mix in with the locals. They had heard of two Canadians, stopped on the road a few months previously, losing their lives for the sake of their cameras and a few dollars. Mike took calculated risks, none foolhardy, and regularly sought advice from locals and in the absence of a tourist office, the police.

They were magnetised by Guatemala's cultural environment from the off. It was as exotic as they come. Ancient Mayan history saturated the museums they visited. The hybrid Catholic religion – a legacy of the conquistadors – was deeply venerated in the churches they entered. People thronged the bustling markets: markets scented by the abundant fresh produce, the bouquet of burritos and tacos and addictive wafts of grilled fish and fried chicken. Markets decked with thousands of vivid fabrics and garments. Markets displaying galleries of hand-painted wooden masks, musical instruments, furniture and other diverse artwork and woodwork. Markets resounding to the cacophony of stall-callers and bartering, pipes and bongos, cocks crowing and dogs barking. Urchin children, grubby but healthy and full of mischief and smiles, swarmed anywhere they went – amicably after a coin or a dollar for a shoeshine. Mike and Ben rapidly adapted to the local customs and food. They even acquired a smattering of Spanish. For days they had been incommunicado with the outside world or their own civilisation, apart from meeting the odd, intrepid, fellow explorer.

And the scenery! One particular morning in Panajachel, they hired a small outboard motor boat to potter around the exquisitely beautiful Lake Atitlan. Magnificent volcanoes surrounded it, sensually veiled by the early morning mist. The little craft puttered along its casual course until they came upon a small Mayan village, set high above the water. A semi-circle of local women standing knee deep in the water, decorated the shore. All were clothed in traditional hand-woven multi-coloured fabrics. The women exchanged smiles and waves with Mike and Ben as they tied the boat to the rickety wooden landing platform.

The human rainbow returned to its baskets and the task of doing the weekly laundry in the lake. The tiny green boat claimed its place in the landscape as they approached the path rising through the verdant grass. It was surrounded on both sides by vibrant acres of maize and vegetable fields that flourished and rose up the fertile volcanic soil. In the distance, one or two local farmers could be observed languidly going about their labours under their typical broad-rimmed, cowboy-style straw hats – the same headgear the two backpackers sported, bought in Chichicastenango's market. They gazed down to the receding shore and tried to absorb the incomparable magnificence of the scene. Saturated with this visual paradise, they entered the village, where they were greeted with the heart-wrenchingly poignant sound of Billie Holiday's *Strange Fruit,* oozing out of a doorway. It stopped them in their tracks. They silently listened. Mike noted the giveaway sign in Ben's eye as his own emotions welled up.

Ben chose Tikal and its ancient temples, set deep in the jungle, as the major cultural site on their itinerary. The internal flight to Flores was *Hobson's choice* on a small, old and rickety Russian propeller plane. Its London Transport-style bench seats would have been enough to deter the most seasoned traveller. Ben had no qualms, thinking it was a bit of a laugh. Mike had none either. His secret fear was unconnected to aviation and, anyway, he was convinced that he was more or less cured after the Grand Canyon and The Eye. In spite of all his anxiety, Mike had only succumbed to his fears once, many years ago: that brief episode in the Lake District.

A guide persuaded they hire him for the morning to tour the ancient Plazas and get a taste of the surrounding jungle. He left them free to enjoy the remainder of the day. They came to the base of Temple II. It was reduced to a small, dark, *triangular* shadow by a mendacious overhead sun. Mike was unreceptive and immune to any warning or mysteries that might reside at this once-sacred site. Horatio or not, he didn't acknowledge Hamlet's philosophy – *or Jungian symbolism.*

Ben suggested they climb the Temple's steep steps and get a bird's eye view of the whole complex and the famous Jaguar Paw Temple opposite.

'If you're up to it, Dad.'

'Cheeky monkey – I'm fitter than you.'

Mike relished that sort of challenge, especially from his own son. He agreed without a moment's hesitation. It was a long haul up the high pyramid in the humid heat and, though pretty fit, they were both glad to reach the top. They sat on the stone platform and reclaimed their breath from the long ascent. The astonishing scenery took it away again.

'Whew! Fantastic! Well – we've done the hard part,' Ben puffed as he snapped smiling photos of his Dad from their lofty position. Ben couldn't have been more mistaken. Unease began to creep into Mike's being, minute by minute. Anxiety competed with the stupendous view. They made towards the stone staircase, for the descent. Mike reached the first step.

He looked down.

The thunderbolt hit hard and true. Sheer panic. Heart thumping, throat constricted, he felt the taut, downward pull of gravity. He could scarcely pick out the slight indentations of the steps they had ascended on that steep, almost vertical slope. People below were like flies climbing up and down, clinging to a flush wall. Overwhelming giddiness in his head sent an accelerating spin sensation through his body. It made his ears pop and stomach churn. His legs weren't jelly: they were liquid. One false move, one involuntary slip, could propel him headlong down to his death. He stepped back into the middle of the stone platform and pushed his head into the corner of the square Mayan archway behind him. Almost immediately he succumbed to the most violent retching he had ever experienced.

'Dad – you OK?'

'I'll be all right in a minute. It must be something we ate in the market.'

Ben waited for a sign of recovery. None came: the opposite, he saw his father's face drain of colour.

Mike was living all his nightmares at once, real time, without the sanctuary of waking. He had no escape. No way down. The ropes had snapped: the ladders had fallen. He would be stuck up here forever. How could he possibly manage that horrendous, long descent? Terrified. Trembling. Adrenalin coursing. Heart pounding. Hyperventilating. Sweating – saturated by fear. In a frozen panic – he was helpless.

'What is it, Dad?'

'I can't... it's hard to explain.... difficult for you to understand.' Mike hesitated in overt distress.

'Is it to do with what happened in the Lake District?'

Bingo. The question jolted Mike; defibrillated his brain.

'You remember that? It happened years ago.'

'How could I forget it? It was *my* fault wasn't it? Nothing to do with the café's food.'

'You thought that? You're partly right,' Mike said, his colour improving.

'I remember the way you stared at me – same as today. Terrified. I must have scared you stiff. You seemed so angry, blamed me.'

'Blamed you?'

'That wild stare in your eyes did – what is it, Dad?'

Mike took a moment to reply then slowly raised his head from his hands. His almost mechanical responses had helped his brain to re-engage. Temporarily at least, away from the edge, he had some respite from his dire situation.

'You must promise not to tell anyone – especially your mother.'

'Not even Mum?'

'Particularly Mum – how upset she gets – I'll tell her at the right moment. You've got to keep it between us.'

'It's a promise. I won't tell a soul. What is it? How can I help?'

'You are absolutely right about Surprise View. I am amazed you grasped it was to do with you.'

They went over that day together.

'It wasn't the lunch that made me sick. You are right. But neither was it your fault.'

An unwelcome vague memory surfaced. He forced it down again into its dungeon. Should he expose everything to Ben; his shame and guilt, his inability to deal with it, his feeble coping ploys, and his failure to cure himself? *My deceit with Helen. What a rotten role model.* Mike sought another answer: another outcome, any other possible option. But he had no choice. He had to unburden himself.

'Ben, I've got to explain. But you must keep it between us.'

'Absolutely, Dad – I'm a man now, aren't I?'

'Yes, you're a man. So it's man to man?'

Ben gravely nodded. Mike noted the bright sparkle in his eye. It echoed his response with his own father. He lacked his father's integrity. He was using this moment for his own salvation.

'I have a secret. I'm afraid of heights,' Mike began.

'How come?' Ben interrupted, 'Grandpa told us what a terror you were as a child: how you were fearless climbing trees.'

'That was true once – then it all changed.'

'But Mum says how you love heights.'

'Grandpa told you about not believing everything you hear.'

'Yes – so do *you*.'

'The truth is I have a sort of phobia. At the hospital they would say it was petty – think me stupid. I've tried to cure myself without bothering anyone else.'

'What about Mum?'

'Her brother Lionel: why she stopped you getting a bike? It would only add to her worries.'

'How? Why? When?'

'Whenever I try to desensitise myself – up mountains, for example.'

'You really *don't* like climbing?'

'And Mum thinks I love heights,' Mike replied, shaking his head.

'Do you *know* why you're like that, Dad?'

'Yes, I think so.'

'You once say that was half the problem – finding the source.'

'It is. I've dealt with it,' Mike lied, curtly, as obscure images of a dark secret flashed before him. His long forgotten crime exploded into life: the police, the courtroom – the horror of it all. Within seconds he re-buried those memories under layers of fear, guilt and shame.

'So what was it?' Ben asked.

'I failed… to keep a *promise*. It caused some trouble,' Mike said, defensively: reluctant to broach the subject any further.

Ben latched on to the word and shot off at a tangent – to Mike's relief.

'So that's why you're obsessive.'

'Obsessive! Who says I'm obsessive?'

'Everyone – Mum especially. You *always* keep promises.'

'Is that so bad?'

'No. But maybe that's why you are as you are.'

'Perhaps. But I'm stuck with a fear of heights.'

'What about your treatment?'

'It hasn't helped. I once believed I had conquered it – but I haven't.'

Ben was sympathetic. 'So tell Mum. Why would she connect that with her brother? If you explain it would make it much easier for you – and Mum.'

'I'll think about it but not a word from you.'

Ben nodded without further comment.

Mike unexpectedly felt some comfort that he had told him. He would love to share that with Helen. With Lionel in the mix, it would be harder to do. Ben carried a small part of his burden but, fortunately, responded calmly. He offered no criticism, no overreaction: merely down-to-earth good sense.

'Of course we'll get down,' Ben said.

'So *stupid* – I didn't even consider it on the way up.'

'We'll do it slowly and surely.'

Mike was more himself but somehow had to make it down. He forced himself to the rim. He saw it wasn't the sheer drop seen in his panic. But it was very steep. *No handrail – nothing to cling to – damn the Mayans.* It was one long, bare stairway, inclined no more than thirty-odd degrees from the perpendicular. According to their visitors' guide they were one hundred and twenty five feet up. The approach to that first downward movement terrified him.

Ben calmly and clinically took charge. Mike gladly let him. It was a relief.

'You're with me, Dad. I'll help you. We'll take it gently – step by step.'

The child is father to the man. Some man: some child. Mike braced himself for the dreaded, long descent he knew he had to make.

The first step was the most terrifying. With no rail to grab, no support behind to lean on, Mike's heart was pounding. If he lost his balance, his hands would only clutch at thin air. Mike's quivering foot reached out for the step: or possible oblivion.

Ben guided him down sideways, and repeatedly ordered him to 'concentrate on the step.' Mike's task became less onerous as they established a rhythmic approach towards safety. Halfway down they paused for a break, seated on the warm stone, scanning the Plaza. Mike felt surprisingly relaxed. He was going to make it. Perhaps, even, he was free from his demon. Maybe this intense traumatic exposure – this enforced flooding therapy – had drowned his fears forever; had cured him. He regained his feet. That notion was short-lived.

He looked down.

The steps reverted to the perpendicular. Somewhere, a tiny switch re-set to 'on'. He was chained to his nightmare again. Worse still, he had no respite at this level. No platform to retreat to: no escape. He glanced up. The wall of hewn stones above threatened to lean forward and push him headlong and down – down the remainder of the stairway. His head spun, seized by nauseous fear once more.

'Dad, Dad – deep breaths.'

'Yes – deep breaths,' Mike said, thinking *blow into a bag*. 'Sorry Ben.'

'It's OK – slowly – sideways again. No, don't look below – eyes on me, Dad. Now, focus on the step.' Ben's enforced rhythm came to the rescue once more.

Relieved, sweaty and exhausted, they at last placed their feet on the Plaza floor. They drained the remainder of their water. Mike and Ben peered up and watched others make their steep descent. They did so sideways – and with great caution. The Temple menaced even from the ground. Most people moved slowly along the length of each stone – reluctant to take the next step down – with one extraordinary exception. A young man made a bounding full frontal descent from the top of the tower. On reaching *terra firma* he casually strolled past them. They gawped open-mouthed as his expressionless, oriental features broke into an ear-to-ear smile. He called out to a friend in Japanese.

Shortly afterwards, the pendulum swung back towards Mike's take on the monument. An overweight tourist in tent-sized shorts arduously clambered up the first forty feet of ancient stones. He stopped abruptly, turned his head, and froze into a terrified statue. He was immobilised by hidden forces beyond his control. Eventually he made his tortured way down on his stomach, clinging to, then releasing, every step with his fingertips until he reached the bottom, his shirt glazed with perspiration.

CHAPTER FOURTEEN

Presidents, vice-presidents, and heads of big agencies are opening their minds to accept psychic phenomena, because they know it works. URI GELLER

Helen was relieved and the girls excited immediately they heard them, hidden behind the screen. They traipsed out of Arrivals – suntanned, smiling, sporting their peasant straw hats, and whistling that Laurel and Hardy tune – a bonded father and son.

'Fantastic. It was great,' Ben told his sisters.

'We had a terrific trip, Helen. Thanks for letting us go,' Mike said. They shared a longed-for kiss.

'Letting you go? We were pleased to have the house to ourselves, weren't we girls?' she ribbed, relaxed at last by their safe return. 'So, tell us all about your adventures. What was the high point?'

Neither cited Tikal. Their exotic stories shortened the journey home and continued well into the night until they were all tucked up in bed. The house was asleep. Mike lay listening to the familiar soft clicks of the cooling radiators and the tippy-toe curiosity and feathery sprints of the mouse in the loft and the muted barn owl calls outside. Imperceptibly at first a discordant sound interrupted the peaceful nocturne. It disturbed Mike's prelude to sleep. Helen was sobbing.

'What's the matter?'

Helen silently shook her head.

'Come on. Tell me,' Mike said, holding her close.

'It's trivial. It's the relief. I was so worried about the two of you.'

'I told you we would be safe and we were – as promised.'

'You were never in any trouble? No dangers?'

'Of course not – safe as houses,' Mike lied. *No way will I mention that.*

'I was terrified one night. I sensed – knew that your lives were at stake. It was horrible.'

'How could you be so silly?' *Could she have? No. That's stupid.*

'All's well. Sorry to spoil your first night home,' Helen said, pressing her lips to his.

Their kisses soon turned to passionate lovemaking, as intense as it had been since newly-weds.

Mike woke the next morning filled to the brim with a warm love of life, eager to return to work. The dark blue 95 coasted through the country lanes, towards town. The stereo randomly selected the bright crystal sounds of Miles Davis playing *So what*. It formed a perfect soundtrack for the scenery around him. Finely drawn trees were budding into life and long-lost rural hues restored by the morning sun. Mike might have chosen *Mahler's Fourth* to accompany this glorious start to the morning. The first movement conjured a picture of a country ride in an open carriage drawn by a happily trotting horse. But the inspired jazz was equally hitting the mark and, with the visual splendour of early March, induced a cocktail of endorphins to suffuse his head.

Mike loved the synergy of music with other stimuli. This morning's frisson triggered a cherished moment from Guatemala. The compressed bud of his memory burst into full bloom as he continued his casual drive through the spring countryside. He recalled the simultaneous affect of *Strange Fruit* on him and Ben. It left them with an indelible impression to keep for the rest of their lives. Mike relived the incongruity and its instant emotional impact. The intense memory was vivid – as if captured on silver by Cartier-Bresson. It condensed all the experiences of their trip into a single moment.

Ben had chosen well – Guatemala was steeped in ancient history. Mike was strangely fascinated by stories of horrendous brutality inflicted over many centuries by invaders and dictators and even by their own customs. These persisted in recent years with the scars of maimed bodies in evidence all around. Men in most villages were either very young or geriatric: the others killed – victims of avarice and alien doctrines. Yet in the old capital of Antigua and the surrounding countryside the human spirit prevailed. However, the splendour of the scenery and the smiles and hospitality were tainted by suppressed pain and suffering. That was a harsh fact: the incongruity.

Mike's memories retracted once more into storage as he arrived at the clinic. Several urgent messages awaited his return. The immediate penance for his days of pleasure focused on the young behavioural therapist, who had been having problems with her patient. Mike had intended to advise her before he left. He had forgotten. She was upset that her adherence to his standardised schedule for treating a spider phobia was making her patient worse. The session went so badly the previous week that the patient, in tears, cancelled further treatment. The therapist was annoyed with Mike for dropping her 'in it' but tried to avoid being judged incapable.

'Perhaps we're giving the wrong treatment.' She had a distinct edge to her voice.

'Wrong? What do you mean?' Mike asked, flabbergasted, unused to criticism.

'We could try an alternative method. Flooding perhaps?' she imprudently continued.

'Flooding? Where did you get that idea? Don't you have any compassion?' he replied. Not simply annoyed with her – he was extremely angry with himself.

'It was in our course.'

'And it can stay there. Nobody uses it here.' He was unusually abrupt.

'But I read…'

Mike cut her short. She had dragged him to the top of Tikal.

'It's all very well in theory. Think of the horrors you would put that woman through, trapped in a room full of spiders until she stops screaming. Flooding! It's useless.'

That was for sure. The mild dose he had experienced at the Canyon point with no safety barrier had no effect. His problem remained. The terrifying experience at Tikal was full throttle flooding. He dreaded ever going through that again. It was the most extreme form of behavioural treatments – hopeless as a therapy. It had momentarily resurrected his suppressed crime. The residual guilt and shame made him doubly cross. Cross with himself, not his assistant. It was his fault, nor hers. *He* had forgotten the patient. He had certainly managed to upset this young therapist further, whatever his excuse.

'But if it could cure her?' she said.

Mike exploded. 'Don't ever mention flooding again,' he shouted. It was completely out of character. Few people had seen him in a rage.

'I can't continue li..ke th..is,' her voice began to break up.

Mike came to his senses and grabbed the reins. 'I'm sorry. Forgive me.'

The apology calmed her down. He was out of order and, he admitted to her, probably stressed. Poring over her records longer than was necessary he checked how she had carried out the desensitisation programme.

'You've done it perfectly correctly.'

'I have?'

Her innocence pained him with some deserved discomfort.

'I'm to blame. I'll call the patient and see what I can do.'

'Thank you,' she murmured, relieved of the responsibility.

'I apologise for being angry with you.'

She shyly smiled. It gained him some comfort – utterly undeserved.

Mike went to his desk. 'Mrs Jenkinson? – Mike Daniels – I'm head of the psychology department at the hospital.'

'Thanks for phoning but I must tell you, therapy's making me worse. I cancelled...'

Mike interrupted her, 'I'm so sorry. My fault.'

She quietened down.

'I intended to sit in on your last session but was called away from the clinic,' he lied. *No point telling her about my great trip.*

Soothed by his calm voice, Mrs Jenkinson was persuaded to listen, and after some resistance, agreed to see him.

The young therapist went through her notes with Mike and gave a thorough appraisal of the patient. She had a long medical history of a relatively minor and manageable nature. Recently it had developed into an acute reaction to spiders. She had seen another behavioural therapist without success some months ago. It had become so severe that whenever a spider turned up at home she had to check into a hotel for a day or so. She reacted to any hint or mention of spiders.

Mike suggested that her condition might have worsened because of some other unattended matter. If so, that could produce free-floating anxiety. And *that* could attach to and magnify her long-standing phobia.

Mike again assured the therapist she had acted correctly. Maybe Mrs Jenkinson would continue her treatment after he had seen her. The underlying motor behind her phobia must have revved up substantially. It was futile to make any further attempts to desensitise her to spiders until he had addressed the why and wherefore of this destructive force.

Mrs. Jenkinson had been happily married for eighteen years and deeply loved her husband. He was some twenty years her senior. Financially they were fine; her husband had a good pension coming soon, for a comfortable retirement.

'Do you have other episodes of anxiety?' Mike asked.

'Yes,' she replied. 'Terror attacks. They come out of the blue. I go into a blind panic.'

'You feel under attack, unsafe?'

'Yes, exactly.'

'Describe how these panics start and finish – how you cope.'

'I don't. They begin at home – alone. They stop as soon as my husband comes in.'

'You must get desperate for him to return?'

'Very. It's unbearable if he's late. It gets worse and worse by the minute.'

Mike noted her chin quiver and a teardrop form in the corner of her eye. 'Is it comparable to your fear of spiders?' he asked. That opened the floodgates.

'Yes,' she answered through sobs. 'It's the same panic, the same terror.'

Mike was intrigued. Why did these disparate triggers provoke similar reactions? He investigated further. In the phobic situation she describes the home as contaminated by the spider – its *presence* the essential ingredient. Her remedy is to leave home and stay in a hotel.

During the panic attacks she feels the home is incomplete – with the *absence* of the husband. Terrified, she remains at home until the attacks are relieved by the return of her husband. The two reactions are, as she said, 'the same' but the conditions are the opposite sides of the coin. The presence of the spider is on one and the absence of the husband on the other. Both produce off the scale anxiety levels.

She exhibited the primitive human instinct of danger and death linked to spiders. However she didn't dwell on features often emphasised by others with the phobia. She scarcely commented on hairy legs or the horror of eight legs creeping along, or rushing about, or hiding, waiting to strike, but was especially anxious about their colour.

'What does black mean to you?' Mike asked.

'Bad things – sinister and dangerous,' she replied.

'You mentioned death earlier. Perhaps black suggests death?'

She accepted that instinctively black, death and spiders were mutually linked. Mike hinted at another connection – the spider and her husband. She gave a slight shudder. He left it at that until the following week.

*   *   *

'We established your spiders represent blackness, covert fears, death. You described your reactions to the spider and your husband's absence as the same?'

'I think you may be right. I've questioned myself a lot about that – they may be connected.'

'How? Are you saying spiders represent your husband?'

'Maybe. I definitely feel threatened by that idea.'

'That's the third *maybe*. Connected? You used the word connected – in what way?'

'I haven't a clue but it bothers me.'

Mention of the age gap with her husband made her panic. His approaching retirement set off a stronger reaction – a torrent of tears. A reservoir of hidden fears and free-floating anxiety fed her phobia, increasing its severity.

'I'm afraid he'll die and leave me alone.'

The anticipation and fear of that repressed portent had terrified and paralysed her for months. Her anxiety had been a shield. With a new, more rational, perspective her panics subsided. Mike sent her for a new attempt at desensitisation. She responded well to further behavioural therapy from her delighted therapist. 'She even held one in her hand!'

Helen was distinctly off-hand as he arrived home that evening.

'What's up?' Mike asked

'Up's the word. I thumbed through your *Lonely Planet.* It carried a warning. Climbing Tikal's temples is dangerous. People have died falling down those temples!'

'We're home safe and sound aren't we? And how many die on the roads?'

'Is that all you have to say? You risked my son's life.'

'*Our* son – and he was fine.'

'Fine! Fine you say. I've spoken to Ben. He couldn't look me in the eye. He was obviously hiding the truth. You dragged him up – you terrified him, didn't you?' Helen was at boiling point.

'Ben was perfectly all right. *I* was scared.'

'You scared – you bloody liar! I saw the photo – you smiling your face off at the top – you were thrilled.'

Helen rarely swore and certainly not often at him. He was shocked and hurt and in a quandary. If he told her what happened she would feel even more insecure over Lionel. Mike was her rock. If he didn't tell it could crumble. She would think him selfish and irresponsible – and Ben disloyal to her, covering up for his dad.

'Helen, calm down, you were not there. It's over and done with.'

'No it isn't. Tell me exactly what happened,' Helen screamed.

'It was a minor incident. I made him nervous over it. That's all.'

'That's all. That's all you can say after risking our son's life.'

'You're so wrong, Mum. I told you – we weren't in any danger.' Ben had come down to find out what all the shouting was about. It stopped at once. They avoided rows in front of the kids. And they both knew it was partly to do with tomorrow. Lionel's birthday *and* Tikal were coming between them.

That evening, in bed, Helen brought up the subject again. 'What day did you say you climbed that temple?'

'Thursday. Why?'

'I checked my diary. It was that ghastly night I told you about.'

'*That night* – so what?'

'So what! You were six hours behind the UK. You said you went up after lunch. At that precise moment – that evening, six hours later here – I *knew* you were scared, desperate for help,' Helen shrieked. 'I couldn't eat any supper. I was a bundle of nerves. After the girls had gone up I had a hot bath and went to bed early. It didn't help. I didn't sleep a wink that night.'

'It was a panic attack because we were so far away.'

'No! No! No! I knew you were in danger – taking risks as usual – getting your kicks.'

'Helen, how could you possibly know what we were doing?' *Coincidence – wasn't it?*

The matter didn't end there – the wedge was driven in a little further a month later. A two-inch story in the papers reported the closure of Jaguar Paw Temple to tourists. A student had fallen to his death. Helen, grimfaced, slammed the story down in front of them. Ben and Mike each read it in silence. They made no mention of it again in front of Helen.

CHAPTER FIFTEEN

(I'll never be the same until I discover what became of) My old flame. SONG: COSLOW & JOHNSTON

M ike was surprised that the carriage was half-empty and pleased to take his place between unoccupied adjacent seats. It allowed him all the space he needed to spread out and read the confidential reports away from any prying eyes. The train was late but the journey gave him a full hour to prime himself for the interview. He gave a cursory glance at his fellow travellers – mostly business types engrossed by laptops and mobiles – a few reading newspapers. One smartly dressed woman read a paperback. Attractive, she briefly caught his eye before he chained himself to his task.

The witness and police statements were unambiguous. After half an hour's perusal he concluded that any assessment he made would be unhelpful to the defendant. He squared the papers together and replaced them in the folder, returning them to his brief case. He raised his head. She was staring at him, and, since she had dropped her hands and the book into her lap, probably for a while. His glance shattered her stare and she immediately resumed reading. He turned to the window and the passing fields. His eyes drowsily closed for a short nap. When they opened again they met her unyielding stare and hesitant mouth.

'Michael?' she gambled at last, confident of an odds-on win.

Mike furiously shuffled his memory cards and re-dealt the hand he held all those years ago – to resurrect Sophie from his past. She'd startled him. He sat as open-mouthed and in awe as Caravaggio's disciples. He had mulled over her for many years after he'd crushed their teenage affair and possibly her heart by going off to Australia.

The train's late arrival in Birmingham limited them to the briefest of exchanges.

'Are you working here?

'Yes. I'm up for the day.'

'Me too – we must have lunch together. I've got to rush. Give me your mobile number,' Sophie insisted.

'I might be delayed getting away,' Mike said. A feeble token resistance: if any.

'That was my line once. Our first date – and I was early! Remember?'

Mike could barely make out Sophie's dissipating reply as she hurried away, late for her appointment, but it registered. He sensed she knew. He was as intrigued to meet her for lunch as he was all those years ago outside the tube station.

In spite of the train he was early for his appointment. He casually strolled the mile towards Winson Green. He re-captured those distant days.

The King is dead – long live the Queen! He was so smitten by Sophie he surrendered allegiance to his deposed sovereign. Beside his loss of interest in chess, he'd fought his last boxing match. That fight may have impressed her, but was spoiled, tainted by defeat and its resultant first minor injuries. Michael had discovered all he ever needed to know about himself in the ring.

Those changes signalled the end of boyhood. His secret liaisons led to late nights, initially un-remarked upon by his parents.

Sophie was attractive and slim – smartly turned out – a girl demanding attention. Her bubbly personality radiated confidence. She magnetised people towards her. And she knew it. Michael couldn't believe his luck. Why was she so interested in him? Was she slumming it? Cocking a snook at society or her parents for some reason? He was a working-class Jewish boy who lived in a council flat, well run, rather than run-down, but nevertheless a council flat.

She came from a well-to-do family. Her father was a family doctor. Her mother dealt in antiques. The truth was she was a free spirit, sexually adventurous, and, after watching his fight, found him compulsively attractive. She was more than a year his senior, had a PA job in the city, and shared a flat with two other girls. Michael had little contact with them. Sophie saw to that. They were rarely home if he was coming round. At first Sophie paid for both of them going out. Michael found that difficult to accept. The job he got checking football pools on Sundays earned his self-respect but ate further into his studies.

Michael discounted his fumbling sexual encounters with other girls. Sophie bewitched him. She was his first true partner. Her lust, her wicked sense of fun, her daring exploits, erased any inhibitions he had held. In retrospect, he was amazed how he was so easily led and how they had got away with so much. She controlled their relationship from the start. He recalled with amusement how he had been helplessly initiated into carnality – seduced by her on a stairwell at a party. His resistance was mainly generated by an attack of diffused guilt and shyness. That was never far way.

'What's all this' Sophie asked, squeezing his tense muscles.

'Someone might….'

'Everyone's here – nobody else to come,' she said with a wicked giggle.

For all his attempts to match her maturity it was Sophie who dragged him – unwillingly, she subsequently teased – into adulthood. He didn't have to resort to the Periodic Table or name American Presidents. The tension over being discovered defied his inexperience.

'That wasn't your first time. Was it?' Sophie asked, churlishly.

'It was,' Michael said shyly.

'Was it really?' She was pleased: that boosted his ego.

Did she think I had cheated her out of her first pristine conquest, he wondered. Maybe she was redressing the loss of her own virginity. She had certainly taken control. Now, so many years later, he felt his pulse hasten reflecting on other erotic risks they had taken. Michael found the heavy emotional price tag attached to Sophie unaffordable. With her around it was difficult to concentrate on anything but her.

What turmoil his fling with Sophie caused at home. He had ignored his A-level studies and his report the year of the exams was damning. Guilt began to set in. He couldn't let down his family or himself. He was the major source of pride to unselfishly supportive parents. He respected them and made allowances for well meaning but unwelcome intrusions into his life – even his mother's annoying homilies.

Mum distilled life down to sayings and proverbs. She regularly shot herself in the foot with her aphorisms without apparent pain or personal embarrassment. She would rouse the boys citing the 'early bird.' His bleary-eyed younger brother once laconically countered, 'Mum. What happens to the early worm?' Mike's regard for him was unbridled that morning.

Yesterday Amy provided a family classic. She had told on Claire. Helen dismissed her accusation with a *glasshouses* warning.

'You don't know what that means,' Claire said.

'Yes I do. 'Cos people can see what you've done.'

A sure sign her grandmother's gene flourished.

Mum got frustrated with Michael's behaviour and Dad's support for him. 'It takes two to tango. Don't put all the blame on the girl,' she told him.

Dad didn't. He was fond of Sophie. He knew, from their long *tête-à-tête* after the fight, how much Michael had grown up. Sophie was more evidence of Michael's increasing maturity. She happened to turn up at the wrong time. Dad suggested Michael take a reality check.

Michael was made of sterner stuff. He felt duty-bound by the sacrifices his parents made. And he had his own ambitions. He made the supreme effort to dam his obsession with Sophie. Determined to get his A-levels, he agreed to stop seeing her for two months. He finally knuckled down to study – so deeply engaged he absent-mindedly consumed a full bowl of fruit in the process. 'Do you think it grows on trees?' Mum screamed.

Mike was still early for his assessment and the regulated prison hours. He stopped on the way for a coffee and Danish. Sitting alone by a window, a perceptible smile warmed his countenance as he continued to reminisce.

His agonising predicament over Sophie came to a head later, after passing his exams and getting a place at university and regularly seeing her again. They stayed several weekends at her family home in the Sussex countryside. During an evening with her parents' friends, she grabbed his hand and led him away. He followed her obediently into the study. He fleetingly glanced about him, noting the bookcase, paintings, the roll-top desk, the armchairs and the deep, leather settee. He turned to Sophie standing in front of the door. She closed it with a coquettish nudge from her shapely bottom. Her hypnotic, deep blue, smiling eyes locked on his and she proceeded to circle him. She was neither his predator nor opponent, as she engaged him and brought another of her entrancing fantasies to life. Michael was spellbound. She managed to unbutton her blouse unnoticed until she slipped it slowly off her delicate shoulders. She calmed his evident panic with a sweet finger to his lips. After a tantalising, languid striptease she laid her warm ivory body on the cool black leather altar. Once again he succumbed unscathed, as they escaped the attention of the noisy host of people in the adjoining room.

Michael recovered from this audacity only to be further staggered by Sophie's astonishing aplomb as she reverted to the innocent Daddy's girl as they re-entered the crowded lounge. She wound everybody round her little finger to get her way. It was more than *her* animal lust; it was mutual and the catalyst for discovering the so many admirable qualities they saw in each other. The relationship changed, maturing into a deeply emotional young love.

Unlike his brother – carefree, sailing through life without fear of unseen traps – Michael was intensely involved. The Sophie saga had a profound effect on him. His parents' disapproval apart, he realised that he had become ensnared. He was too young to make any further commitment, yet too besotted to lose Sophie. How was he going to get through a degree? How was she going to accept his absence? The situation became even more fraught after his A-level passes. They magnified and advanced his distress. He was no longer his own master.

Mike's best friends noted he was in a bad way and tried to help, but it was Dad who helped assuage and dissect his angst. In another marathon *Buberian* exchange, he came to the rescue. He listened quietly to Michael talk himself out until the early hours. His confusion gelled into more rational ideas. More tangible. Shaped by the enforced organisation of communicable speech. Dad succinctly summed up for Michael.

'Do you love her enough to let her go?' was his killer question. The old sage.

He did – and needed a period apart from everyone to reclaim his own freedom. He had to find his true self and define his goals in life. In those days gap years were unusual rather than the norm. He joined P&O and went to sea working in the purser's office. It was exhilarating to be a free man; free from family, free for the moment from his studies, and no longer a slave to an all-consuming love.

Not free, but locked up – Mike remembered the man he was due to see. In one gulp he swallowed the remainder of his coffee and left the cafe.

A raw starkness pervades prisons. It echoes in the voices of visitors, prisoners and warders alike. Here, in the depressing old Victorian buildings, with the unyielding clank of iron doors and heavy-duty locks and keys, it resounded. As he entered, the immediate impact of being cut off from the rest of society halted any further daydreams about Sophie and the past. The duty officer checked off Mike's name against his list and signalled to a warder to lead him to the interview room.

The prisoner sat across the table and the warder leaned against the far wall, out of hearing. Mike began the interview getting his history and a personal account of events leading to the man's committal. He responded to questions as any patient might – hardly different from them. It was difficult to visualise this mild-mannered man as a violent criminal. The facts, and his current guilty plea in court, proved he was. The casual way he spoke of his crimes and his evident lack of remorse were damning. Mike's report would have some influence on the man's sentence and treatment. He had to be certain of his findings. The meeting went on long after the two hours set aside. They took a break for lunch.

Mike's mobile rang as his foot touched the first paving stone outside.

'Sorry I can't make lunch. I'm not free for another couple of hours,' he said.

Sophie would have appreciated his turn of phrase if she knew where he was. His words lingered – *would I be free thereafter?*

'I'll be done by four. We must meet.'

Was that desperation in her voice?

'Of course, give me a call when you're finished.' he replied evenly.

A limp salad baguette and forgettable coffee from a nearby café had to suffice for a snack lunch. To clear his head, Mike wandered down to Summerfield Park and through to the reservoir, where he sat on a bench watching a pair of great crested grebes diving for their more appetising fare.

She never made contact after his harsh rebuttal split them apart.

Did Sophie hold a secret?

He had intentionally hurt her because he loved her. It was to release her from him, from love, from the impossible.

'We must meet.' Did she emphasise must?

Panic. A surge of hot blood filled his head.

Perhaps there was a child. No, I'm becoming neurotic.

Mike evoked anticipation as worse than events to gain the same comfort it afforded his patients. He would, of course, meet her as promised.

Mike remained an extra hour in the gaol. It produced no further evidence to alter his assessment of the prisoner. Concurring with the other referees his report would mirror theirs. At three forty-five he was finished. Sophie called.

They met for coffee. Sophie insisted they catch the same train back: her later one that stopped for Mike before St. Pancras. 'I didn't get to eat. I turned down a good lunch for you,' Sophie said in mock anger.

'Sorry. I only had a snack. We'll get a bite – we've got hours yet for the train.'

Sophie was incredibly poised in her navy business suit and sharp stilettos. She was a venture capitalist and had spent the day assessing a possible investment for her group.

'It's strange seeing you – how much you've changed. Are you married?'

'Divorced, with two grown-up children,' Sophie replied.

He could no longer see her as the girl he was once so madly in love with. Sophie also noted the change in Mike.

'What happened to those two young lovers? You're so different,' she said wistfully. She instantly plucked Mike's heart with her once so familiar tilted glance. The moment passed – short-lived.

'I had a job believing it was you,' he said.

'I was told you'd emigrated to Australia after you ditched me.'

'I had no choice, Sophie. I had to get away from it all – space to think.' Diffidently, he remembered the ruthless way he had quelled her love.

'Goodbye, no use leading with our chins,'

The opening lines haunted and tormented whenever his parents played that record.

'This is where our story ends – this is where the pain begins.'

It had been years since he last heard that song. Belonging to another era, dated, it nevertheless stirred the old emotions and the echoes of that tortured decision.

'It was ages before I could admit you were right – realised why you did it – how it must have hurt you,' Sophie said quietly as they re-lived the past.

A confused shame – for shunning her instead of softening the break-up – surfaced. 'It was cruel. I should have been gentler,' Mike said.

Why didn't I wish you love? *'So with my best, my very best, I set you free.'* Those few plain lyrics, so succinct, saturated with bittersweet memories, drew Mike into deeper contemplation.

'Cruel? Never. You did it to release me,' she replied to his pensive silence.

'Is that what you thought?'

Like the old days, Mike was staggered by Sophie's remarkable radar for the truth. *If I had wished her love she would have loved me even more,* he told his conscience.

'Well, didn't you?' she asked.

After a further longer silence weighing up any repercussions, he confessed.

'Yes, I had no option. It's hard to get away with anything with you.'

Sophie smiled; that same dazzling smile that lit up darkened rooms and grey skies.

Mike felt a pang. Those blue eyes still hypnotised. The old feelings were stirring.

'More coffee?'

He brought two more large coffees from the counter.

The afternoon drew on. Their diverse current lives receded. The old memories flooded back. Compelling core traits they each possessed, once so irresistible, were again bringing them closer – embers that could easily be fanned into flames.

Mike was fully alert to the danger of eternal *triangles*. They start with a minor incident and end in a major accident. So often he had witnessed the damage caused to those left in the wake. How many times had he listened to the regrets of people who had embarked on that first, exciting step? How often had he secretly held dynamite entrusted by one partner, or both, that could blow a relationship apart? Then, again, he had also seen some people happily manage the most complicated of love lives.

It wasn't cold feet – Mike was hardly risk averse – Sophie professionally assessed risks. Was any relationship riskier than monogamy – one basket? Both trod with care. They slowly retraced the days shared together and the paths they had chosen since. Sophie flirted – Mike responded. It was in their natures, their history, nostalgic rather than romantic and kept in perspective by current responsibilities.

Mike was unswervingly loyal to Helen, but sometimes, unaware and casual, he made eyes at other women. He could be quite insensitive – do it right in front of her. It was usually after a glass of wine – fun or plain vanity. Occasionally he fancied them. It was no threat to their relationship. It was so out of character it usually generated Helen's amusement rather than offence. Sophie was a danger, but he could not resist exploring the 'ifs and buts' and the roads they had travelled.

'Michael.'

'It's Mike, these days.'

'I once called you Mike. Your mother disapproved. I prefer it – more informal, but stronger. It suits your need to control.'

'Stronger? Control?'

'You tried to control me,'

'What?' Mike exclaimed. 'Me control you? Impossible.'

'Well you were determined to get your own way.'

She's right. We wouldn't have stayed together.

'Where do *you* want to eat?'

'Fancy a curry?' Sophie replied, turning to the Indian over the road.

'You crafty devil, you saw me glimpsing over your shoulder.'

'I noticed it earlier. Let's go.'

Their conversation turned oddly cool and platonic over the shared spicy Madras vegetables and Tandoori chicken. Yet Mike warmed to this changed Sophie. He admired her unchanged self-assurance and utter honesty – qualities that appeared to be intact. She had clinically chosen her career over her marriage and become freer and even more ambitious once her youngest began secondary school. Her husband struggled but failed to match her earning power. He found it unacceptable. She could not sacrifice her independence but, pragmatic, ensured that they both remained friends and good parents.

Mike respected her attitude though alien for him. They had matured into different people. At the end of the meal Mike noticed the physical change.

'What's happened to your nose?' he blurted out to his surprise discovery.

'I had that corrected years ago.'

'Corrected? But that's what first attracted me to you. You've blown it.'

149

Sophie put her hand over his and gave him a pout of mock disappointment.

He no longer felt any remorse over his handling of the break-up. They would eventually have split up with a great deal of extra pain and regret. Sophie realised that. She was baffled by his choice of the NHS.

'You could have made a fortune in Harley Street.'

'Pander to the neuroses of idle wealth?'

That dichotomy alone would have torpedoed any chance of a stable relationship.

The train journey and the public farewell brought their brief encounter to a fruitful end: more so for Sophie. For all her insight and dignity, she had taken the original parting badly.

'I'm so pleased we met – and to find closure – certain at last why you left.'

'Closure – after all these years?'

Mike bent down and affectionately kissed her on the cheek and whispered, 'Love is clearer looking back.'

Cheerily, he called out, 'Take care of yourself, Sophie,' as he left her, and the train, to follow their destined paths.

He walked to the car park wrapped in sadness. Not because Sophie was again out of his life, but because he had not been as honest as she had been. '*Love* is clearer....' He had intended to say 'life'. It was complicated. So long to grasp how cruel and hard he had been. He could have called it off gently and honestly. She would have understood. He had proof. She would have accepted his decision without all those years of uncertainty. Even today, he lied over sharing the agony of separation. He spared her any further pain with the truth – his own closure barely six months after they parted.

Aboard the P&O liner from Colombo to Sydney – the longest leg of the voyage to Australia – Mike was struck by a whirlwind romance. Leila was the rebound he had found to express his frustrated feelings for Sophie. Her Eurasian beauty, a product of her Sino-French mother and Indian tea-planter father, dazzled him. His white uniform played a big role in doing the same to her. For almost three weeks he projected his bereaved feelings for his lost love onto Leila. She was a delight – a young romantic, fuelled by her exotic upbringing. They were at sea, isolated from life's practicalities. Within days they became lovers: lovers untainted by responsibility. They had a cruel price to pay on reaching Sydney, Leila's destination. Reality shattered their impossibly perfect union. Inevitably, in the exquisite agony of their final days together, they were forced to bring their doomed affair to its conclusion. Darling Harbour, aptly named, witnessed their last goodbye, as the ship turned round for home after five days in port.

The foghorn resonated through the ship's hull, vibrating his rib cage. Michael drew a length off his bright orange, paper streamer. He threw the remaining roll straight and true. She jumped up on the quay. Her delicate hands caught it. The ripple of water separating them first became a wide river then slowly swelled as the liner eased away towards the ocean. Michael clung tightly to his end of the streamer. Long before Leila had fully un-reeled the tape they could no longer pick each other out from the masses. They saw scores of other coloured streamers tear apart, as their own held to a perfect arc, mirroring the magnificent bridge over the harbour.

The breeze finally captured theirs. It too, snapped and shot upwards, a brilliant fluttering flame against the cobalt sky, signalling their affair's conclusion in sight of the whole world. Michael watched every millisecond of every last twitch of their love's death throes waft into the ether as the paper zephyr fell, floated, and at last sank beneath the waves.

An icy shower; porridge hitting cold milk; a camera click; the end of young love; his goodbye to Leila; his closure for Sophie. After the swift catharsis that followed Mike felt – welcomed – a sense of relief.

He started up the Saab. Its secure, comfortable, practical, unadventurous cocoon so accurately reflected his character. His car was a pragmatic choice, as ever, for a boringly organised man who needed to have control. Would he tell Helen about the day? Possibly, in outline: probably avoiding the detail.

White lies are often less harmful than the stark truth. He was envious of Sophie's uncomplicated honesty, yet wary of its pitfalls. She didn't take any responsibility for truths. They were fixed components in her life. What are truths anyway? They are not definitive. They vary from one observer to the next. Mike had to take responsibility in revealing truths, particularly to patients. Not conceit – he hoped he was frank and approachable. He accepted he could not match Sophie's openness.

'Hi, Darling – how did it go?' Helen asked, puckering her lips for his kiss.

'As I said it would be – a bit of a wild goose chase – my report is superfluous.'

'You did manage to get a bite?'

'Yes, with an old friend I bumped into.'

'Anyone I've met?'

'No – mover and shaker in the city – changed a lot over the years.'

No lies. But a tinge of guilt fluttered across his face.

She studied him. 'Old girlfriend, wasn't it? I can read you like an open book.''

'Yes. Guilty as charged. Am I that transparent?'

Mike offered a silent smile. Helen returned it, shrugged her shoulders, jutted out her chin, and left the room.

Some minutes later she called out 'Who was she?'

'Someone from long ago – in my teens.'

'Well, are you going to tell me about her?

Curiosity got the better of Helen. She was no longer as sanguine.

CHAPTER SIXTEEN

A journey of a thousand miles must begin with a single step.
LAOZI

Mike approached the urban sprawl. The roads widened but traffic increased and slowed to a halt. It was unfair to blame mums with kids. He and Helen ferried the children several miles to and from school coaches. It was one of the prices they paid for rural living. In today's world Helen, in particular, was cautious over child safety.

He studied the stationary drivers around him. His Mondays used to be in accord with Bob Geldof's Boom Town Rats. The despond could take as long as Wednesday to lift – helped by the cavalry due over the horizon at the weekend. He peered into the cars. *Complain! Lobby for schools to start earlier. They do it abroad.* It was directed at 'them' – he had made his change for Mondays.

Phyllis greeted Mike with her usual efficiency. A mug of Darjeeling and two dark chocolate digestives followed him into his office.

'Someone called Harry from your garage phoned about quarter of an hour ago,' she reported, innocently confirming her diligent early start. 'Please could you call him?'

Did I forget his bill? He phoned. No. It was personal. Harry needed to see him urgently. Phyllis had told Harry she had a possible cancellation in the afternoon.

Mike, on his lunch break – a sandwich and an Americano in the café along the street – welcomed the quiet twenty minutes. He caught up with the news and sport and did the quick crossword in *The Daily Telegraph*.

153

Phyllis slotted Harry into the confirmed cancellation, the second appointment of the afternoon. Nervously, he entered Mike's room. He wasn't his usual self. Mike had never seen him out of overalls. A slimmer Harry had bought his suit, but rarely worn it. Mike suppressed a smile. Harry fitted precisely *that* PGW character who poured himself into his attire and forgot to say 'when'.

'Thanks for seeing me, Dr. Daniels. I've got into a bit of a mess. I hope you can help me. My brother is in hospital. He's had a heart attack. It's a shock.'

The brothers had run the family garage together for years. 'I'm sorry to hear that. How's he doing?'

'They haven't said yet. He looks normal. They're doing more tests.'

Aside from his brother's welfare Harry found himself in a pickle at the garage. He was happy in the workshop and office. This week, no longer confined to those duties, he had to take on his brother's job in the sales forecourt. The mechanics carried out most of Harry's chores without a hiccup. His problem – delivering and test-driving vehicles – was the issue. His brother had always done this in the past.

Harry was unwilling to use motorways. He was secretly afraid of them. His lifestyle had been dictated by this fear. He developed a reputation for being devoted to his family and his job. He found a myriad of excuses to avoid motorways, and made longer journeys on other roads 'to avoid the traffic'. The phobia was mild on minor roads and tolerated, as he could easily turn around for home. Motorways gave him no such choice. He was terrified he might get blocked between junctions, by an accident or congestion.

His reticence for test-drives had put off some potential buyers. If others remained interested he delegated the task to his mechanics. Inexperienced, they were nervous salesmen. Harry had probably lost the garage one or two sales.

'I could refer you to the hospital – be on a waiting list though. Besides, your brother's coronary will take some months for treatment and convalescence,' Mike warned.

'That's the trouble: time.'

'Your brother: any idea how long they'll keep him? Did they say?'

'They said, whatever they find, he will have to take it easy.'

'We cannot hang about. Let's see what we can do.'

Mike soon discovered Harry's anxiety was attached to a need to return home. A short précis of his history revealed two misfortunes. One day, he returned home from primary school to find his mother had left the family. She had run off, never to return. If that wasn't enough to destabilise his childhood, he suffered a later trauma. He arrived home as a latchkey child to discover firemen dowsing the family home – gutted by a fire from the kitchen. Unsurprisingly, he became anxious on return journeys home from school. These two events were related in a most matter-of-fact manner but – surprisingly unrelated – unconnected by Harry. Motorways had replaced school.

'Re-examine your two childhood shocks during the coming days.'

'What about driving?'

'Try taking short motorway trips – one junction at a time – turn off if it gets stressful. I think the panic will reduce quickly now you've found its source.' Mike said.

The next session Harry arrived as his old cheery self, but still testing the seams of his suit. He had braved the motorway as Mike suggested. His aversion even to longish drives had almost vanished in the course of a week. He had little trouble taking on his brother's responsibilities and was relieved his heart attack was considered mild – he would soon be returning to the garage. The doctors told his brother to treat it as a warning. He had to change his diet and take life easier. Harry was happy to help out.

155

But, exploring his childhood memories, he had stirred up old, long-forgotten emotions. He recalled that, even though he hadn't seen her since she left, he felt closer to his mother than his brother did. Deep down he missed her desperately. The memory of her disappearance rekindled anxieties over returning home.

'Why? Who do you think could be next to leave – your wife?' Mike asked.

'No, of course not – it's that hollow feeling inside.'

'We'll go over that in detail next week.'

'I'm going to try and find her,' Harry said. 'One of my customers is a private detective.'

'What will you do if he does locate her?'

'Dunno yet. I'll wait to hear her version of what happened.'

'If he does, hold fire before you contact her – we ought to talk first,' Mike said.

'Thanks. I've no idea what I would say.'

'Good luck – see you next week.'

The week passed. Harry arrived, pleased. The local detective agency had traced his long-lost mother without difficulty. She was living less than thirty miles away. Excited, Harry contacted her. She sobbed, overwhelmed by his initial phone call and asked him to ring later. She needed to get over the shock. With the return call they bridged some of the space that had separated them, and she gratefully accepted his offer to meet. Although it was four junctions up the motorway, it was no longer a problem. He was comfortable facing that journey. Harry had come for advice on how to approach the reconciliation.

'Bear in mind you were a child when you last saw her,' Mike said.

'I've kept a vivid image of her,' Harry said.

'Your memories might be somewhat distorted or idealised. She, and you, must have changed dramatically,' Mike said.

'What do you suggest I do?'

'Keep your expectations low and the conversation as neutral as possible. Listen to what she has to say about leaving.'

'She abandoned me. I mustn't accuse her of that.'

'Try to stay calm with her. She probably feels guilty,' Mike cautioned.

'I've wondered about that. I won't get angry,' Harry said.

'Bear in mind she was a teenage bride. She was catapulted from a naive childhood into a harsh adult world.'

Off Harry went on his quest. He returned a week later.

'Did you recognise each other?' Mike asked.

'Immediately – her hair's grey and she's old, but I knew it was her the moment she arrived.'

'How did it go?'

'It's fantastic,' Harry replied, 'she's as happy as I am to get together. We had a great reunion. We're going to take it slowly, as you said, but see each other regularly.'

'That's terrific news.'

Harry described in detail how their meeting went: the words rehearsed so often he recalled it without a pause or any of his usual glances at the ceiling.

'Did she say why she left or why she hadn't contacted you again?' Mike asked.

'Yes – another man and money – a lot of it didn't make much sense to me.'

'Anything in particular?'

'Yes – something odd – she hoped I would forget her after she left.'

'Why she made no contact?' Mike asked

'Yes. She said it was because she loved me.'

Mike empathised with a brief pang of longing.

'Dr. Daniels,' Harry, like Phyllis, insisted on respectful formality, 'the last few weeks have changed my life. Thank you for all your help.'

'Not at all – thank you for your help over the years. You saved me having to change my car last month.'

If only. If only I could help Helen so easily. 'Lionel days' are far worse since Tikal. Ben's right – it could benefit both of us if I first shared my problem.

*   *   *

Apart from 'Lionel days', Helen was content – carefree even – taking breaks with Mike. They both worked and played hard. It masked their unresolved problems but Mike remained wary. His zeal on Mondays diffused into a massive increase in overall job satisfaction. Content – he had drawn a curtain across attention to heights – he gave out no distress signals to Helen. Her expectant doom was nearer the surface. She had reacted badly on her recent visits to Lionel. She was down – depressed even – for some days afterwards. Mike cautiously monitored her over the following weeks. Passively. If he interfered he might direct her attention to her dread and shape it up. He didn't see any sign of her fear of another family tragedy – not a hint. It was best left for the moment, and soon forgotten.

Mike was relaxed at weekends. They were reserved strictly for leisure. Sunday mornings were spent at the tennis club and he played golf at least twice a month, but alas, with no improvement on his 18 handicap. Those days off were a welcome relief, uncluttered, unspoilt by anybody.

It was rather that way, *even with Helen*, on precious day trips or down in London for an evening out. Those activities, and sport, kept Mike's mind off Lionel. He forgot about him most days.

Tonight they were off to the Proms. Mike was unusually chatty on the way down that evening.

'Odd, isn't it? They're employing music therapists at the hospital. I suppose it is *the* most profound form of communication,' Mike said, unprompted.

'Maybe, but what does it say? Does that do any good?'

'Say? Zilch. It transcends language. It can chime with their emotions'

'Come off it, Mike. Can that really help anyone?'

On the false assumption that everyone found psychology equally intriguing, Mike could be a trifle trying.

'It has proven effective with some people.'

'How?' Helen snapped.

'For starters, calm, classical music can reduce anxiety.'

'I suppose it can,' Helen said, thinking that was blooming obvious.

'They have measured increased alpha waves in the brain that reduce stress,' Mike said, reading her mind.

'Music can increase stress – cause excitement in films, theatre, TV, adverts. How often have you complained out shopping?' Helen said, cuttingly.

'What's shopping got to do with it?'

'Mike, you do go on about people being exploited by the power of music in shops.'

Helen had a knack. She simplified, Mike agonised. Plain common sense – no deep analysis – that is all she needed. She let him have the last word. He got onto his pet subject – motoring. That obsession had no limits – music even figured here – he was certain it dramatically influenced driving behaviour.

In their courtship days Mike was a bit of a romantic. He remained so, particularly over the piece they were about to hear again tonight: the Brahms D minor piano concerto. Whether or not it was written by the composer smitten with Clara Schumann he had not checked, but he *knew* the piece described the detail of their relationship. He was sure the first movement expressed Brahms' turmoil caused by his growing affection for Clara and his conflict of interest and guilt towards her husband, his good friend Robert.

Mike's amorous assertion occurred those many years ago. He accepted his destiny to spend his life with Helen in the middle of the second movement. The gentle passage was a few bars tinkled on the piano. Cued – the whole orchestra vigorously took up the theme and sent it and Mike's bolt of lightning reverberating through the hall.

'That was the precise moment Brahms surrendered to love,' he said, afterwards.

'What makes you say that? Helen asked.

'It's Clara's theme.'

'It wasn't in the programme notes. Who said?'

'Dr. Zhivago,'

'You fool,' Helen said, and giggling squeezed his knee.

'I dedicate it to you,' Mike said in earnest, gazing deeply into her eyes, 'I love you.'

From then on Mike was forever bombarding Helen with his appreciation of music. He may have bored her, but she was a staunch ally on the subject in company. Some years ago at a party, he had a heated discussion with his Jewish friends. They were upset with Barenboim. He was playing Wagner in Tel Aviv.

'How could he?' they asked.

A virulent anti-Semite, Wagner's grandiose music had accompanied much that occurred in the death camps. Mike was no great Wagner fan. He found most of his works, particularly the Ring Cycle, long and tedious, and his racist writings utterly obnoxious. However he did find some of his music sublime – and made a strong argument for it to be judged on its merits. It wasn't music that perpetrated those crimes against humanity. Nor did it spout bilious offence. He attempted to argue his point without causing more hurt. He expressed his opinions as sensitively as possible.

'Try and accept it *is* art,' Mike said.

Immediately he came under attack.

'You call yourself a Jew?' one said.

'In Israel of all places,' another added.

'People aren't forced to attend those concerts, but they do,' Mike said.

'And what about Holocaust survivors?'

'Music is innocent of atrocities.'

'So you would hang one of Hitler's paintings at home, would you?' one of the friends asked angrily.

'No. I would not,' Mike replied, firmly.

'Why not – what's the difference?'

'In the first place it's hardly great art.'

'And in the second place – if it were?'

'Well,' Mike said, playing for time, bowled middle stump by the question.

'Well, what?'

'Well....it's physical. Too close to the monster.'

'Physical, shmysical, musical: what's the difference?' the friend asked. He turned to the others with a shrug and raised both hands, his arms forming a W for *What*.

Mike's objective approach to life had innocently swamped his inherent compassion for people. Helen rescued him. Seeing his dilemma she diplomatically intervened and adeptly changed the subject.

Their night at the Proms rekindled the old romantic notions in the Brahms. The soft passage in the second movement found its mark, and the late stroll through Kensington Gardens in the balmy night air set the seal. Idyllic moments such as this reminded Mike how lucky he was in life to find his true soul mate. Their relationship was a personal benchmark to compare with the many miserable stories he encountered daily. He wasn't complacent about that. Life can be brittle. But it was an added impetus to his aspirations to change people's lives for the better.

CHAPTER SEVENTEEN

Dreams are the royal road to the unconscious. SIGMUND FREUD

Mike assessed new patients cautiously. Many minimise major problems to minor ones. Mild symptoms or trivial ills can hide profounder issues.

Jennifer arrived – her first appointment – ostensibly for marital counselling. She had attempted to resolve her concerns with the local vicar. Once an easy-going partnership – it had changed. No children. Her husband had his own business, with Jennifer attending to administration, initially as an employee: eventually marrying the boss. She described their bonding as a slow but sure build-up of friendship, mutual respect and inter-dependence. An unromantic love developed over the years.

In recent months she had become increasingly agitated, uncharacteristically irritable, and critical of her husband over small matters. No apparent reason. Financially they were secure and had reduced their hours with more days off for leisure and holidays.

Jennifer was an intelligent, somewhat introverted, anxious woman: quietly spoken – she blushed fairly readily – a modestly attractive and slim forty-three-year-old. Her introversion and routines were non-neurotic. Lately she was sleeping poorly and 'had butterflies' over even minor changes in her life. The vicar's initial chats were comforting. He was good company. He, as she, was an avid reader. They exchanged views on authors they had read. A quiet and mild character, he empathised with her introverted traits. She considered him a good friend and his visits therapeutic.

Her husband blamed himself. His unsought compensations made matters worse. Jennifer's angst, true to character, formed set patterns with regular, anxiety-driven, dreams waking her at night. Mike would see her again next week.

He had a busy schedule to contend with at the hospital. The unit's backlog had increased significantly in recent months. He was coping at the limit. His life was rushing past in a grey blur. The years were accelerating. He dreaded facing the breakfasts every fifteen minutes, promised in old age.

Another week passed quickly. Jennifer had done as he had bid and unearthed all she could to cast light on her anxiety. Mike pursued then discarded unproductive avenues to focus on the one area that had captured his attention – her dreams.

Jennifer's disturbing dream occurred almost nightly. It started pleasantly enough with her serenely gliding through the sky. Then her flight abruptly veered and she was whooshed away on an anxious, uncontrollable, pre-determined path. Mike stayed off Freud – dreams of flying and sexual matters. After soaring over indefinable land and sea she landed on a lonely island. Once on *terra firma* she became calm and relaxed. She described it as a place of peace and quiet. Gradually, mild anxiety set in and after a slow build-up, turned to panic. At this point she awoke in turmoil.

'Your dream could be a subconscious link to your marriage. The island might be a clue,' Mike said.

'I think it was the Isle of Man,' Jennifer said.

'Why do you *think* it was the Isle of Man?'

Jennifer had no answer.

Mike had a map of the Isle of Man at the next session – it could hold the key.

'Have you ever seen one of these?'

'I don't think so. I had no reason to – not having been,' Jennifer replied.

'Take a peek. Does anything register?'

Jennifer took a minute or so perusing the map. She shook her head.

'Do the towns of Castleton, Douglas or Ramsey mean anything to you? Somebody's name, perhaps?'

'No.'

Discounting the map, Mike sought other features in her dream.

'I have strong feelings for the Island. Mixed emotions. If I fly away from it, it's with both remorse and relief.'

'Can you recall any features in the landscape? Any landmark on the Island?'

'None.'

'Anything else – any people?'

'I do remember seeing the odd glimpse of a shadowy figure, faraway.'

'About this figure: would you have spoken to this person if you could?'

'Yes. I would have asked *him* why *we* stood here.'

'Do you think the shadowy figure in your dream could be someone you know?'

Instinctively, or because of so few contacts in her life, Jennifer suggested the vicar. She had turned to him as her amateur therapist. This squared with her potential question for the unidentified man.

Jennifer recalled her conversations with the vicar. Mike had come to a tentative conclusion about him, observed through Freudian eyes. Her account was proof. It provided a logical explanation why the Isle of Man caused so much anxiety.

In dreams she was uncontrollably whisked off to the Isle. Mixed emotions fused into a high state of anxiety, waking her. For some months, she had thoroughly enjoyed her chats with her vicar. Lately they caused her anxiety. Mike saw why. The answer *was* in her dream. He guided Jennifer to that solution.

'Repeat the words *Isle of Man* over and over please,' Mike said.

'Sorry, how do you mean – why?'

'Try it, but do it without thinking.'

She did so until it sounded like a Buddhist mantra.

'You need to find a hidden message.'

'Sounds fun – a secret code perhaps?'

'Good – treat it as a game. See what comes to mind.'

'*Isle*: was 'Isle' a reference to 'aisle' and the marriage?'

'Possibly,' Mike said. 'You're on the right track. Any other meaning in the sounds?'

'Isle of – *I love.*'

'Yes, go on.'

'Isle of Man: *I love man, I love man.*'

'Exactly. That's it. You've got it.'

'But was does that mean?' Jennifer asked, puzzled by her relief at finding the answer.

'Have you heard of transference?'

Jennifer's transference during her 'therapeutic' encounters with the vicar had been misinterpreted. She didn't love him or want to spoil her marriage. Her subconscious had cunningly used the *Isle of Man* to vent her anxieties as a veiled warning. It was a classical Freudian interpretation of a dream.

'Your marriage was built on friendship and partnership. You yearned for romance. Your husband can fulfil that need – he's certainly been attentive – all those presents and fuss.'

'I made him feel guilty, didn't I?' Jennifer said.

'Perhaps, but it shows he can provide the romance you craved for subconsciously.'

'But I wasn't aware…'

'Exactly,' Mike interrupted.

Mike was pleased: pleased he had helped Jennifer, but even more so finding such a perfect Freudian answer. Many modern psychologists discounted Freud as out of date. Mike put his theories in context: the early twentieth century held scant information on brain function. Neurology. Psychoanalysts held no monopoly on Freud. It was satisfying to find such a neat lynchpin to define what, initially, was a diffuse case. It was a unique NanoMO to add to his research papers.

CHAPTER EIGHTEEN

Only those who will risk going too far can possibly find out how far one can go. T.S.ELIOT

Good news yesterday: management had agreed to sixteen sessions per patient – another victory for Mike's independence. He was benefiting on all fronts. His status with management had risen in line with its empirical results for CBT. Junior members of the team were taking on the responsibility of proven behaviour therapies, with the gusto of youth. These formulaic procedures almost without exception produced positive results and were a great help to patients and satisfying for newer psychologists. Mike was frankly bored by some of this repetitive stuff but was intrigued and happy to help clear unusual hurdles. His role was mainly advisory or administrative in this area.

The hospital had become as fulfilling as his private practice. CBT requires more than experience and training to be effective. Apart from an analytical mind it was indubitably dependent upon an ability to communicate, empathise with, and love your fellow beings – to walk in their shoes and feel their pain. Mike could do that. Whether angst, depression or fear, he could experience it strongly enough to share patients' needs and help them carry their burden. His prized reward was their progress.

Unsurprisingly, Mike had come home in a good mood. That was quickly shattered. He had a fierce row with Helen. He could deal with his patients' problems calmly. It was a different matter with Helen.

'I've wangled a couple of days free – first week next month – it will make a long weekend. Let's go away somewhere,' Mike said.

'I can't that week. I think I'm booked in at Greenway pharmacy,' Helen replied.

'Check your diary.'

'Yes, I'm their locum on the Thursday morning.'

'Is that all? Cancel it. They'll have time to get another,' Mike said.

'No. It's impossible,' Helen shouted.

'What do you mean impossible? You've done it before with far less notice.'

'You expect me to drop everything to please you.'

'Alright we'll go off after lunch that Thursday.'

'No!'

'What do you mean – no?'

'I said no and I meant it,' Helen shouted.

'Do you have any idea how difficult it was to arrange?' Mike shouted back.

'You always try to get your own way, Mike. For once you can forget it.'

'For goodness sake, Helen, be reasonable.'

'You be reasonable,' she screamed again, and rushed out the room slamming the door.

Mike pirouetted around, hands clasped behind his head, angry and frustrated. He came to a halt in front of the side table. Helen had left her diary on it – open at the date. The local pharmacy was indeed marked in for the Thursday morning. *Damn it, damn it, damn it – how did that come around again so quickly?* Lionel's birthday was entered on the Friday. He found Helen, sobbing in the lounge.

'Go away. Leave me alone,' she responded as he entered the room.

'This can't go on,' Mike replied.

'What can't go on?'

'This fixation with Lionel.'

'You sound like my father. You think I'm ill. I'm perfectly well!'

'Have you ever allowed yourself to mourn Lionel?'

'Mourn him? Of course I've mourned him.'

'Partially maybe – what do you feel after you visit him those days?'

'What do you mean *those days*?'

'They increasingly put you under the weather.'

'How do you expect me to be?'

'Better – some improvement – it's been a long while.'

'It stays the same. I can't change,' Helen insisted.

'Helen – tell me – describe your emotions after visiting.'

'I'm not one of your patients. Stop trying to analyse me.'

'I'm not analysing. How do you feel – physically?'

'Physically? How does that fit in?'

'It might help me understand.'

Mike quietly gazed at Helen during the long pause that followed. Sheepishly, she made eye contact.

'I'm in no mood for this. Can you leave me alone please?'

Mike gently held her shoulders and drew her closer, eye to eye.

'Describe your reactions – give me an impression how you are – so we can share it.' Helen querulously scanned his face for a moment then relented.

'It feels as if I am carrying a heavy load inside.'

'Inside where?'

'Here,' Helen replied, pointing to the centre of her chest.

'What sort of load?'

'It's like a taut balloon inside, filled with cold liquid, weighing me down.'

I'm right. Helen hasn't fully mourned. Her tears are trapped.

'That must feel pretty bad,' Mike said.

'Do you appreciate why I can't go away that weekend?'

'You are compelled to visit – I realise that much.'

'Yes I am. And I'm *not* ill.'

'Sorry darling, I forgot the date. I'll swap my days.'

Mike had to help get those tears to flow. Helen needed to fully mourn Lionel. *I'll catch her with her defences down.*

*   *   *

On morning autopilot, he put last night's row behind him and started to shave, making his usual ornithological studies of the garden outside. It was remarkable how a few handfuls of birdseed could create so much happy activity. Such a tiny contribution on his part and yet it was so eagerly appreciated. NanoMOs were everywhere. Cartier-Bresson froze them; Caravaggio painted them; and Brahms composed them.

Helen's locked tears entered Mike's thoughts again. He empathised – certainly – but was he helping by pussyfooting around her problem? If he revealed his own weakness, it could help as Ben suggested. Or hinder and fortify her defences and make matters worse. Anxious that he might do exactly that by accident his attention turned away from his minor fear. Protected, caged by safety barriers – or unprotected, clinically confronted head-on – his mild phobia remained unchanged. And hidden – it was two years since the involuntary *flooding* in Guatemala. He had not been in a similar situation or been tested or needed help since. *I'll find my answer one day.*

*   *   *

Mike was under immense pressure lately. He had forgotten his motto – work hard and play hard – until someone pointed out that he was due four days holiday. He had to take his remaining entitlement for the year, next month, or lose it altogether. He and Helen both needed a break. Four days – that meant they could get a full week away with a cancelled Monday. He checked for obstacles. Helen presented none this time. Her parents were locums for the kids.

'You choose,' he told her.

'It's been years since I last went skiing. I wouldn't mind doing that. What about you?'

'Never done it. I could give it a try. Sounds fun. Let's do it.'

And so Mike went skiing with Helen. They started the week with two days on the nursery slope. Helen re-acquainted herself: Mike learned how to snowplough and turn. After day three they were ready to take on a gentle run. Helen warned Mike to be careful to drop off the *Poma* lift at the right place. She insisted on leading the way to indicate. He sat on his button seat behind her and nonchalantly viewed the long row of skiers tracing the snow ahead of her, as they stuttered and swayed their leisurely way up the mountain.

On reflection, it was stupid – done on impulse – he fancied a piece of the Toblerone that Helen gave to keep him going. He trapped the glove in his armpit and pulled out his hand, holding firmly onto his ski poles with the other. He ferreted the pack out of his side pocket. Either the unexpected effort needed to bite off that frozen *triangle* of chocolate, or the group of seasoned skiers who alighted, or *something else* distracted him. Whichever, he unwittingly slipped off his seat and comfortably joined them on his skis. He called to Helen. She didn't hear. The loud, almost panicky shout, his second attempt, did carry. Helen turned. She saw his empty seat, then his distinctive ski suit in the distance. He appeared to be teasing, jovially waving: not calling for help. Annoyed, she continued her ride up and around to the other side of the mountain.

Mike had come off at the wrong point at the top of a black run. The gentler blue and green slopes, and Helen, were on the other side of the mountain.

He looked down. Where they had come from – with deep crevasses and thick forest – offered no safe way down. The alternative was upwards, downwards and round, impossible to fathom out where. Again out of the question. The only option was the impossibly steep *piste noire*. Mike's stomach reacted to his plight then his head started reeling. It was Tikal all over again, but with Ben absent apart from echoes of his voice. The incline was as daunting as those stone steps, but it was covered in snow, deep and soft.

An image of blood in the snow shot into his head. *Where did that come from?* Mike searched through his past. *My great-grandfather! The Cossacks stormed through his farming village on horseback and beat the Jews over their heads.* All his great-grandfather, then a small boy, could ever remember of Russia were pools of blood seeping into snow. The story chimed with Mike. He examined it no further – he could break an arm or leg on his way down – but that would be *bloodless.* The connection was superficial – deeper down he was disturbed for another reason.

The wind was icy. Mike went into a cold sweat – did that help him keep a cool head? Perhaps. Anyway, in control, he took stock to clinically devise a safe method down. For starters, if he got into trouble he could sit on his bottom in order to brake. Embarrassing and uncomfortable maybe, it was nonetheless a safety net. The task was manageable.

Other skiers took off and zigzagged their way down into dots in an instant. His eyes followed their path. It looked even steeper. He remembered Ben's injunction and turned away. He went through the skiing routines he had learned. *Don't, whatever you do, point the skis downward.* He went over, again and again, the position of feet and poles on turns. Determined – he would make the descent whichever way he could.

He aligned himself sideways to the run, his skis, poles and body angled against the pull of gravity. He began his long journey. He moved slowly and deliberately with chessboard concentration. The early turns were rigid. He dug his poles in too deep, but they were effective. He made four or five zigzags against each one taken by passing skiers. His measured descent was ponderous but safe: his progress marked by the black icons at regular intervals. Around halfway down exhaustion hit him. His legs went into painful spasm. He stopped side-on for a breather. He summoned up strength to continue. His skiing improved. His turns became more relaxed – two-thirds of the way down – almost casual. The run gradually flattened out with no more warning signs. His tiredness vanished. He began to enjoy himself.

It was then that Helen spotted his royal blue ski-suit and bright orange helmet. She had taken her moderate slope down and made her way around to the base of the black run. She was relieved, astonished – and jealous. She watched as Mike, with no experience at all, descended as skilfully as any of the experienced skiers. He prolonged his run with languorous turns, as he basked in the afterglow of his newly acquired skill – his scare at the top forgotten.

No longer concerned for his welfare, Helen became impatient, watching what she reckoned was a show-off display. He reached her waving his poles aloft in triumph. She lost her temper and accused him of taking the black run deliberately.

'You can't resist the challenge, can you? You have to get your kicks.'

'Let me explain.'

'Explain what? How you couldn't care less about me, Ben, anybody, when you are chasing your thrills?'

Mike smiled at her. 'I slipped off my seat. I didn't mean to.'

Helen got angrier – he was openly smiling – the story behind the smile untold. He had enjoyed the last bit of the run, that was undeniable, but more importantly, he had found a way round his fears. *Perhaps I've conquered them at last.* He felt cured. He was ecstatic, and it showed.

'Nobody 'just slips off'. You knew exactly what you were doing.'

'Helen, I.......'

A longer argument was nipped in the bud. Some crazy guy, crouched in a ball, came hurtling straight down the run at phenomenal speed, to brake at the last moment in a blinding snowstorm turn in front of them.

'I'll bet he's Japanese,' Mike said.

Helen assumed he meant *kamikaze* – not the echo from Tikal.

Exposure to the steep alpine heights did produce a strong echo of his fear. But it was manageable. After Tikal's trauma partly shared with Ben, Mike deemed the worst over. *Achilles healed?* His smile drifted away. Deep down, he deceived himself. He needed a solid belief, the last piece of a jigsaw, a sharp click of a perfectly hit golf ball. It was none of those. He didn't paper over other people's problems that way. Internal angst, together with Helen's burden in the equation, impeded complete salvation.

Mike viewed a world susceptible to tiny changes. A flutter of a butterfly wing in the West could cause a hurricane in the East. Minimal inputs on his part had made dramatic changes to some people's lives. Such changes went unverified in private practice. It was insular. Any feedback came from patients, voluntarily. At the hospital it was slightly different, and recent follow-ups by both his team and management had unearthed some rich seams of appreciation for almost negligible efforts on his part. It was most gratifying.

Mike covered a large sphere of people at the hospital. Many social dramas were played out before him. Social workers sought his advice on family matters or individual predicaments originally referred to them. They occasionally revolved around patients' core cognitive flaws masked by domestic squabbles. Misconceptions or mistakes blighted counselling. They had to be identified and addressed before it could continue. Mike found this more interesting than his auxiliary staff. He enjoyed being a consultant detective. They thought it a slog. A few months ago such a social worker came to him for some guidance.

'Dr. Daniels, I'm making no headway with a family case. Could you possibly lend a hand?' she asked. Mike was happy to oblige.

He arranged to see the family and anticipated one or two long sessions hearing everyone's views. The young daughter arrived first. Her boyfriend had been hanging around outside, waiting for her. Her behaviour was evident from the outset. The lad meekly asked where she had got to, and she silently flinched. He became annoyed. 'Don't you have a go at me,' she said, and glanced at Mike for sympathy.

Mike focussed on the crucial clue. Her body language was the marker of subtle aggression. The young lady slightly, but consistently, flinched her head even to his neutral questions.

The family arrived and offered their accounts. The father regularly lost his temper and threatened to slap his daughter's face. Mike made no reference to her regular flinch. An uncritical observer, he turned to the boyfriend.

'Were you angry she was late?'

'No. I was simply asking.'

'You were criticising me,' she said.

'No I wasn't.'

Her response – the silent flinch – was almost imperceptible. It promoted her as a victim, falsely accusing others of attacks, so inviting aggression. Unaware how it had subconsciously irritated him, her boyfriend became angry.

She turned on Mike – and the tears. She argued and tested him with the flinch. He pointed it out to her.

'What do you mean?' she asked.

'You aren't aware you're doing it?'

'No. I suppose it's me being nervous,' she said.

Unconsciously used, to get her own way, her flinch made people angry then sorry. Her father had been hoodwinked. It triggered his further threats or uncontrolled slaps. Chicken and egg – he felt obliged to make amends after losing his temper. Mike's neutrality was met with the same petulance. It required some effort not to be intimidated.

With a key source of their arguments exposed, the family screened the daughter's behaviour and she actively avoided flinching. Their relationships improved and the counsellor pursued her role to a fruitful end.

Mike's single intervention was the norm in these cases, but not the last he heard about their progress. He had forgotten that one. Yesterday the counsellor mentioned it. This large unit had that advantage – it was unusual to hear about his ex-patients in his private practice. At the hospital, management, with all its faults, did follow-ups routinely. Whilst their goal was a cost-and-value equation, the spin-off was vocationally rewarding for Mike and his team. His contributions were tiny but they undoubtedly helped auxiliary staff to perform their tasks. Successful results were a shared satisfaction for all the team.

The contrast between what were once his onerous hospital duties and his exciting and almost privileged private role was fading. His *Independence Day* helped to justify and accelerate funding and improvements for his NHS clinic. Whilst Mondays remained valuable days to explore cases more fully, the rest of the week was proving to be equally enjoyable and fulfilling.

If the NHS, with all its management and costing controls and large turnover and demand was the supermarket, then Mike's private practice definitively served a niche market. Not in an elitist sense – his fees were minimal. He saw some people wishing to distance themselves from the medical world and GPs – the usual first port of call. Those people didn't appreciate being labelled with obscure illnesses – or having their cards marked officially. Others saw him simply on recommendation or by self-referral.

Mike started the car and let the Clifford Brown CD conclude the exotic *Night in Tunisia* – Brown's last. He died aged twenty-six in a car crash after that very session – genius extinguished by a NanoMO of the mundane. *How fickle, how brittle, how unfair life could be.* How difficult it is to accept life's random injustices. He had heard the morning news at least twice, and the droning, moaning, interim dialogues on Radio Four would continue until 9 o'clock. The crisp and bright March morning soon lifted his spirits. Spring was well on its way.

One downside to living in the sticks was the English Winter. The rest of the year, away from the city, the sky grew larger. In winter it shrank, lowered by dreary grey clouds. And the countryside was colder and unrelentingly damp.

Mike was reinvigorated by the skiing holiday. Winter got him down if he went without a sun-filled break in the middle. It was bad enough for him. He knew better than most people how hard it must be for sufferers of depression or SAD syndrome.

His early morning introspection came to a halt at the surgery car park. Today's new challenge was Roger, a businessman. He had fallen victim to the current economic crisis. As a long-standing managing director, fifty-three years of age, he had seen his firm been forced to merge with another. To reduce costs in the hostile economic downturn, the staffing was pared back. This applied to all levels of management as well as company directors. His counterpart in the other company was his junior by some ten years, on a lower salary, but equally capable. The inevitable result meant that Roger's world was turned upside down. In the cruel world of commerce he'd had to clear his desk the moment he was made redundant, take his severance package, and gear himself up to a different style of life.

Mike had witnessed people distressed, both psychologically and financially, by such shocks. The most balanced of people could succumb to intolerable stress and rendered impotent to redress their plight. Contending with screaming spouses, distraught children, school fees, mortgages, creditors and perceived loss of respect with colleagues and friends hardly induced clear reasoning. Stringent objectivity was the most important, and often the most elusive skill that people required in these situations.

Having been used to his past dependable and generous income, Roger urgently required new employment at a similar level of remuneration. He was responsible for university fees and living expenses for his children and serviced a heavy mortgage on his home. These burdens and the inference of personal failure could have incapacitated him. But Roger coped well, using his undoubted business acumen to buy the company car for a trifling sum, and keep his finances on an even keel.

He came ostensibly to address the difficulties he was having at interviews in his search for a new job. He dressed immaculately, grey pinstripe suit, glazed black shoes and a white shirt, its collar sharpened by a blue, solid woven silk tie. That gave an impression of being in control, but Mike guessed he was suppressing a mountain of stress. Roger was well qualified to take on any management position. He knew several companies who would benefit from his wide experience. However, at interviews he was intimidated by the competition from other applicants. Each, without exception, was his junior. Companies affected by the recession veered towards younger applicants. They were eager, energetic and on lower salaries. Roger felt at a distinct disadvantage and interviewed poorly. 'I'll do all I can to help,' Mike said.

Roger was skating on thin ice. One crack – an unsympathetic bank, a repossession order, panicky creditors or an unsupportive wife – could place him in a critical position. Such toxic cocktails can wreck lives. Mike had seen the domino effect leave men without a wife, children, home, a job or any remnant of self-respect or hope for the future. He had to keep Roger in a positive frame of mind.

'At least you're in good health.' He immediately regretted the comment.

'That's the bottom line,' Roger half-joked.

'Sorry. I didn't mean it to come out that way. You have a good attitude and you can plainly handle financial pressures.'

'I suppose,' Roger concurred. 'But I have never been put in such a predicament.'

Retaining his self-esteem and determination to find suitable employment, he rejected two offers at a lower grade. His refusal was neither false pride nor over-confidence. He wished to minimise his trauma over the long term. Panicking into any job was the wrong solution. His logic was perfectly sound. Mike examined his situation objectively.

'Roger, you could take this crisis as an opportunity to better yourself. Why restrict the search to your old level of employment?'

Roger pondered. He had all the credentials necessary to move up the ladder.

'Those jobs are scarce, Mike.'

'But plum jobs – you could turn the tables. You'd be competing with people who were probably your senior. They would be at a disadvantage to you.'

'Yes, yes I suppose they would.' Roger tuned into this new wavelength.

'Could success in such posts lead to extended contracts and even to being headhunted?' Mike asked.

'You could be right. Those positions tend to be short-term contracts but they are more lucrative.'

Encouraged, Roger noted the plusses in his favour. With his experience – composure in a crisis and confident abilities – he *could* compete at senior management level. He interviewed well for those top, highly prized positions. With the tables turned, he held the aces over his rivals and was soon snapped up for a post superior to his lost one.

A tiny quotient of insight helped this capable chap meet his challenge. Mike was delighted. Once again, a minimal intervention had effected a massive change for someone. It was one of the reasons why, against Helen's advice over encouraging spongers and drug addicts, he would press the odd £1 coin into a street beggar's hand.

'Tell him to get a job,' or 'He'll waste it on drugs,' Helen would say, angrily.

'It might make a difference,' or 'Better a fool than a pig,' he would reply, borrowing one of his mother's quaint observations.

Conversely, Mike appreciated the joy people had condensing reservoirs of information into a handful of symbols – succinctly representing complicated ideas. Picasso created beauty and truth with just a few strokes of a brush or a bicycle handlebar and saddle. Einstein distilled his complex theory of relativity down to $e = mc^2$. Four amines produced our very existence.

CHAPTER NINETEEN

'Tis the privilege of friendship to talk nonsense, and to have her nonsense respected. CHARLES LAMB

After nearly a year all six friends got together again. It was a special occasion. Alice and Archie were both playing at the Festival Hall. John's suggestion that they all go and make an evening of it appealed equally to his wife, Liz, as to Helen and Mike. The concert was a sell-out: the programme, Mozart's *Jupiter* and Beethoven's *Pastoral*, a popular choice.

Helen would have had trouble persuading Mike to go but for seeing their friends. The pieces were frequently played and the *Pastoral* especially was ruthlessly exploited in commercials. Helen was pleased he had agreed to make the effort – for her. She was eager to see Liz in particular, and Mozart and Beethoven were two of her favourite composers.

Mike had managed to get the afternoon off to avoid a rush-hour journey to London. It turned out to be one of those treasured, sunny March days: a perfect overture to the concert and a prelude to the long-awaited end of winter.

'Take the Mazda?' Helen asked, as she rustled up a snack lunch.

'Sure. You drive down. I'll drive home.'

'I can do both.'

'We'll see,' Mike said, rather keen to have a turn in the sports car.

Hood down, wind deflector up, heater on, dressed warmly; they hummed their way on empty lanes towards the M1. It was one of the least busy periods of the day but, with a section under repair and the warning of a minor accident ahead, they rarely exceeded 50mph on the motorway.

'Could you do this daily?' Mike said, off again on his hobbyhorse.

'All those cones – no thanks. Roadwork signs – no workers!' Helen replied.

Traffic came to a standstill. Frustrated, Mike fought the impulsion to get Helen to creep into the hard shoulder lane as they approached the slip road.

'At last,' Helen said as they left the M1.

'London – is larger and livelier in a convertible,' Mike said.

'Hmm, and smellier – phew – that uncollected rubbish.'

'Don't be so negative – smell that coffee,' Mike countered.

Helen stopped for Mike to pay the dratted congestion charge. She studiously ignored a couple of builders' flirty remarks, but was secretly flattered and amused by their continued attempts to attract her attention, in spite of Mike's return.

'What are you so happy about?' Mike asked.

'Can't I be happy?'

Helen was in the best of spirits crossing their favourite bridge to park at the South Bank for the day.

'I fancy a nice long stroll along the Embankment,' she said.

The walk came to a halt. A jetty timetable had caught Mike's eye.

'Let's take the river. A round trip to Greenwich leaves in ten minutes.'

'It's for tourists,' Helen replied. 'You stay clear of them abroad.'

'The boat – it's empty. It'll be fun.'

The boat chugged off with no more than a couple of dozen people sharing perhaps two hundred seats. Mike and Helen sat alone on the rear bench.

'This is so...' but before Mike could say 'romantic' the loudspeaker croak of the guide assaulted their ears, harsher than a collapsing slate roof.

They laughed at their misfortune but in doing so must have encouraged the persistent corn and atrocious puns that punctuated what were genuinely interesting facts about the passing sights on the Thames. In spite of the racket, they did enjoy themselves. As they left, Mike dropped some small change into the guide's cap, which raised Helen's eyebrow.

The evening air quickly cooled. The falling sun painted a Turner sky. The city's slick silhouettes were a fine contrast. Perfect for the walk towards Hay's Wharf and to sit outside in their loosened warm coats, sipping coffee. Ibrahim Ferrer's distinctive voice achingly drew a melancholic *son*, out of the door of the bar.

'What you smiling at?' Helen asked.

'You. You're smiling too.'

'Isn't this the best city on earth? I could happily live in town,' Helen sighed.

'Perhaps when we're pensioners,' Mike replied.

'That's when people move out of town. *You know*, retire to the country,' Helen said, as if it was news to Mike.

'We could be different. Free bus passes,' Mike said, his furrowed brow contemplating the suggestion. 'We could roam anywhere in London.'

'*Here* we go,' Helen said, alerted to a new brainwave.

'I mean it. The countryside's no picnic in winter – it's much warmer in town – think of our bones creaking in old age.'

'I'll buy you another '*round tuit.*'

It was Helen's name for the pottery she had bought during their tour through Somerset one summer – a model of the circular 17th century Yarn Market in Dunster – it was a token consolation for his inability to *get around to it* with some of his schemes.

The sun had set – its masterpiece gone. The evening chill set a brisk walk to the Festival Hall to meet their friends in the foyer. It was filled with concert goers and weary city people sitting around the bar, unwinding, relaxing, soothed by a drink and an insouciant trio playing mellow jazz.

'Helen!' Liz called out with a loud giggle, having failed to attract their attention with her eager wave. Helen and Mike responded, simultaneously realising they were ten minutes late. Unforgivable – they had spent too long meandering around. Where had the day gone? Their friends had managed to arrive early, coming directly from work through the rush hour. But the delighted couple warmly greeted and congratulated them.

'You did so well to get here on time with your long journey,' Liz said.

'The traffic was appalling,' John bellowed.

Mike and Helen exchanged glances without comment.

It was an exciting evening. Alice and Archie had gone off to change and would pop back before the start. Mike brought a bottle of chilled *sauvignon blanc* and six glasses to the table. The couple returned in full evening dress, standing out from, and getting the attention of the crowded bar. They were vibrating – charged with nerves and electricity – thrilled their friends had come.

'You both look so smart,' Mike said, pouring the wine.

'Just a sip please – we're on in twenty minutes,' the musicians said, shy as ever.

'Same for me,' Helen said. 'I'm driving later.'

'Noooo – I am,' Mike said and poured her a full glass.

Her shrug confirmed her partiality to the Marlborough wine.

'We must be off.'

'Hope you enjoy it.'

'See you in the interval.'

'We'll wait for you by the bar.'

With that gentle duet Alice and Archie departed.

The full auditorium applauded vigorously at the end of the Mozart. For all its familiarity it was brilliant played live. No matter how good CDs and hi-fis were, they failed to force the sound into Mike's bones like live performances. Whether it was the visual orchestral activity or the finer separation of the instruments – the piece sounded almost new. He sensed an extra gusto from nuances unnoticed before: why people flocked to concerts.

The foursome made their way down to the hospitality bar to congratulate their friends and meet other members of the orchestra and the conductor. The air crackled. Faces glowed with the sheen of perspiration. Excited, lighthouse eyes flashed in all directions. They were champing at the bit to play the second, larger symphony.

The Sixth was played superbly and transcended the commonplace. Its commercial exposure apart, Mike usually treated the *Pastoral*'s fixed narrative in each movement as a barrier. He disliked having his imagination dictated to, even by Beethoven. It was different tonight – magnificent. Poets describe spirits soaring: Mike felt his corpuscles redden, endocrines squeeze, heartbeat strengthen, vision sharpen, as undefined aspirations rose within him.

The concert over, Alice and Archie emerged.

'That was superb,' Helen said.

'You played brilliantly,' John said.

Both sets of eyes shyly peered downwards.

'Thank you, we're exhausted,' Archie replied.

Alice concurred with a sigh.

They coagulated and moved away from the noisy crowd and their canapés and drinks.

'I can't hear you,' Liz said.

'No it's impossible here,' Helen replied.

The sponsored spread was more than ample, but John's more than amplified voice was unable to overcome the surrounding hubbub for an intelligible conversation.

'Let's move on,' he called out, gesturing to the exit door.

'How about a bite?' Liz asked.

They agreed to a late snack at her *great* Turkish restaurant nearby.

'Brrr – it's turned freezing cold,' Mike said.

'What were you saying about it being warmer in town?' Helen asked.

They walked briskly, away from the river and past The Old Vic, towards the restaurant. At eleven o'clock it was busy with the theatre's exodus and other London night owls.

'Table for six, please,' John boomed.

'Be about ten minutes, sir.'

They patiently waited, their hunger sharpened by the walk in the night air and the excitement of the day.

'Ooh. I fancy that,' Liz said, as a waiter passed by with an aromatic dish.

'The food or the waiter?' Helen whispered.

'Both!'

Alice and Archie quietly scanned the tables and studied the appreciative nodding heads as they savoured the food. Once they were seated, the proposed meagre snack changed to starters and main courses.

'Mixed mezze for six to start,' John told the waiter.

'With some extra tarama, please,' Liz added.

It arrived sooner than expected. They ate at leisure, catching up with news and gossip.

'My,' Liz said, 'I didn't notice earlier. You've both got a tan. Where've you been?'

'Does it still show?' Helen asked. 'We went skiing last month.'

'How long have you two been into that?' John asked.

'Helen used to go with college friends. It was my first go,' Mike replied.

'He frightened the life out of me,' Helen said.

'Take no notice,' Mike protested.

'You loved it. Admit it, you daredevil,' Helen said.

'*What* did you get up to this time?' Liz asked admiringly.

Mike pursed his lips and lowered his head.

'He was brilliant. He thoroughly out-skied me,' Helen said.

Mike tried to steer the conversation away from skiing, to no avail.

Helen went on to relate in detail her version of his feat. It was different from Mike's. It was *very* different from the truth.

'After three days' practise, Mike decided he could ski,' Helen told them.

'I keep telling you. It was an accident.' Mike said, again protesting his innocence.

'It could well *have* been. You can't resist danger, can you?'

Mike tried to explain to their friends. Helen countered his attempts with *her* truth of events. He vaguely hinted he was nervous about heights. Helen's frustrated riposte was devastating.

'You would have gone to the open edge of Grand Canyon if I hadn't stopped you,' she shouted. Helen rarely shouted. She was irate. That was extremely rare.

'You've got it all wrong.'

'*I've* got it wrong!' Helen said, sarcastically. She turned to the jury. 'You should have seen his disappointed expression.'

'Helen, it wasn't like that.'

'That's what you said on our climbs in the Lake District.'

'I wasn't keen at all.'

'And I suppose you weren't that keen in Tikal.'

'I wasn't, Helen. I've told you umpteen times.'

'He says he was scared. Can you believe it?' Helen said.

'I was,' Mike pleaded with them.

'Thrilled! Thrilled! That's the word. That's what you meant.'

'Please. Let's drop it.'

'Drop it! You risked Ben's life up that bloody temple.'

187

Helen grew angrier with each plea. Trapped again! Every occasion Mike, or fate, tested his resolve his reputation as an adventurer increased. Helen saw his past desensitising attempts as a genuine love of heights – Tikal seasoned with extra bravado. The friends interpreted Mike's protests as modesty – his smiling photo atop the temple giving proof to all. They had no idea how wrong Helen was over that day's skiing or of Mike's frustration that evening.

'I believe Helen. Mike's like all men: naughty boys at heart,' Liz said, trying to lighten the mood. John, laughing, pointed a finger at Mike to let him see he was in good company. Neither was aware how they added to Mike's irritation. But they did help calm Helen. Alice and Archie kept quiet.

So once more the myth grew. Helen had given her version to the kids. It added to the many exaggerated accounts of Mike's exploits from their grandparents. Even Ben had barely raised an eyebrow. He had not skied and had no idea how steep a black run could be. Relating it to their friends was a different matter. They had sympathised with Helen – sided with her, even – to Mike's further annoyance. Once she had calmed down, they were more neutral.

'I can see why you get so angry. He's a handful,' Liz said, blatantly displaying her admiration for Mike.

'Few people could do that – I certainly couldn't,' John said, truly impressed.

Mike continued to dig his hole. He tried his best to correct Helen's portrayal. It made matters worse. John accused him of false modesty. Mike tagged fraud to his embarrassment. Helen gradually began to sense the hurt in his eyes.

'Sorry, everyone – my fault – I didn't mean to spoil the evening,' she said.

'You haven't, Helen. We all have our little tiffs,' Liz said.

The main courses arrived. The discourse had moved up in step. It revolved around deeper topics: highbrow issues. Mike had been unusually silent until lamb chops and spicy koftes, grilled to perfection, alerted him to his hunger and their conversation. Archie and John were discussing what a gestalt was.

'A few bars will soon identify a pop song or a classical composer,' Archie said.

'You can recognise Beethoven, Mozart or Mahler almost immediately,' Alice said.

'What do you think, Mike. Aren't gestalts in your field?' John asked.

The sextet's conversation followed a set score. Mike was often their reference point playing a solid bass rhythm to the lighter fantasies of Archie and Alice and Liz. They ignored his didactic streak – it never bothered them.

The musicians had cottoned on to the gist of a gestalt.

'Music *is* a good example,' Mike replied. 'An orchestra is greater than the sum of all its instruments.'

'And a chord gels into more than its individual notes,' Alice added.

'You've got it. That's perfect,' Mike said.

'Yes, and John can identify almost any make of car on sight without seeing its badge. That must be a gestalt,' Liz said, stretching its meaning.

'She calls me an auto-twitcher,' John said with a mock scowl.

'Yes, he's like my cousin. He can spot birds by the way they sound, move, rest, or appear, even from a distance,' she replied and giggled.

'He says it's their *giz*. Would you call that a gestalt?' John asked.

'Could do,' Mike replied.

As a student he had found gestalts weird and wonderful. He later discovered how common they were, despite the mysterious name. Liz and Helen noted how a few combined brush strokes often suggest far more than is actually painted. They went on to discuss how people easily recognise and distinguish between a

Van Gogh and a Renoir or Turner, or identify composers, gestalt or not.

'Another bottle of the house red, please,' John called, his voice louder and more boisterous; his cheeks and nose noticeably redder.

The waiter made to pour for Liz.

She and Mike put a hand over their glasses.

'So we're the drivers.' She nudged him.

'Some can take the Tube home,' Mike replied with mock jealousy towards the musicians.

'We've got to thread through the blessed cones again,' Helen said.

'I was chatting to a time and motion official the other day,' John said, as he contentedly drained his glass. 'One analysis of road maintenance showed some men were occupied no more than fifty seven minutes in an eight hour day.'

'Are you surprised? We didn't see a soul doing anything all the way down,' Helen said. Her despair unintentionally primed Mike for his pet grouse.

'Too many cooks; too much sub-contracting,' John said. His dismissive boom set off the fuse.

'You're right,' Mike said, 'They could easily reduce frayed tempers and long queues.'

'How?' Archie asked, nervously.

Mike ignored the feebler voice – he was addressing John. It discouraged Archie from further engagement.

'Road maintenance is all cockeyed.'

'And how would you change it?'

It was a perfectly sober question, from a somewhat inebriated John.

'Use massive teams – concentrate on one major project at a time.'

A frivolous response, but Mike's compressed, telltale frown said otherwise. Maybe it was an attempt to restore his self-esteem from the sham Helen had innocently foisted upon him earlier. If so, he took full advantage of the opportunity.

'Labour is quantified by man-hours, material and machinery costs, ignoring any inconvenience. Take a 100,000 man-hour job. If two hundred people were employed they'd need around three weeks. If a thousand were used, it could be done in four or five days,' Mike said.

'You're ignoring the logistics of getting men and machinery in place.' The well-lubricated voice was louder.

'No. I'm talking about macro projects that might take weeks even with a large workforce,' Mike said.

'Where's the benefit?' John asked.

'You agree the costs to the taxpayer will remain the same?'

'Probably,' John nodded, trying to follow.

'Say you had five similar projects all using two hundred people over three weeks. That's fifteen weeks of motorway misery for the public. If forces were combined on each of the five projects it would cause no more than about three weeks of disruption to complete all of them,' Mike said, triumphantly.

'It has to have a downside,' John said, no longer attempting to keep up.

'Not at all – people would readily forgive a short upheaval.'

'Utopian,' John said. A benign smile crossed his face: the new bottle had arrived at the table.

'No. A well publicised prior warning – perhaps call it Mega roadwork – would encourage people to avoid the disturbance and chaos.'

'It's simplistic or tomfoolery,' John said. He could no longer focus on deeper matters. 'I sense sleight of hand here,' he continued. He finally dismissed the argument with an expansive sweep of his arm.

'Magic?' Mike asked.

'Magic. Who believes in magic? You claiming you can cast spells?'

Many glasses of wine were speaking. Mike shrugged his shoulders and ignored John's aggressive response.

'You two still at it?' Helen asked. She had turned away from her quartet to take her coat from her chair. 'Mike, you're obsessive. It's getting late.'

'We mustn't miss the last train,' Alice reminded Archie. She adjusted her woollen scarf.

They settled the bill and walked together towards the car park, the musicians saying goodnight at the Tube.

'I can't put my finger on what's wrong with your idea, Mike,' John said, his head clearing in the cold night air.

'Must it be wrong? Ask your time and motion man. See what he thinks of management.'

Helen and Liz discussed plans for a day out together.

Both conversations shortened the walk and soon turned to goodbyes.

On the journey home Helen, warmed by the heater and drowsy from the wine – their row forgotten – was soon asleep. Mike was exhilarated by the drive in the open sports car and the clear night sky until dictated by cones to a single lane on the M1. He re-tuned to his theory – *any hidden penalty?* Motorways are national lifelines. *Essential journeys could be made.* Costs and total man-hours stay the same for each project. *Any snag?* The materials required stay the same. The more economic rotation of operators and machinery would cut unnecessary duplication and costs, he concluded.

Halfway home, in his head, he was advising the Dept. of Transport. The logistics – moving large workforces and machinery around the country – are minimised by geographical planning. A macro approach in a sequential Mega roadwork programme was superior to smaller schemes run concurrently. Costs and public inconvenience would be greatly reduced.

As he drove he promoted himself to Minister for Transport. In his first, impassioned, speech to Parliament he demanded they instigate this revolutionary system.

'Constraints for structural engineers and other professionals will insist upon minimum intervals to monitor each stage. Minor modifications can satisfy those essential controls. Mega Roadwork will reduce delays for drivers, with lower costs for taxpayers.' It is truly a win-win situation and a vote winner for the Government, he informed the PM.

Mike's political career evaporated as he negotiated the familiar bends in the last narrow lanes of the journey home. The surrounding countryside was bathed in chilly silver. The pitch-black sky and full moon underlined Mike's sense of isolation and reminded him how late it was. Helen remained snugly dozing until Mike switched off the Mazda's engine – awakened by its roaring silence. He guided a tottery Helen to the front door. They sank into bed and deep sleep.

'I'm sorry I lost my temper last night,' Helen said, over breakfast.

'It was my fault. My little contest with heights.' Mike's attempt to *share* was abruptly halted by Helen.

'I don't want to go through all that again. It's over. Let's forget it.'

Mike gave a sigh in surrender. 'It *was* good seeing them again,' he said, defensively.

'We ought to do it more often,' Helen replied. 'But you two were going on a bit about motorways. John must have been bored to tears.'

'Well he wasn't, and he couldn't produce any flaw in my idea. I was trying to find one. I can't.'

'Engineers must have their reasons to operate as they do.'

'Do they ever take in the big picture for transport? Remember how cheap and efficient the railways were in Italy and how they got us to the smallest villages?'

'That's Italy.'

'It's the same in other countries – Spain that year. What have we got?'

'So you're going to change the railway as well?'

'Railway! Since Beeching, it's just main stations connected by increasingly congested roads. And high charges at full car parks – and crammed passengers – and exorbitantly expensive fares,' Mike said, building up steam.

'And? And? Will that be your moan when we next see John?' Helen asked.

'Sorry. It's *so* annoying. Moreover, you say the same.'

Helen secretly shared his view even if he was out of his depth. She accepted the demands of shareholders and others – the downside of a capitalist economy – far more readily than Mike. He was no businessman.

'No. We're talking hard cash, materialism here, not people's *private lives and emotions*,' Mike said, peeved by the skiing row.

'One extreme to the other – from Nanos to Megas,' Helen said.

'Sorry – what's that?'

Helen repeated herself.

Mike had noted the medical journal open at Helen's article. He was too engrossed reading to respond.

'This is good,' he said, lifting his head, changing the subject.

'Thank you,' Helen replied pausing for a mouthful of cereal. She silently wagged her spoon at him as she swallowed, then added 'I hope others think so.'

'Would that reduce costs and waste that simply?'

'*Yes*. And make my life a lot easier.'

'How come?'

'Whole packs – easy to monitor and repeat for patients.'

'*If* they order multiples of 28.'

'Precisely – that's the magic pay-off.'

'Last night, talking to John – I mentioned magic – he blew up.'

'A bit the worse for wear, wasn't he?'

Helen's article was dressed as a fable entitled *The Magic Square*. A grandfather tells his grandchild how a clever young doctor notices a wet, unused, little box earmarked for 'days' at the top of a prescription. It was crying. 'Nobody takes any heed of me and I have so much to offer,' it pleaded. The medic enters 28 in the box. His sympathetic response is rewarded with the square's secret. Written in earnest for GPs, the story concludes with the child asking the vital question.

'Will the others use the square now?'

And the grandfather replying,

'I doubt it. Grown-ups don't believe in magic.'

This grown-up does. Mike found it in people, in psychology, and in the medical world. The subconscious; subliminal suggestion, hypnosis, the placebo effects of homoeopathic medicine, acupuncture, even the latest technologies like MRI scans: all were touched by magic.

CHAPTER TWENTY

I'd rather have a bottle in front of me than a frontal lobotomy.
DOROTHY PARKER

'Can I have a peek at my diary for this month please,' Mike asked Phyllis as soon as he arrived. His list was almost full. It was brought with her usual efficiency, accompanied by the Darjeeling and two plain chocolate digestives.

'You asked me not to take on new patients until I checked with you. A gentleman rang urgently for a private chat.'

'What did you tell him?' Mike asked with a raised eyebrow.

'I pencilled him in for the four o'clock you left free last week.' Phyllis was even less confident she had acted correctly.

'That's fine. But no more appointments until the end of next month,' Mike said.

'I'll ring him to confirm, Dr. Daniels.' Phyllis picked up her phone – relieved.

At four o'clock Mike made his acquaintance with Simon, whose first words were, 'I don't think I'm normal.' New patients frequently made such remarks.

'Forget normality – it's statistical – have you got a fingertip missing, one and a half cars in your garage and about one and three-quarter children?' Mike asked. Normal, non-pathological behaviour covered a broad span of eccentricity and idiosyncratic traits.

Simon insisted on confidentiality. He felt that people were acting oddly towards him and were wary of him. Recently it had come to a head. Mike must conceal his problem from everyone. 'Especially my GP – it could jeopardise my job if he put it in my medical records.'

At the end of a busy day he would sip a quiet pint in his local and read the newspaper. It was nice to have a rest, wait for the rush-hour traffic to subside for an easier journey home. He wasn't a heavy drinker but this became a regular habit in recent years. In spite of his entrenched opinions Mike made no criticism. Simon was perfectly sensible and limited himself to one drink and at least bided his time before driving.

It was at one of his locals, as he sat alone in a corner, that Simon first noticed the barman surveying him. He had repeatedly done so recently. It made him apprehensive – guilty even – for no good reason. He knew the barman had to be watching *him*. He had also been treated in a brusque manner. The barman was happy to see him leave. In recent weeks, feeling unwelcome at this particular one, he tried another pub. Similar things started to occur at that one. Simon became even more stressed. Once again he was treated in an odd manner and made uneasy.

Initially Mike discounted Simon's description of those publicans' behaviour. He sometimes got served that way himself. Barmen could be offhand if overstressed or in a bad mood. Dealing with the public can be stressful. Someone as quiet and sensitive as Simon could be made a scapegoat for other customers. Mike was more interested in Simon's reaction and he concentrated on that. His probing questions inadvertently increased Simon's anxiety.

'Do you think I'm paranoid?'

'The man who left Twickenham after the first scrum?'

'Sorry?' Simon asked, puzzled.

'The players were talking about him.'

Simon smiled. He gradually relaxed and continued to present himself as a pleasant, somewhat introverted, but intelligent man.

'You are possibly reacting to stress of some sort. What may have caused that?'

'I've no idea. I've got no other problems.'

'See how you go after our chat. If you have to see me again, give my secretary a call for another appointment. The earliest she could fit you in would be next month.'

Mike stopped his eyes following Simon too closely as he rose to leave the room. He was about as abnormal as any normal person. *I doubt if I'll hear from him again.*

Everything had run surprisingly smoothly that month. Mike didn't have to re-arrange his schedule one jot. He did have one concern, however: Simon had made several phone calls, desperate for an appointment. Phyllis said he sounded distressed and agitated last Friday. Mike managed to squeeze him in for today.

'I hoped our little chat last session had given you some perspective.' Mike said.

'Me too.'

'So, are you feeling any better?'

Simon's expression tensed. His forehead perspired slightly – his hands overactive. 'It's got worse.'

He was fully convinced he was being victimised. He went on to relate the past few weeks' events.

'It makes no sense. Why would unconnected strangers take offence?' Mike asked.

'I have no idea. That's what bothers me. Am I going crazy?'

'You don't seem crazy. You're under some sort of pressure.'

'That's for sure – but why – what?'

'Who can tell – a hidden trauma from the past – suppressed? Stress can exaggerate problems – even non-existent ones.'

'You mean it's my imagination?'

'Not necessarily – you've heard of mirages in the desert?'

'But it seems so real.'

'Take heart. People are rarely mentally ill if they're aware of their odd behaviour.'

198

'So where do we go from here?' Simon asked, gratefully aware he was aware.

'I'll see you again next week. We'll start with a brief résumé of your past, so give it some thought.'

Simon told his story. It was unremarkable until he mentioned a family tragedy in his childhood. He was brought up in one of those run-down boroughs of London. He and his older brother were playing on a demolition site that had flooded to form a large pond. They created adventures for themselves by making commando raids to enter the area, thwarting the security hoardings. One day they chose to play pirates using loose doors and other debris as rafts to cross the water. His brother slipped. Neither of them could swim. Simon was left screaming for help. None came. Hidden behind the hoardings he couldn't be seen or heard above the outside traffic. His brother drowned in front of him.

That set off alarm bells and Mike's empathic response, dogged by a similar trauma throughout his marriage to Helen. He silenced the ambient noise. He keenly latched onto Simon's story, amazed how he had coped so well dealing with his tragedy.

Simon was fully alert to his feelings of guilt. He had accepted it and made no attempt to rationalise his inability to save his brother. He had worked through it unaided. He did however, during the later discourse, use the phrase 'drowning my sorrows'. *That's it!* Mike did not point out to Simon its probable connection.

The initial assessments had produced enough material for Mike to sift through for the moment. He wandered through his notes trying to find structure in Simon's behaviour. It was fruitless. Further minor matters emerged from Simon's past. Mike ignored them. Simon's day-to-day life increasingly dominated the sessions as his reported encounters worsened over the weeks. One evening, a publican told him he was limited to one drink, which was strange as that was all he ever had. Another day customers moved away from a nearby table where, apparently, they stared and talked about him. He was absolutely certain they had taken strong exception to him. Several such stories pointed to Simon 'drowning his sorrows'. He was adamant that he was not a drunk. In Mike's presence his demeanour was generally mild-mannered, if anxious. It made no sense at all. Mike was making no headway. Simon was getting more uptight about 'normality'. *Is he imagining it all?* Apart from his pub stories, he was perfectly reasonable and lucid in sessions. *That tragedy must be gnawing at his subconscious.*

Simon was seriously stressed on his next appointment. During the week a barman had rebuffed him at one of his locals. The more he protested – the worse things got. Finally the publican told him to leave.

'Sorry, you can't come in here anymore,'

'Why not?' Simon asked.

He got no further reply – other than; 'Ask yourself.'

He left the bar feeling thoroughly confused and depressed – even guilty over his mystery crime.

This, together with the 'one drink' restriction and the tales of other customers' attitudes, suggested he was either paranoid or hysterical, or was unaware of his own behaviour causing offence of some kind. *Is he in denial?* Substantial evidence pointed to drinking or 'drowning his sorrows' as the source of his problems. *Could he be paranoid?* His general demeanour led Mike to dismiss that idea.

Matters finally came to a head the following week. He was refused service at *The Swan*, a place he rarely used. Dropping his natural mild manner he challenged the landlord. What followed was extraordinary. He was told that he had been violently drunk the previous night and had smashed a chair and threatened several customers. Simon insisted he hadn't been there the previous night or anytime in the past six months. The landlord became irate, telling him he was a regular troublemaker, and he couldn't put up with it anymore. They ended up having a flaming row. Once again he went through the shameful experience of being ejected from a pub.

The aggression alleged by this landlord and Simon's admitted reactions in *The Swan,* were out of character – neither introvert nor placid. He had been accused of no particular misdemeanour up until then. He failed to comprehend how he could upset so many people. The specific charge of violent conduct had turned him extrovert and angry.

The picture was murky. Mike's theory, that 'drowning his sorrows' was a window to Simon's troubles, was disproved. The brother's death caused remorse without a trace of anger. *The Swan* episode was unconnected to sorrow or tragedy. Simon was certain he was being victimised. *Was it paranoia?*

That idea was unsupported unless his denials of drunkenness and visits to *The Swan* in the previous weeks and months were fantasy. Mike consoled and assured Simon he seemed perfectly fine in sessions. But puzzled he decided to do some covert research.

The Swan, an Elizabethan Inn, was a local landmark just a two-mile detour from Mike's journey home. He couldn't recall ever entering it. He frequented few pubs apart from the gastro ones – for food rather than drink. Along with many others, this one had smartened up its act recently and was promoting its family-friendly image and new restaurant. Far from being the dreary, smelly beer-house, with regular sops and uninviting staff and surroundings that Mike had conjured up from Simon's tale, it was pleasant. So was the jovial landlord, who welcomed him with a bright 'Good evening'.

Over a glass of plain tonic water Mike casually engaged him in conversation over the recent troubles. The publican described Simon to a tee and confirmed his drunkenness.

'You sure you aren't a policeman?' he asked, for the second time.

'I'm not a policeman,' Mike said, firmly.

'What then? Why are you so interested?'

'I'm someone trying to help, professionally.'

The barman tilted his head and scrutinised Mike and his drink for a moment.

'Ah, I see – AA counsellor.'

Mike smiled. The landlord relaxed and got chatty.

'Your man started coming here, regular like, the past few months.'

'Did he behave strangely from the beginning?' Mike asked.

'No more than one or two others I could speak of. He comes in, sits over in that corner until he's 'ad a few. Then he pesters me at the bar.'

'And you don't consider that a little odd?'

'S'pose not. Some do that.'

'How would you describe him?'

'Lonely – moaning about the world and its troubles – aggressive to anyone who disagreed with him. A bit of a depressive if you ask me. And he downed plenty.'

'Good customer, then?'

'That's the last I'd call him.'

Mike also discovered he invariably ordered a taxi home. He had been getting more obnoxious over the weeks and was regularly rude, both to customers and staff.

'I don't want him giving my pub a bad name. I've built up a good class of clientele here. Last week I decided to put a stop to it,' the landlord said.

'I heard about that,' Mike said.

'He became violent. He smashed a chair to the ground and swore and threatened me and my staff.'

'Why? What did you say to him?'

'I told him he was upsetting my customers. I called a taxi and told him never to come in here again.'

'And after you barred him from *The Swan?*'

'Blow me,' the landlord continued, 'if he didn't turn up next day – bright as a button and all spruced up, butter wouldn't melt in his mouth – and expect me to serve him.'

Mike could scarcely believe his ears but here was proof positive. Could Simon be unaware of his behaviour? Could he forget all his episodes of drunkenness; even his regular visits to *The Swan*? The two wildly divergent accounts of the same events were remarkable. Something was amiss. The publican had no axe to grind, but he described someone acting differently from the person Mike knew. Yet he unshakeably identified him as Simon.

Someone else was drowning in this case. Mike felt out of his depth. He was as astonished by the barman's solid evidence as he was confused by Simon's insistent denials. He accepted his dilemma and concluded Simon needed to see an expert in psychopathology.

Over lunch Mike bemused his hospital colleagues with Simon's case. They agreed he should be referred to the psychiatric department.

'It isn't as if you can ignore it, Mike. He needs a full clinical assessment.'

'I promised him full confidentiality. I'll have to ask him,' Mike said.

This puzzling case and Mike's moral *Catch-22* became the topic of the day at their table. Then – a chink of light. One young doctor mentioned a rare condition he had heard of in medical school. It fitted Mike's patient. As far as he could recall, it was named *pathological alcoholism*.

Mike sifted through a range of references. *Cheat*, he muttered. As on the odd occasion when he was stumped by the last enigmatic clue to a crossword it did not feel satisfying or noble. The Merck Manual had the answer to Simon's symptoms.

In America it was called *pathological intoxication*. It occurred in a tiny number of people susceptible to the smallest amount of alcohol. They suffer a profound reaction with 'acute drunkenness, aggressive and violent behaviour, followed by a deep sleep and amnesia.' It explained both Simon's story and the landlord's contradictory one. The combined syndrome could account for all his bizarre encounters with other publicans. Neither Mike nor any of his colleagues had ever heard of this rare condition, and yet here in this modest practice he had discovered a full-blown case.

'I told you, the other day, I'm simply a crossword man.'

'It certainly wasn't simple to me,' a colleague said.

'All right, it was slightly complicated – I missed the solution. But that one factor clarifies the case.'

Mike saluted a finger towards the young doctor in gratitude.

Whilst Mike's concern for Simon was paramount, he was somewhat elated by his discovery. His confidence was modified though: by one doubt. *An endogenous condition should have come to light earlier. Why had no similar incidents been reported in the past? Simon may be unable to recount them with the associated amnesia. But surely others would have been affected and told him?*

As a matter of urgency Mike had to verify – or dismiss – his findings. *Can I confront Simon without destabilising his fragile equilibrium?* He had discussed the case with colleagues. He felt awkward about that having given his word. It was in Simon's best interests, he consoled himself, and he had at least concealed his identity.

Nobody sought Simon's arrest for public disorder – hardly surprising – publicans were reluctant to summon the police and risk their license. *What solid evidence have I got to present my diagnosis to Simon?* Mike had no proof whatsoever that he suffered from this rare condition. *Can I risk a referral to confirm it?*

He put every area of Simon's life under the spotlight. His personal relationships with his friends and colleagues or how he behaved on holiday, at parties or weddings, or such – failed to bear fruit. Simon was adamant that he rarely drank much. He had admitted to having been 'truly blotto' merely once or twice in his whole life. Nobody since could accuse him of being obnoxiously or violently drunk.

Mike concealed the outside discussions and the unusual diagnosis. He went over all recent events with Simon again. He tried to get him to recollect any other small detail he may have missed. He disguised his tenuous opinion that Simon suffered from pathological intoxication. He tried a hypothetical approach, suggesting the symptoms and a scenario that would answer the problem.

Simon was sure what did or didn't happen in those pubs. How could he forget the embarrassment and sense of alienation from those false accusations? To suggest he had been violent without knowing was, he insisted, outrageous. He didn't get drunk, never used taxis, and was sober at home the night he was accused of being at *The Swan*. And he was not one of its regulars.

Mike had to concur that he hadn't so much as mentioned that particular pub at the surgery, until reporting last week's happenings. Simon was so certain – so unwavering in his accounts – that Mike began to doubt his own observations. He found it difficult to distil all the symptoms and facts into this newly discovered and rare illness. Nothing gelled – no sharp click – no solid reason to counsel Simon about an outside consultation. For the present it was impossible to refer him to a specialist. Mike decided to keep his powder dry until the next session. It proved dramatic.

Simon arrived out of control, hyperactive, exhilarated with a grin from Cheshire and crazed eyes. The word *manic* invaded Mike's head and made directly for the landlord's *depressive* diagnosis. Mike united them. Simon stopped him in his tracks.

'It's all over. *I'm normal*,' he screamed into Mike's face. 'Wait 'til you hear this.'

Mike remained silently bewildered. Simon raved on about how he had gone into a pub the previous night.

'Guess what? I saw myself sitting at the bar.'

Simon silently perused Mike's expression before explosive laughter almost threw him off his seat.

Mike's valiant efforts to stay composed and conceal his instinct for self-preservation sent Simon into further painful hysterics. Mike veered towards having him sectioned – immediately – he had finally lost it.

'Believe me – it's true,' he spluttered, his ruddy features convulsed. 'The guy's my double! My spitting image! My doppelganger!'

And so he was.

Mike's amazement even surpassed that of the landlord's seeing the two together.

They got over the shock of their close resemblance. Curiosity – and amusement – replaced it and the two men became chatty. Simon's double had had a marital break-up, left home, and arrived in the area some months ago. He was depressed, but Simon's misfortunes cheered him up no end. 'Sorry mate, I wasn't laughing at you – it's the situation,' he said.

'Forget it. One day I'll think it funny,' Simon replied. Relieved, he couldn't get angry with this culprit.

Simon had come to Mike with a healthy disregard for psychologists and psychiatrists. It was no doubt fortified by this experience with one.

'What can I say?' Mike murmured, weakly.

'Say? You tried your best. And it did help a bit,' Simon replied, generously.

'So much for…'

Simon stopped him.

'Where can you spot a psychologist?'

'Do tell,' Mike said, primed for the riposte.

'Front row of a strip club – head turned – observing the audience.'

It was Mike's turn to laugh – he did so feebly – but not for long.

'My double told me that one.'

'You told him about me?'

'Yes. Sorry. You have to see the funny side of life,' said Simon with the last laugh.

Mike had neutrally listened throughout this extraordinary story. It was debatable that he had helped Simon – even to cope with the stress. Simon had remained remarkably sane because of his own inner strength. The signposts pointed to a pathological diagnosis. If Mike had continued to follow them – would he have referred Simon for further assessment and treatment? Fortunately he sought solid evidence to justify that radical route. *What a disastrous decision I could have made!* That single step could have put Simon on a treacherous path. *Thank goodness that double turned up.*

Mike accepted this as a cautionary tale. Psychotherapy is not foolproof. Initially, in Simon's case, it had erroneously directed him towards the childhood trauma that he eventually dismissed. Mike had wasted much time and energy running down avenues that turned into cul-de-sacs. He had rejected all manner of possible psychological answers. All he was left with was a medical condition – the far-fetched idea of *pathological intoxication*. The actual solution was no less mind-boggling. Even he could drive down *Cognition Road* without headlights. How strange, he mused, that a case so full of the features he had itemised in his student tutorials had emerged so soon, to prove his fallibility. Once more, it brought him down to earth. It also triggered another bout of guilt and self-criticism with further doubts about his integrity, honesty and competence.

Helen was first to hear the outcome of Simon's case.

'Can you believe it?' Mike said, dejected by his failure.

'Yes, you often take the scenic route.'

That flattened him further.

'I suppose I do. Did you guess a double?'

'No, of course not.'

'Thank goodness for that,' Mike said, heartened that Helen's instinct had failed on this occasion.

'But it's a fascinating story.'

'Is it?'

Pragmatism had set in before his arrival at the hospital the next day. He made no mention of Simon's case – until the young doctor raised it at lunch.

'Had any more thoughts on that patient of yours, Mike?'

'He's fine. He's a different person,' he answered, laconically.

'What?' 'How's that?' The table stopped their chatter.

He laid down his hand, poker-faced. The answer sunk in. Their responses, hoots of laughter and banging the table as he filled in the details, drew attention from others in the refectory. They related the gist of the story to the inquisitive adjoining tables. The same responses echoed to each replay.

Mike pondered. He casually picked up his fork to prod and play with the shepherd's pie. The Simon case had certainly punctured his ego, in more ways than one. But, thinking positively, as he instructed patients, he began to salvage his pride. *It is useful material – good for a student talk. People remember episodes like that.* It was a story told against him but that was irrelevant to Mike. *I'll embroider it into an instructive NanoMO.*

Mike went off for the afternoon 3M – Monthly Management Meeting. The Chanel suit was once again soporifically droning on about her evidence-based hospital performance stats.

'She does go on,' whispered the colleague beside him.

Mike, fixedly gazing at the waltzing crane outside, muttered a dry reply.

'One more elephant in the room and the floor will *physically* give way to her.'

That was the current catchphrase. *How many more could they come up with?* Over the years he had cringed in agony over the umpteenth; 'getting our ducks in a row', 'joined up thinking', 'singing from the same hymn sheet': not to mention all the 'lessons to be learned' and the 'fit for purposes'. It was enough to hear politicians on Radio Four endlessly lay claim to the same regimented, self-important watchwords. *How much longer to suffer?* He disengaged. At the end of her appraisal she flattened Mike's alpha waves with his name.

'Dr. Daniels – if you could spare me a moment please – a quiet word.'

I wasn't asleep. My eyes closed – that's all. What is she going to do? Give me a detention?

'I hear your last lecture went well. Could you give another someday soon?'

'Perhaps. If I could fit one in. I'll see what I can do.'

'I do hope you say yes. This *is* a teaching hospital.'

Mike dismissed compliments. This one competed with recent self-doubts. In contrast with structured professionals he was often the static bystander; an observer, an astronomer, a silent twitcher, no more. The activities occurred outside and around him. *I'm an inert tripod that helps sharpen perceptions.* Thus Mike labelled himself dull. But it was more than the singularity of the new that people found attractive. They appreciated stability and steadfastness. His repetitive routines and bland reliable self, formed reference points and benchmarks that his patients, colleagues – and Helen – depended upon. Even during initial assessments people did derive some comfort from his presence. They were not privy to his inner analyses. As far as they knew, he was merely listening to their anxieties: someone to talk to. That alone gave perspective and solace.

CHAPTER TWENTY-ONE

Avoiding danger is no safer in the long run than outright exposure. Life is either a daring adventure or nothing. HELEN KELLER

Helen glanced at the kitchen clock. Mike was late.
'Sorry darling – I got held up with some paperwork,' he said as they kissed hello.
He put down his briefcase and settled into his kitchen chair in front of the mug of tea.

Helen's ESP had let her down. She had put the kettle on long before he had entered their village. She was convinced they shared telepathic messages – *in extremis* sometimes – like her reaction to Tikal's temple. Mike failed to convince her it was more to do with subliminal cues, habits, or coincidence.

The tea had cooled, awaiting Mike's arrival. He politely drank a few mouthfuls and poured the rest into the sink behind Helen's back.

'Where did this come from?' he asked, sliding the *Lonely Planet* towards him.

'The Library,' Helen replied, nonchalantly.

'Who said anything about actually *going* to Australia?'

'No-one, I thought it would be interesting to thumb through.'

'You're conniving, aren't you?'

'No. You suggested we might go,' Helen shyly whispered.

'I said, I can't make a decision yet,' Mike said grimacing at her affected innocence.

'I'm preparing, just in case.'

Helen and her 'just in case's' – she had set her sails on a course.

'Please don't bank on it.'

'Of course not,' Helen said wrapping her arms round him from behind the chair.

Her childish teasing bore fruit. Mike's features softened.

'We'll see,' he said and smiled.

She had made first base.

Helen returned to her cooking. Mike wandered into their lounge nursing a gin and tonic. He stopped in front of one of Helen's watercolours. It was his favourite; Palladio's 16th century wooden bridge over the Brenta River in Bassano. The scene had entranced both of them a few years ago. Helen had sat engrossed on that grassy bank for a full afternoon sketching and mixing her colours.

She popped her head into the room.

'It's ready. We'll have ours before the girls get home.'

'That's not like you,' Mike said.

'Claire could be late and, anyway, Amy will need a shower.'

'I love this picture.'

'Dinner will get cold. You can love it later.'

'Now and later – you're talented.'

Helen moved towards him and rewarded the compliment with a kiss.

Mike slowly sat down at the table, brooding over his lack of any artistic flair.

The rich casserole was Mike's favourite. Helen served it bordered with bright orange carrots and vivid greens.

'Thank you,' Mike said in a voice so flat it turned the food grey.

'Mike you're so down in the dumps lately. You need a holiday.'

'You're conniving again. Am I getting on your nerves?'

'Why do you say that? You don't – in fact, you inspire me. We both need a break.'

Helen found the best ploy to snap him out of one of his dips was a little flattery.

'Inspire?'

'Yes. How you appreciate that picture. Remember when we came upon it?'

'Sure – I loved the place at first sight. It was the year we were in Verona.'

'That was such a romantic trip,' Helen said.

They gazed at each other and shared *déjà vu* smiles.

Over dinner they relived the week spent around the Opera. They had each chosen a day's excursion. Helen had her heart set on going to Padua, particularly to see the Giottos in the Scrovegni Chapel. Along with a score of other privileged visitors, they had gazed in awe at the realism and the three-dimensional effects in the frescoes. Mike chose to see the Teatro Olimpico in Vicenza: Palladio's masterpiece. After that visit *he* decided to drive into the Veneto countryside. Then serendipity lent a hand and they found themselves in Bassano for lunch.

'So you see, Mike, you helped me find that scene.'

'Come on. I am not going to take any credit for that.'

Helen dismissively turned with the empty plates towards the kitchen.

'Lovely stew – delicious,' he purred, following her.

'That day, you gave up your afternoon for me,' she said, countering Mike's change of subject.

'Willingly. Other than spotting that bridge I didn't do a thing.'

'But it helped – like one of your NanoMOs. You were as critical as a catalyst in a chemical reaction.'

'The heck I was. You've got rose coloured glasses,' Mike said.

'You once told me people don't see themselves as others do. Well you're the perfect example,' she said and handed him the dishcloth.

As they silently finished the washing up together Mike reflected on that episode.

'What are you thinking about?' Helen asked.

'Bassano.'

'You were hanging about for me for hours. You must have been bored but you didn't complain.'

'No. I went for a long stroll. On my return I watched you from the bridge, engrossed with your sketchpad.'

'That must have been a thrill,' Helen said, deadpan.

'You eventually noticed me. Our eyes met and you gave me one of your special smiles.'

Helen studied him silently.

'What?' Mike murmured, defensively.

'You're smiling. What are you smiling at?'

'You – so lovely by the river.'

'See? You encouraged me,' she teased – pleased she had lightened his mood. 'At least admit you helped a weenie bit.'

Mike left the room, still smiling at the images of that day.

'Anyway, Mr Doom-and-Gloom has exited, stage left,' Helen called after him.

Within the hour the Saab pulled out of the drive again, its engine still warm. It was a short trip to pick up Amy from the station. Claire was making her own way home from school.

'Damned cones – they're everywhere. We're going to be late,' Helen muttered.

'Relax. It'll soon clear.'

Congestion brought the traffic to an infuriating stop-and-start procession.

'You're right.'

'About what?' Mike asked.

'Mega roadwork.'

On the way home Amy gushed about her team's lacrosse win and how she had got her black eye.

'What have you guys been up to today?'

Yes, it was *guys*. Internally cringing Mike let it go with a pained smile. Helen jumped at the opportunity to reveal the plans she had been making for Australia. Mike made no attempt at any sort of smile on that news.

'We've been organising a trip,' Helen said.

'You scheming minx,' he said, 'I said I've yet to decide. What about the girls?'

'I told you – Mum and Dad will stay with them again – they love doing it,' Helen said.

Amy instantly turned peevish. 'You'll go, Daddy. You will. You always give in at the end,' she said.

Amy told Claire about Australia the moment she arrived.

'That's not fair. It'll be another year gone,' Claire screamed.

'We want to go with,' Amy demanded.

'I'm *so* jealous. You were supposed to take *us* on a trip this year,' Claire shouted.

'Yes Daddy,' Amy frowned. 'It was the same last year – and the year before – and you *promised* you would this year.'

'You did,' Helen agreed.

'Why isn't Ben here? Three to one against – I need him,' Mike said in mock despair.

Whilst Ben had his own life, having started university, the two girls continued to be dependent on their parents. And they were right. Ever since his trip with Ben he had said he would take them on an adventurous holiday one day. This year he had promised.

'I'll think about it. It's different for girls. It can be a bit tricky.'

'What? My father's the chauvinist? I'm nearly thirteen. I had my bat-mitzvah last year and you promised, even then,' Claire shouted, and promptly left the room – slamming the door.

How am I supposed to take the girls on an adventure? He would be fully responsible if plans went awry – with no stalwart Ben-at-Tikal beside him. With the girls, and Helen worrying over them, it needed to be risk free.

The girls pressed him harder by the day for a firm commitment. Although a mild sense of guilt may have helped tip the balance, the idea became attractive. It would be fun. They would soon outgrow family holidays. He knew Helen would regret that even more than him. Soon the girls would spread their wings and go away with friends. Then gap years. How often would they see them after that?

'We can leave Oz 'til next year,' Helen said. That sealed it.

'If we went on an adventure as a family, would that suit?'

'With Mummy as well?' Claire asked.

'Is that dissent?' Mike replied.

'Of course not, we'd love Mummy to come.'

'How about after Christmas – could you both squeeze it in before school starts?'

'Yes,' Amy screamed.

'It's good with me. I'm free 'til mid-January,' Claire said.

'Where shall we go?' they asked.

'You two come up with some ideas, then we'll all decide,' Mike replied.

Helen and Mike exchanged amused glances as they listened to the girls effervesce.

'I have to see jungle,' said Amy.

'What about the Amazon?' Claire asked.

'South America – cool.'

'The Galapagos?' 'Peru?' 'Macchu Pichu?'

It was extraordinary how these two young ladies came up with so many ideas.

They took and changed flights of fancy to each faraway place with increasing excitement.

'Sooo many choices,' cooed Amy.

Mike shrugged his shoulders and offered Helen his trademark plastic clown face with raised eyebrows. Helen jutted her chin forward as she smiled and shrugged in reply.

'It's time we were all in bed. We'll talk about it in the morning – 'night.'

Their goodnight kisses failed to interrupt their two daughters' breathless scheming.

'Mike, have you realised what you've done? Let yourself in for?'

'And you. I'm curious what they're going to come up with.'

'They can't get over-adventurous – I won't let them.'

'Darling, stop worrying – they'll be fine.'

The girls' discussion continued over breakfast, as if night hadn't intervened.

'Have you both got your costumes and towels?' Helen called from the top of the stairs. They had.

'Right, we're going. When will you be home from tennis?' she asked Mike.

'One, one-thirty?'

'Try not to make it any later. Remember Ben will be home – ravenous as usual.'

Triple 'byes and kisses and they were off.

Mike, dressed in tracksuit and trainers, was almost ready to leave. He finished his second coffee and read the team news for the afternoon's football. The phone rang.

'Police? What's the problem?'

'Is this Dr. Daniels?' the officer asked. The flat emotionless tone immediately set Mike's nerves on edge. *Had the girls had an accident?*

'We've got a critical situation at the hospital: potential suicide.'

'Suicide? Who?' Mike asked. His relief masqueraded as calm.

'A patient of yours – Tony Clayton.'

'Clayton? Clayton? I've seen him once – last week,' Mike said, aware he was trying to disown him.

'That's as maybe, but we've been given your name as the one contact who can help.'

'Surely you have people specially trained for this?'

'We've tried. We've got nobody local and it is the weekend.'

Mike offered other suggestions. They were rejected.

'All right, I'll come,' Mike replied wearily. 'Be ten minutes.'

On the way, he commiserated with himself. *Damn it. It's perfect weather for a game: light breeze and mild.* He drove up to the three police cars parked in front of the entrance.

'I'm Daniels. Where's the patient?'

'Over the other side Doctor, follow me,' the sergeant said.

They turned the second corner and walked straight into a group of around a dozen police mingling with a junior registrar and some auxiliary staff.

'Where's the patient?' Mike asked to nobody in particular.

'He's in the tower.' The words echoed about as the group pointed to the crane dominating the half-built new wing.

'I can't see anyone,' Mike said, hoping they were mistaken.

'He's about halfway up – see him? – he's moving up again,' a senior officer said. He tutored him in a strangely incongruous, matter-of-fact manner. He sounded like the one who had phoned.

'How the hell did he get up there?'

'Easily, apparently: no builders at the weekends.'

'Why did you suggest *me*?' Mike asked the junior registrar.

'Clayton came in earlier insisting on seeing you. I told him you were off duty. He went berserk and tore off, screaming abuse. Then one of the nurses reported seeing him on the base of the crane. I got her to call the police.'

'I see,' Mike said and turned towards them..

'One of our men went over to him. He started to clamber further up. We tried to calm him down but he continued climbing. We decided to hold off and wait for our Chief to arrive,' the sergeant said.

'He then threatened to go to the top and jump if he couldn't talk to you. So I thought it best to await your arrival,' the officer in charge said. 'What can you tell us about him?'

'Hardly anything. He's in his late teens. His girlfriend jilted him for his best friend. His GP put him on paroxetine – it's for depression – and sent him to me. I have no other information.

I've briefly seen his medical history and done no more than make preliminary notes.'

'Well, it's you he demanded,' the policeman insisted.

'What do you expect me to do? Have you got any contact with him – a mobile?'

''Fraid not, Doctor.'

'How can I talk him down?'

The officer's eyes scanned his men to warn them off untoward sniggers.

'How are you with heights?'

'Me – go up t-there?' Mike said. He hoped he had covered his slight stutter.

'It could be his best hope. He climbs up higher if we approach him. He's determined. Perhaps with *you* making the effort he'd come down and talk.'

Mike pondered for a moment.

'He appears to be using a sort of ladder inside. Is it secure?' he asked.

'Yes. The crane's walkway is enclosed up and along by a lattice of steel. It's pretty safe as long as you don't slip off the rungs going up and can stand heights at the top,' the officer replied.

Mike felt a thump within his chest and tried to dismiss it. It was adrenalin. Quite normal, he assured himself. More adrenalin, butterflies, pulsating temples – he ignored them. *This young man's life is at stake*. Mike had heard anecdotal reports of suicidal reactions with paroxetine. They hadn't had one at their unit, but it was a possibility. Whatever the cause, this lad needed help – and fast.

'Leave me with him. Keep your men well away. I'll call on my mobile if I need help. What's your number?'

Mike walked slowly towards the crane. He reached the base and waved. Clayton stayed where he was, watching. 'I'm coming up, Tony. Meet me halfway,' he called out, through cupped hands.

Mike jumped up onto the platform and entered the tower. Inside it, he glanced up and saw Clayton's head peek out over his shoes. He looked much higher up from here. Mike considered the long climb to reach him and his glands secreted another shot of hormone. He maintained control. Yes, it was daunting – but protected by the *triangulated* metal framework do-able by him. Five years had passed since Tikal. He hadn't suffered a twinge since – apart from his escapade skiing.

He started upwards, fortunately ideally dressed for the ascent in his tracksuit and trainers. At about fifty feet, a third of the way up, he paused for a breather. He lifted his head but could no longer see any sign of Clayton. Mike felt a gentle movement within the metal structure. *My imagination?* The early morning breeze had strengthened and sang eerie ghostly music in the metal framework. *Can Clayton hear me through this noise?* He shouted louder. Again his missive fell short. It was pointless. Trying to hit two hundred yards with a putter. He continued upwards and stopped at the two-thirds point. Not his imagination: the crane was definitely gently swaying. The wind rush was much louder. He saw no sign of Clayton, either in the tower or along the crane's arm. *Has he jumped?*

Below, Mike's eye was drawn towards a *triangle* formed by the three parked police cars. They stood blocking the front entrance to a growing crowd, now joined by a TV unit. *No reaction from them. He must be on the jib by the tower, masked by its vertical lattice.*

'It's me – Dr. Daniels – come down to talk,' he called out again unconvinced his shot would find its target even from here.

Near the top he saw the slim figure start to move along the jib. Adrenalin coursed through Mike's body. He was no longer its master. The tower occasionally gave a slight shudder like a train over tracking points. The wind had developed into a gale. It growled at him as he raised himself onto the long jib arm.

Clayton drew halfway along and started to wriggle out of the passageway formed by the latticework and the safety wiring. The jib violently jerked as a strong gust of wind hit the flat side of the concrete ballast at the other end. Clayton almost shot off the frame. Mike's head and shoulder were thrust through one of its apertures. Along the jib was Clayton with his arms and legs entwined in the metal framework.

Mike looked down.

The crane's tower was behind him, out of sight. Just thin air – all the long way down, between them and the ground – and that was it. As the terrifying downward force of gravity pull at him his buried beast came surging up with the howling wind. The jib gently jostled him from side to side. His legs melted as he slowly sunk to his knees on the trellised walkway. His head swirled around in a fierce eddy. The nausea rose from his stomach. He was in crisis. Helpless. Paralysed.

CHAPTER TWENTY-TWO

The greatest obstacle to being heroic is the doubt whether one may not be going to prove one's self a fool; the truest heroism is to resist the doubt. NATHANIEL HAWTHORNE

B en arrived home earlier than expected. He sat reading the papers over a late breakfast. Kelly, his girlfriend, had had hers. She had gone into the lounge and switched on the TV. She rarely watched it in the morning. She had regularly told Ben those who did so would watch anything on the box – unlike her. The station reverted to the local TV studio after the National News. She remained watching.

The link girl gave an update on the day's local events then switched to live coverage of a serious situation. What a treat for that large swathe of dedicated viewers who loved accidents or emergencies – particularly live ones. They thrived on videos of police car chases that ended in tragedy, insensitive to any injuries to either felons or bystanders. And they feasted on bombings and earthquakes without a moment's compassion for victims. No doubt the TV producer was cheered that he had an exciting show for those ghouls that quiet Saturday morning.

Kelly found the broadcast tedious with its continuous inaction on camera challenged by the persistent commentator insisting that something was happening. As she reached for the off switch the camera panned away from the inaction. She became immediately involved and interested.

'Ben, come here quickly.'

'What's the matter?'

'Is that your father's hospital in the background?'

'Yeah – what's going on?'

'Apparently some maniac is trying to kill himself. Someone from the hospital is trying to talk him down.'

'Down? Where is he?'

'Up on that crane – they're zooming in again.'

The reporter dramatically pieced together the snippets of information coming down his earpiece as the camera moved in.

'The police have told us a Doctor Joules from the psychiatric department, has persuaded them to let him try and reason with the patient. He's gone up to coax him down.'

'Dad's never mentioned a Dr. Joules. I'd remember that name. He did say Joules?'

'Yes. I think so,' Kelly replied.

Think so. Perhaps the producer thought so. Perhaps the reporter thought so. Perhaps they *said* Dr. Daniels. Perhaps he only caught the end of the name. Perhaps he *heard* Dr. Dan Joules. Panic set in. Ben feared the worse. It couldn't be Dad? He left a note saying he would be at tennis this morning. He tried to calm himself as he clicked on his mobile. It rang. It kept ringing.

Mike recognised his ring tone under the noise. Pressed down on all fours, overcome by fear, he forced his hand to move. He held on tighter with his left hand and reached for his mobile with his trembling right. He desperately needed help and would have to rely on the police. He located and pressed the green button with his thumb.

'Yes?'

'Dad?'

'Ben?'

Mike, surprised it wasn't the police and momentarily overjoyed to hear his son, loosened his tenuous grip, and dropped the mobile. It bounced on the metal walkway grid. His frantic attempt to catch it knocked it upwards. Static, at the top of its parabolic flight, Mike made a desperate effort to grab it. He reached it with his fingertips but they failed to grasp it. Instead, it hit a metal spar and span off the crane. He watched it rotate.

Down, down, down it went. In slow motion – forever – confirming the long drop before hitting the concreted ground.

'Dad. Dad. Where are you?'

Ben got no answer.

The TV reporter excitedly whispered into his microphone. 'A small item has fallen from the crane. Could be a mobile.'

'They must have tried to contact the guy but he's thrown his phone away,' Kelly called out.

'What! I've got to go to the hospital. Wait here.'

Mike had stubbornly ignored his fears on his ascent. Ghastly nightmares, replays of past panics and futile efforts to cure, flashed in front of him. He had successfully stifled all the warning signs, oblivious to any danger: until the moment the wailing wind sent that shudder through the *triangular* tunnel. The sharp clang of metal traumatised him. The lost mobile isolated him with the threatened suicide. Both of them urgently needed help. His desperate plight tipped him into a maelstrom of irrational fear, guilt and shame. He suppressed that but couldn't move. Clayton could – he aggressively wriggled, thrashed and squeezed through the metalwork.

'You're like all the others. You don't care either,' he screamed above the noise. Outside the frame, primed to jump he held all the aces.

'I can't…' Mike dragged out of his throat, as loud as he could.

'Can't what? Stop me?' Clayton shouted angrily.

Stop him. How can I stop him? Both their lives were in the balance. In paralysis, Mike was helpless. First Clayton would jump; then, shaking with fear, he would lose his footing and fall to his death in the tower. It was ordained. His dread – a fall from a height – would happen today. His life would end aided by a willing accomplice. *My family! They would blame themselves: Helen for rejecting his truth, Ben for concealing Tikal. Both permanently stained by guilt.*

'Help me,' Mike pleaded. He was living his worst nightmare – a fall ending with a dull thud. Would that be Clayton's fate? A young life lost in a split second? *It would be my fault.* He could barely suppress the guilt that churned his stomach: the fear that strangled his throat, the shame that drained him physically.

'Help me,' he pleaded again, desperately controlling the hair-trigger reflex to vomit.

'Help *you*. Trying psycho tricks, are we?' Clayton screamed, with a hollow laugh.

'Help me, *please*. I'm petrified by heights.'

It wasn't the pleading. It wasn't the pretty-please. Clayton was shocked by Mike's contorted expression. He gazed, transfixed, and felt the full force of the sheer horror in those bulging eyes. Bamboozled he searched his mind's blank screen for his deleted menaces – in vain.

'You're really terrified,' Clayton said in a measured voice. 'You risked this for me?' He took a long intake of breath. Held it. Then burst into tears.

Minutes passed. What would Clayton do next? Would he try to jump or was it a turning point? Mike did not speak: chance the wrong words. He waited and watched. Clayton methodically thrust his arms and head, and squeezed his body, back inside the jib. He could scarcely believe that Mike had risked his life for him. Someone terrified. Virtually a stranger.

Mike's panic subsided – relieved by Clayton's move from the brink. But he intentionally maintained his twisted features – they kept Clayton under control. It was his one opportunity to save them both.

'Tony. I need your help to get down,' he said with a quivering voice.

He watched that request register with Clayton and saw his sense of worthlessness slowly fade away to be gradually replaced by some semblance of self-esteem. Clayton was no longer overwhelmed by an imminent desire to leap. This was a calmer Clayton. Mike noted another change – in his own perception. In spite of all the noise and shuddering in the weathervane jib, as it fought the wind, the iconic passageway was secure. His worst fears over, he hammed up his anguished appearance as a defence against Clayton changing tack.

'I can't make the descent,' Mike said. It was a convincing lie. 'You can help me. And be on television.'

Clayton was mystified.

'See the TV crews? You'd be a hero. I could manage it if you went in front of me.'

They moved down, slowly. Clayton bore his new responsibility with great caution. It deflected his mind off his personal angst. He regularly stopped and turned to check on Mike. Around halfway he saw no further need. Mike was at ease.

Mike revealed no more than that. He was actually pleased with himself – as on the second half of that black run. Once more he had overcome fear – and possibly, at last, cured himself. It was certainly a move in the right direction. He hadn't been sick. If nothing else this experience, as at Tikal and on the Alps, had put his reactions into perspective to give him temporary, if not permanent, respite from his phobia. This time he had the added satisfaction of saving someone's life. Towards the bottom, he paused and put his hand on Clayton's shoulder.

'Thank you, Tony – you saved me.'

'We're even, then.'

'Not quite: I owe you one. We've got a lot to talk about.'

'I suppose we have. Now?' Clayton asked.

'First, we could both do with some rest. We'll speak tomorrow.'

The registrar and two policemen seized hold of Clayton as he stepped onto the concrete base and escorted him off to the hospital.

'Super job, Doctor – well done,' the Chief said, shaking Mike's hand as they walked towards the applauding crowd. Ben sprinted forward.

'You OK, Dad?'

'Sure. How did you get here?'

'It was on local TV.'

'Hmm, I saw the crew. Does your mum know?'

'Yes. I got her a moment ago as they came out of the pool.'

'Did you mention Tik…?'

Ben stopped him.

'No way,' he replied and concluded their secret exchange.

After a short de-brief, the Chief emerged to give interviews. The news teams surrounded him. He lauded Mike, as well as his men, for their professionalism. Mike, his son and the Chief walked away and the crowd began to disperse.

'Can you believe it? He expected to be on television. He's a nutter,' the Chief said. 'He's telling them he saved *you.*'

'He did. I told him I was afraid of heights,' Mike confessed.

'Clever ploy, Doctor – and he fell for it,' the Chief said admiringly.

'*Did* he?' Mike said. His voice was flat and resigned. He was irritated by the misplaced regard.

'Very droll, Doctor,' the Chief said, on another planet. He left, his head tossed back, chortling to himself.

Mike responded with pleading eyes towards his son. He noted the mixture of pride and apprehension in Ben's eyes.

'How could you risk going up there?' Ben frowned. 'It *was* like Tikal, wasn't it?'

'A bit,' Mike replied. 'Can I borrow your mobile? Mine's a gonner.'

Ben handed it to him with a half-smile. Mike rang home.

'Ben, Mum says to remind you about lunch today. And you'll want to say hello to the girls – they're going out later.'

'I forgot – and Kelly's waiting for me. I'd better dash.'

Ben shot off. 'See you at home,' he called out, running backwards.

Mike responded with a raised hand, the other holding the phone to his ear.

'Yes, I'll be home by one thirty. Love you, too.'

Helen greeted him with a silent kiss and tight hug. Mike sensed that was more to do with relief than affection.

'The phone hasn't stopped ringing. It's driving me mad,' Claire said.

'Mine has,' Mike said, reminding his son.

'If you've finished with my mobile can I have it please?' Ben said. His outstretched hand insisted.

'Dad, you're a hero, going up that crane,' Amy said. She was bubbling over with excitement. 'Weren't you scared?'

'I'll bet your Dad enjoyed every minute. Grandpa used to tell you how he loved climbing,' Helen said sharply.

'He also told you,' Mike began, 'believe nothing you hear…'

The usual family chorus added '…and only half you see.'

'But they all saw it on TV,' Amy protested.

'So it must be true?' Mike replied.

Ben looked askance at his father. His lips remained sealed. He realised how easily his Dad got trapped in this double bind. Today's exploit had cast his reputation in stone. It was absolute. How could anyone possibly comprehend the dilemma he had faced? The girls, Kelly included, were staring in awe. He glanced at his Mum. He first assumed she was gazing at Mike with pride. He was wrong. She was glaring. He turned again and caught his father's eye. Mike noted Ben's deep sympathy. It was writ large on his face.

Helen stared deep in thought, perturbing Mike. Why did he have to continuously flirt with danger? Selfishly, without any regard for her feelings – was he that insensitive – ignoring her fears? She again misread him. He warmly gave so much to other people – why so diffident with her? Why was he always so reserved on her bad days?

Helen's 'Lionel days' weren't helpful to either of them. Mike kept his distance on those anniversaries. The barrier Lionel created between them had grown higher and wider in the past year. Helen remained obsessed with his memory – worse – it triggered her negativity over today's shenanigans.

The girls left. Ben and Kelly went off for a walk. Mike braced himself for the raging onslaught – the predictable reaction in her eyes. Helen gave full vent to her anger. 'You can't resist, can you? Not satisfied dragging Ben up bloody temples, you go climbing cranes,' she screamed.

The same pattern emerged over and over again; first the fear, then the relief, and then the anger. Mike could no longer tolerate these Lionel-inspired rituals. They unnerved him. They began to corrode his love and respect for Helen. He had to tackle matters and get Helen to accept her loss. She was getting worse. 'How could you risk your life?'

'I had no choice.'

'No choice! You couldn't resist, could you? The police said you volunteered.'

'No, Helen, I *did not* volunteer. They were desperate – their counsellor was an hour away. I had to do it. A life was at risk.'

'Yes – yours – you didn't think about the children and me. Did you?'

Mike pleaded but failed to convince her that his actions were in the line of duty, not pleasure, and taken with great caution.

'Helen, please.'

'Please what: it isn't enough to have lost my brother!'

'Helen, I'm not a drunken driver,' Mike shouted, as if he had been accused of killing Lionel.

'What? What did you say?' Helen screeched.

'You can't keep dumping all your anger onto me.'

'Are you trying to analyse me again?'

'I don't need to. You have a fixed pattern,' Mike snapped.

'What pattern?'

'First you're scared someone will die; then you're relieved they haven't, and finally you lose your temper and blame it all on me.'

'Do I?' Helen snapped.

'Yes, I'm afraid you do.' A touch of uncharacteristic nastiness crept into his voice.

'Mike......... I'm sick to death of all your theories.'

'It's not theory.'

'Yes it is. I'm sick of your probing – your mumbo jumbo.'

'It's not mumbo jumbo.'

'And I'm sick of you and your – your – your *fucking* psychobabble!'

Helen stormed out of the room, slamming the door so hard that bits of plaster fell from around the frame.

*   *   *

Mike was shocked – Helen never, *ever* swore like that. He had alienated her. A solid stonewall of silence separated them. He assumed Helen was partly aware of her behaviour. He was wrong. She was not. For years he had failed to address the problem right in front of his nose. It could threaten their marriage if handled insensitively.

His world was at stake – on the table – and he was not a gambling man. *It's my fault.* He went to the kitchen and put the kettle on. It boiled. He ignored it. *Why did I lose my temper: feel so guilty about Lionel?* For several minutes he sat stunned. He examined the events leading up to their argument and its outcome. Yes, their marriage could be in jeopardy, but Helen's outburst meant he had hit a nerve. He had breached her defences. If she were a patient he would rejoice. He was in another double bind. *I've got to settle this once and for all.* He had ignored the

230

unwritten law not to treat family, friends or oneself. *If Helen won't listen to me she'll have to seek outside help.* He switched the kettle on again and made two cups of tea. In the rear room Helen lay face down, her body still shaking the sofa.
'Have a cuppa. You'll feel better.'
'Go away. Is that all you can think of – tea?'
'We need to talk.'
'Talk! Talk! Talk! I've had enough of your tea and talk,' Helen snapped.
'Helen, we can't go on this way.'
'Dead right!' Helen screamed, thrusting her contorted face at him.
Mike calmly sipped his tea. Helen stopped shaking.
'Your tea's getting cold.'
'So what.'
'We need to sort this out – together.'
'Sort out *what*?' Helen snarled.
'Your obsession.'
Helen shot up.
'*My* obsession – you're the obsessive one!'
'Helen, why do you insist on special days for Lionel?'
'Why? I've told you why.'
'I can't accept that any more. It's over thirty years ago. Why haven't you come to terms with it yet? Why are you so determined – no matter what – to visit his grave on those days?'
'I've always gone.'
'I'm not disputing that. Maybe you're afraid to tempt fate by not going.'
'What on earth are you on about now?' Helen demanded.
'Superstition.'
'I'm not following.'
'Walking around ladders.'
'I'm still not with you,' Helen said, irritably.

'*Superstition* – disasters might befall you if you didn't go?'

'Do you think I'm stupid? I'm not superstitious.'

'I may be right – I may be wrong – but it's possible.'

'I don't avoid ladders. I don't touch wood.' Helen was more thoughtful, calmer, as she attempted to rationalise her inner reaction to *superstition*.

'What do you feel on your visits? Loss, anger, deep sadness?'

'Of course – sometimes all of those – perhaps not as strongly these days.'

'So why, then – why are you so inflexible?'

'Inflexible? It's just twice a year,' Helen replied, impatiently.

'Why keep so rigidly to those days? Remember how you made me change that weekend break because of Lionel's birthday?'

'So what are you saying?'

'You were adamant, angry, *frightened* even, to go away. Your urge to keep visiting is akin to throwing spilt salt over your shoulder, touching wood. It's superstition. Magic if you like. Perhaps you think it protects us.'

'What nonsense – I've had enough of this – I've got jobs to do in the garden.'

Helen marched off to the shed then began to water the flowerbeds. She paused. She stood motionless for some minutes. A drip fell from the can. Teardrops ran down her cheeks and off her chin. She brushed her cheeks with her forearm and resumed watering. She stopped again. She turned her head slowly towards the window and stared at it in a trance. She did not see Mike, motionless, shielded by the curtain, watching. *What is she thinking?* She resumed watering until she had drained the can a second time.

Mike watched her pain. *Is this the start of our endgame – a slippery slope to separation, then even divorce? That would be unbearable. Or have I got through to her?*

Helen re-entered, eyes reddened but in control – the calm and practical person familiar to Mike. 'Suppose you are right, what then?' she asked.

Mike was relieved, but Helen's face had aged ten years in an hour, yet she acted as vulnerable as a teenager – unsure what to do next. He could not stomach seeing her distress. He went to her, held her, felt her warm response – thankful they had closed the door on that icy void. Their long, tight embrace turned the key, sealed it shut.

'We'll sort it out,' he said.

Helen was less amiable the next morning. The red tops carried their usual exaggerated and inaccurate accounts of the incident. It also made a few lines inside the broadsheets. When the local rag came out, later that week, Helen became incensed once more. 'SPIDERMAN STOPS SUICIDE,' ran the front-page headline. Inside, pages of tosh and old photos from heaven-knows-where added to Mike's embarrassment. And he had to placate Helen all over again before he could re-address her fixation with Lionel's grave.

Helen was resistant to therapy from Mike. No matter how well he disguised his attempts, Helen saw through him.

'You sound exactly like my father when he sent me to your hospital. You think I am ill – that I need counselling.'

'That wasn't such a bad move,' Mike said.

'What do you mean? You disagreed with him.'

'He did right by you, though,' Mike said, teasing with his clown face.

'Right! How can you say that?' Helen shouted.

Ouch. Idiot! 'I meant it was fortunate – we wouldn't have met otherwise.'

'He's got a lot to answer for,' Helen said with a faint smile.

Mike, wary of causing any further resistance, gently cupped Helen's head in his hands and kissed her brow.

'Yes he has – you, the kids, our happiness,' Mike said.

'Are you sure about happy. What about yesterday?'

'That's over. I told you darling, we'll walk under those ladders

233

together.'

'What ladders?'

'Give next week's visit to Lionel a miss.'

'Merely the idea of that makes me nervous. I need to go.'

'We can go the following day. You won't get struck by lightning.'

'Maybe. I'll think about it,' Helen said, unconvincingly.

*   *   *

Helen slept badly during that week. She woke exhausted from another poor night on Lionel's day.

'Helen, I'm afraid I do have to go in early,' Mike said that morning.

'Mike I'm desperate to go,' Helen pleaded.

'Hold out until I get home. Promise?'

'I'll try. After that?'

'If you insist later *we'll* have the rest of the day to visit then.'

*   *   *

After calling Helen after lunch and speculating the remainder of the day how well she had coped, Mike arrived back that evening.

'Thank goodness you're home. Let's go,' Helen anxiously greeted him.

'Hold on a minute. You've managed to stay away all day – you've done well.'

'Enough is enough. I can't stand the stress any longer,' Helen replied.

'May I have a cuppa first?'

'Sorry – yes – then we'll go?' Helen pleaded, reaching for the kettle.

'Helen, what do you think might happen if we decided to leave it until tomorrow?'

'I haven't a clue and I have no intention of finding out.'

'Find out what? How can your absence have any influence?'

'It will. I sense it. Just because you don't believe in….'

'Believe! Helen it's all nonsense – there is no ESP, sixth sense or whatever you call it.'

'But I've given you proof – remember that night ……'

'I've told you before. It's your mind-set, selective memory or elective bias or coincidence – it's never proof.'

'I'll have to go on my own.'

'Come on – you've managed all day – we'll see out the last few hours together – and go first thing in the morning.'

After much persuasion Helen nervously stayed home. She couldn't get to sleep that night. Soon after midnight she got up, downed a tablet and then slept. Mike's early morning tea roused her.

'Sleep well?'

'Finally. I needed a temazepam. My head's all fuzzy,' Helen replied.

'You are anti-hypnotics. How come you had any?'

'I kept a few – for long haul flights – remember?'

'That was not long haul.'

'Says you.'

'It must have felt much longer than twenty-four hours,' Mike said sympathetically.

'But I managed to do it,' Helen said, groggy.

'You did! I'll go with you before work,' Mike said, honouring his pledge.

'I don't feel up to it. Let's go after you get home,' Helen replied. Mike was astonished. *No urgency – is it solved that easily?*

*   *   *

Mike phoned home to check at midday. Helen sounded fine. *That's a relief.*

Helen's attitude was somewhat different when he got in that evening.

'I must visit Lionel,' she said, quietly.

Mike concluded it was the drowsiness from the tablet that had dampened Helen's fears earlier in the day. *She's on the mend, though – no sign of panic.*

'You've proven you can do it – that's enough for the moment.'

'Shall we go?'

'No disasters have occurred. Have they?'

'I'm still anxious.'

'We'll go shortly. I'll check my e-mails – and have a cuppa first,' Mike said nonchalantly – stretching Helen's resolve intentionally.

*   *   *

On the way Helen made no complaint about the rush hour traffic. She strolled, more casually than usual, up the long winding path and past the many well-kept flowerbeds, towards the graveyard. They stood in silence. Helen's long shadow, cast by the evening sun, reached out and caressed Lionel's headstone. Mike noted her moistened eyes as she turned to meet his gaze. She gently smiled.

'Helen, you're a star,' Mike said on their return home.

'It was strange reading his name – the date – calmly for once at the grave.'

'What were you thinking about?'

'Good memories – it was different today – none of the usual stress.'

Mike reached out and squeezed Helen's hand. She burst into tears. Uncontrollable tears. Her entire body vibrated. Mike held her close. They moved to the settee. Copious tears soaked Mike's shirt. Without a word he continued to hold her. Her long muffled sobbing was punctuated with periods of painful wailing. It lasted for over an hour.

'Sorry Mike, I can't think what came over me.'

'I know exactly what happened.'

'How can you? It was as if Lionel had died last week.'

'Precisely. I saw someone like that some months ago – depressive. She'd been on tranquillisers and sleeping tablets for over ten years after she lost her husband.'

'And she broke down like me?'

'After I got her off all drugs she confronted her loss.'

'How did she react?'

'The same – she also said it was as if he'd died yesterday.'

'Why? How can it be so vivid after so long?'

'You both suppressed it. The sub-conscious has no clock,' Mike explained.

'But it felt so...so fresh.'

'You've de-frosted it from your mind's freezer at last.'

CHAPTER TWENTY-THREE

*When we love, we always strive to become better than we are.
When we strive to become better than we are, everything around
us becomes better too.* PAULO COELHO

At 7.25 the radio came to life, as ever on cue for 'Garry and Sport'. Helen murmured in her sleep and turned over. Mike slipped out of bed and the bedroom. The third stair greeted him with its usual reluctance on his way down to the kitchen. He switched off the alarm, skated barefoot over the cold tiles to set the table and make the teas. He brought them upstairs trying not to disturb Helen asleep. He slid back into bed and sipped his tea, listening to more dire warnings over global warming and terrorism. 'Morning,' Helen muttered from under the covers, somewhere between a dream and waking. Mike stroked her cheek, watched her drift off again, and got up.

He shaved; his eye on the frantic bustle at the bird table. Their early start to the day – the dawn chorus with its strict order of precedence – had fractured his sleep hours ago. Bird breakfasting had a hierarchy, too, with its expected random interruptions. A squadron of long-tailed tits made a short raid. A couple of bullying magpies went away foiled again by the squirrel-proof feeders. The green woodpeckers, as ever, drilled their heads into the lawn. These regular patterns were so reassuring. They produced harmony. He was projecting his own inner sense of wellbeing. Without question, that had grown in the past year or two. *I've made the breakthrough with Helen!* He reached the shower as *Thought for the Day* tried to intrude on his. Mike 'Sinatra' had the *World on a String* this morning. He

238

switched to cold; paused singing as the icy cascade hit his head, then ended the song.

Leaving the bathroom, he kissed Helen as she sleepily passed him. He dressed in his unchanged sequence – left sock first – but from a blue striped pair he had got last Christmas. Would he get similar ones this year? For no particular reason, this morning he felt compelled to take stock. He noted his attitude to life had changed. He was at one with himself. Recently out on the golf course he was no longer determined to win every game. The strong urge to improve and reduce his handicap had vanished. He was happy to participate and take home a handful of pars and delighted with a brace of birdies. At the tennis club he rarely played singles nowadays and settled for the more sociable, less competitive, doubles. He remained involved in road safety, but no longer obsessively. He stopped badgering people with his notions.

Although his life in general had become more mundane, Mike didn't mind. He was content and relaxed. Yes, he kept some targets, and as yet unfulfilled goals, but none of the fraught struggles of the past. He enjoyed the hospital as much as his private practice. Many changes had been made in the past few years. The atmosphere was different: radically so compared to thirty years ago. Conflict had melted away. He was able to delegate the routine stuff, which produced a welcome benefit. He had moments to reflect, choose his cases, share his expertise with newcomers and no longer felt obliged to undertake tasks that others could handle. Life was no longer a contest. He had made the right decision to blend his private practice with his NHS duties. His current incursions into academia with his NanoMO papers were the icing on the cake. He enjoyed the variety. Perhaps he was on the brink of another small change. Conference and other guest lecturing could feasibly become a permanent feature in his life; one Helen would certainly welcome.

He helped himself to a strawberry-flavoured yoghurt from the fridge and a banana for breakfast. It was difficult to pinpoint exactly when the routine of porridge *every* weekday had been breached. Perhaps it had run out – an empty carton responsible. It was a tiny alteration in behaviour but it was significant. Each step contributed towards his unshackling. It also made him oddly happy to note the changes.

Helen had welcomed the transformation over the past few years. Mike was a particularly happy bunny this month after their fierce argument – today more so with *her* progress. Secretly he had blamed Helen's obsession for magnifying his fears. Not anymore. *It was my fault all along – I should have dealt with it earlier.* He was not a free agent yet – he had some more work to attend to with Helen.

'I had an odd dream last night,' she said as she wandered into sight. 'About you – your face was blank.'

'You think I bore you,' Mike said, smiling.

'No. You had no features at all. I had to paint them in.' Helen's fine fingers performed imaginary brushwork.

'I've often said you made me what I am,' Mike said.

'Don't be silly. I think it was to do with that conversation we all had about bare canvases and emptiness and Cage's 4.33. Do you remember?'

'Yes,' Mike said, with a puzzled frown.

'Well I think it solves your problem.'

'*What* problem?'

'Myopia. You can't see in front of your nose. You think you're boring. You're exactly the opposite. I think you're a closet introvert.'

'Whoa – who's the psychologist?'

'You're forced to conceal your methods and emotions.'

She poured cornflakes into her bowl with an eye fixed on his clown expression reply.

'With patients you mean?'

240

'Forget patients. I'm talking about me – and Lionel. In the past you used to appear so remote in the churchyard. You were there for me all along. Now I can see into you deep down.'

'And how am I, *deep down*? Mike asked.

'Personally involved in everything – music, art, sports, politics, nature, travel – you name it.'

'So are you,' Mike said.

'It's mainly how you deal with people – *you're committed to improve their lives.*'

Mike's clown expression face with extra-raised eyebrows marked his reaction. It was hard to believe she had begun to see Lionel in a different light. This morning's evidence suggested she had. *I've finally burst her bubble!* He dismissed the partial success immediately and changed the subject – his triumphal conceit short-lived.

'I can't wait to get away from people and for our next holiday.'

'Mentioning travel reminds me. We'd better start making plans well before Christmas.'

'Do you think the girls genuinely want to go away with us?' Mike asked.

'What do you mean? We've told them.'

'Well, they're both going to have gap years one day. Freedom, independence…'

'And?' Helen stopped him.

Mike had tried to avoid patronising the children as they grew up. He was aware of his strong trait – older brother perhaps – that made him do so: even with Helen. The girls continued to call them Mummy and Daddy. In other respects they were rather mature. Should they address them as Mike and Helen? No. That didn't ring true at all. Even Ben, who had proved his equal, still called him Dad.

'With us tagging along, might they find it a bit babyish?' he persisted.

'No. It's a freebie. And they *do* expect you to keep your promise.'
'Really?'
'Yes, *really*.' Helen was adamant, 'We're going.'
'Where? We've yet to agree where. They were making a list,' Mike said.
''I've got it upstairs. We'd better check it out.'

*   *   *

'So you reckon Costa Rica?'
'Yes. It fits the bill perfectly. And safe – they don't even have an army,' Mike said.
'Do you think it will be exciting enough? You promised them an adventure,' Helen reminded him.
'They'll be excited whatever the choice. It was on their short-list. It'll have as much adventure as they can handle. What was it? Jungle; river trips, mountains, wildlife.'
'And hot weather in January,' Helen added. 'Should we do it without telling them?'
'Why not? You go ahead and try and hold four economy flights.'
'What if they set their sights on somewhere else?' Helen said – her turn to be cautious over the girls' independence.
'That's why I said *hold*.'
The morning post dropped through the letterbox with a thump.
'More junk mail,' Mike called out as he sorted it on his return to the kitchen.
'One letter for you – one for me.'
Mike opened and read his. He gazed at Helen, transfixed by her expressions of pleasure as she caught up with a friend's distant news. He re-scanned his letter and put it down.
'Is it good or bad news? You look puzzled,' Helen asked.
Mike rotated his letter around and pushed it forward.

'What next?' he asked.

'What's wrong with that? Sounds like a good idea to me – you'd be good.'

'Good? I would bore them stiff with NanoMOs.'

'They're asking for a talk not a lecture.'

Recently Mike had given a lecture at the hospital to psychology post-grads. It was set in stone, dictated by his recent paper, *NanoMOs and the Subconscious.* They could easily access it online. *Weren't they bored by the stuff?* He failed to see how a talk to other university students had any purpose.

'Darling you may have upset me, but to them you're famous.'

'Fifteen minutes of notoriety because I climbed a crane!'

Helen accepted status or pecuniary rewards weighed light on Mike's scales. She loved his attitude to life but he could go overboard.

'It will do you good – a bit of recognition,' she said.

'I'll think about it.'

Mike gulped down his last drop of coffee. A quick kiss, 'Bye, darling,' and with a short trot to the Saab, he started the day. Four weeks to Christmas. Where did the year go? He still had much to do at the hospital. And he also had to prepare his private patients and other people for the break. He certainly wasn't free at present to organise some frivolous talk. He could draft one for future use to shorten the long flights. The earliest he could possibly deliver it would be late January. So, first things first: he would have a brief meeting with his team this morning and work out responsibilities for the most vulnerable patients.

'Hi Spiderman,' the hospital pharmacist said. His meeting over, she had caught Mike sitting alone in the refectory. She had recently returned from a visit to her family in India and was after a first-hand account of Mike's exploit.

'Enough already,' Mike replied. The gentle humour failed to mask his irritation.

'I hear your girls have got you tied around their little fingers. Do you need any holiday tips?' she asked, quickly changing the subject.

'I can't see how I'm going to sort out schedules over Christmas, let alone a holiday.'

'You will – and you'll love taking them.'

'We'll see. How did your holiday go?' Mike asked. 'I haven't seen you since. Didn't you have a big family to see outside Delhi?'

'Yes, we have. It all went well but was exhausting. We also had a lovely week afterwards in Kerala.'

'How did you manage to fit in Kerala as well?'

'We *needed* that week's break at the end. Not that that was any easier. Hotel guests found out what I did. 'Is this dose right?' 'Can I take this with this?' 'Are these that expensive?'' Her head wobbled to emphasise each intrusion. 'They drove me crazy at the pool with their medicines.'

'It used to be the same for Helen on holiday until she reversed it.'

'How did she manage that?'

Mike paused to sip his tea and take another biscuit.

'She lets on what *I* do. We get a no-go area placed around us: peaceful solitude.'

The pharmacist lowered her head and pushed it forward, subversively.

'They think you'll find out their guilty secrets and fears?'

'Precisely,' Mike said, as seditiously.

At the end of that afternoon's 3M meeting he was again buttonholed by the Chanel suit. Surprise, surprise – it was about a student talk. Her sights were raised. She had received a letter from the university's professor of psychology. He referred to his invitation to Mike, who had kept the request for an end of semester talk to himself.

'I'm pushed. I can't possibly do it until after Christmas.'

'Yes you can. I'll see to it. Other people will have to muck in and help.'

'Why's it so important?' Mike asked.

'It's your heroics. You're high profile.'

'Heroics! It can wait until January.'

'It can't. Strike while the iron's hot. It will increase the hospital's prestige.'

'So that's it?'

'No – it's the student intake. It's important we attract the best people here.'

'They aren't all post-grads. Some will have started this term. NanoMOs will be meaningless to them.'

'Who stipulated a topic on psychology? Reading between the lines it's a light celebrity type talk they're after for *all* students.'

'Grief, you'll have me on talk shows next.'

'Well, we got one request.....'

'Yes I got it as well. I refused them point blank.'

'Please do the talk.'

Helen and the Chanel suit – a two-pronged assault – I might as well. Mike sighed in surrender. 'Don't blame me for any backlogs.'

Mike got home that evening to find Helen had been busy. And she had told the girls. They were on tenterhooks waiting for his arrival.

'Confirm the reservations. We might lose them,' Claire and Amy insisted.

'We guessed you wouldn't fancy going,' Mike said, and put on his clown face.

They rushed over and mugged him with joyful hugs – toddlers again.

'And you'll let *us* decide what to do?'

'Of course – it's your trip. Mummy and I will be along for the ride.'

CHAPTER TWENTY-FOUR

I'm just preparing my impromptu remarks. WINSTON CHURCHILL

Mike and Helen were spending their limited spare hours apart for a change. While Helen was having fun with the girls, arranging the car hire and hotels, and listing places to visit, he was engrossed in planning his talk.

For the girls it was difficult to pick which toffee to chew. It was such a vast confectionery. They started to refer to having *only* two weeks; not ungrateful for them, but the logistics of covering even the must-sees were formidable. But Helen was a natural organiser and kept Mike's involvement for the trip confined to their meal tickets.

His talk developed entirely outside hospital hours. He couldn't reduce his input whatever the Chanel suit had said. The task became an interesting challenge. They were putting on a buffet for the heads of departments and the medical and psychology students. The informality had Mike pondering what was expected of him. Obligated by all the fuss he made a special attempt to conjure some magic.

In childhood, Mike had planted a bulb that produced, to his surprise, a bright yellow crocus. It was his first encounter with magic. It was iconic. If he could germinate similar images in those young students' fertile minds his talk could be useful, whatever they were studying.

Daily, on waking, shaving, showering and driving, he searched for ideas to conjure up one memorable hour of material for his talk. He reflected on what stuck in his student days. He must avoid baffling theories and NanoMOs to create an indelible impression – pithy and memorable.

A BIRD STUCK ON THE SKY

Churchill had that knack. *Their Finest Hour* or his *Iron Curtain* speeches attached to the memory like Velcro. One speech, to boys at his old school, had three words repeated three times: *Never give in; never give in; never give in.* It was iconic – recorded by some as his entire address – and seen in folk history as courageous.

Courage; courage; the word reminded him of a more prosaic incident. Ben came home from school one day, miffed at getting '*only* an A.' He had spent hours writing pages on 'Courage' for a mock English paper. Another boy got an A+ for a single page, blank apart from three short words at the centre. His teacher suggested he avoid such bravery as *This is Courage* in the real exams.

Mike was going to require a different sort of bravery to impress those legendary boisterous students. What was expected of him? He hadn't taught students, apart from small groups of graduates in tutorials. This was far more daunting than familiar lectures to his peers at conferences. *Sang-froid,* Miles Davis cool – that is what he was going to need.

Mike extolled simplicity to solve problems without relying upon it to produce the most beneficial or long-term solution. CBT was currently in vogue; it was effective, but it had its limits. He wanted to open doors and minds, without limits. How could he succinctly present what were his somewhat complex ideas?

Astronauts and cosmonauts had difficulty writing in space. NASA used massive investment and technology to create ballpoint pens that wrote unfailingly in any orientation, even under water, without leaking or smudging, in a gravity- free environment. The spin-offs produced worldwide benefits and profits for manufacturers. The USSR, with limited resources in a non-capitalist economy, focused on the big picture in their space race with the USA. They gave their cosmonauts a pencil: a neat solution, but with no long-term benefit.

Mike had to go the American way, with his introduction pinpointing the key issues he wished to convey. His pocket diary became more of a Hemingway Moleskine. His notes on lateral thinking, observation, prejudice and, of course, cognition, neatly entered in its pages, crossed off the days preceding his talk. His paternalistic streak was rampant – he had an opportunity to influence a whole new generation. His parents had been ambitious for him, but sensibly so.

'Get qualified in a profession,' Mum said.

Dad took him aside.

'Choose what you enjoy doing and it will never feel like work,' he said.

He did both. Dad's promise was essentially realised. Apart from the dismal Mondays and the restrictions of the past, he embraced his career. How influential those few words of Dad's had been. He was determined to promote similar ideas with the students. The same sentiments obtained. Making a happy choice was as relevant today as then. Mike, obsessed by his target, prepared scrupulously. He applied lessons learned as a therapist to help create a core structure for his talk. *What is my best strategy?*

Some of his most complicated cases were resolved by detailed attention to, perhaps, three or four important features. That held true in almost all circumstances, no matter how complex. *Be objective.* In his most difficult cases he determined what their worst features were and concentrated on them to promote the best possible changes. Most secondary factors were dependent upon those key items, and were more or less neutral. Combined with strongly negative core areas, problems became entrenched and widespread. Once key items were addressed and changed, the picture reversed; troubles evaporated, even neutral factors turned positive. That rule of thumb held in any crisis. Operating one-to-one with patients, Mike developed a rigid objectivity. It proved useful outside that arena to help cope with any business or non-domestic difficulties.

He needed to select three or four key items to produce the seminal moments he sought – it would probably take less effort than searching amongst the diffuse intricacies in therapy. *I'll target my choices. Things will fall into place.* So he hoped.

Helen, on the other hand, was wading through the girls' long list of must-see places, trying to prune them down into a sensible plan for Costa Rica. She had difficult choices and had to limit driving journeys to maximise *adventure* time.

'Mike, you must help me here,' she called out from her computer seat.

He picked himself up from his chair in the lounge and wandered into the study. Helen was deeply engrossed in the map. She felt his hand on her shoulder.

'I've got to plan around three or four main stops,' she said.

How odd. Same formula. 'Sounds right to me: unless we prefer to spend all our holiday touring by car.'

'Have you got any preference? It might help me choose.'

'Stay away from tourists,' Mike replied.

'Impossible. Come on, give me some help here.'

'That's their list of places? You said they had shortened it.'

'They have! It's still too long – I can't fit it all in.' Helen turned to Mike in despair.

Mike had no answer and returned to the lounge to format his complicated notes. He sat upright, wide-awake, his mind focused on the task. He scanned through the ideas he had amassed in the four pages of abbreviated diary scribbles. He read them through, highlighting and connecting items with pencil lassoes, until he had organised them into more structured groups. A framework evolved with items, one to twelve, on the fifth page as cues for his informal talk. It would be chatty – suitable for this more social occasion. A memory stick determined his academic lectures. Next week's casual address would be more difficult.

Churchill once excused a long letter, citing lack of time for a short one. The last grains of sand settled that evening leaving Mike with a presentation longer than he intended. He had no idea who or how many would turn up, or what kind of reception he would get.

A revised plan evolved over the following couple of days. *This is exactly what I'm after*. It risked failure and student barracking if it went down badly. *I'll do it*. He would brave their hostility. Once Mike's mind was set – that was it: no change of tack. *Be sure you get it right, mister*. It was certainly courageous.

He had made a strenuous effort, putting far more into it than other colleagues would. They told him so. They would have treated it as a courtesy and have been more casual. Some academics started leaving the campus towards the end of the term, to return home for Christmas. Perhaps a dozen or so people from the psychology unit would remain to attend his talk. It was promoted heavily on notice boards and in newssheets at the university but with no telling how many other students would be interested.

Mike, secure at formal conferences, started to feel strangely vulnerable. Unlikely to be embarrassed by an empty room, he was nervous about speaking to perhaps a hundred people who might be on a different wavelength. He was scheduled to speak for about an hour with an extra half an hour for discussion from the floor.

'How's it going?' Helen asked.

'Coming on. And your plans?'

'We're doing fine. What you going to talk about tomorrow?'

'The usual: tell 'em what I'm going to tell 'em – tell 'em – then tell 'em what I've told 'em.' his clown face said. Helen shrugged – chin out – eyes smiling.

'I overheard you talking to the girls about the trip,' she said.

'They know a lot more about it than I do.'

'They do. You said leave it to me to organise.'

'I did. Was I being critical or fishing? I was referring to their excitement.'

'Well it's only three weeks off.'

CHAPTER TWENTY-FIVE

The correct didactic analysis is one that does not in the least differ from the curative treatment. How, indeed, shall the future analyst learn the technique if he does not experience it just exactly as he is to apply it later. OTTO RANK

By twenty to four all the seats had been taken. More people came in to stand at the far side of the hall. Mike was more nervous than ever as he entered the lecture theatre. He had no inkling he would be facing *several hundred* strangers. They are here because of that ludicrous publicity over Clayton – mentioned in the posters – nothing to do with CBT turning mainstream, he mused.

A brief panic set in. Unlike at heights – he felt no nausea, or giddiness, or weak limbs – this was purely the effects of adrenalin, and manageable. He had prepared his talk mainly for students actively pursuing careers in psychology. Were they a majority in this audience? Clearly not, even allowing for outside students. He had expected a much smaller group. *Will I get away with it?* Too late for changes – he would have to suck it and see. *One deep breath – here goes.*

'Good afternoon, ladies and gentlemen, I am flattered to see so many of you here today.' *Nervous – you mean!*
'I usually find my reputation precedes me. My last lecture attracted five people.'
Mike got in his early laugh – so important in public speaking.
'I appreciate that although some of you have an interest in psychology, many of you are here out of curiosity. Dangerous to cats but not to you, I promise. Whatever your motive, I aim to help you choose a fruitful career. The psychology students will, I

hope, get a taste of clinical practise and how satisfying it can be.'
He proceeded to his next cue card.
'Many of you will be familiar with tests for creativity.'
He paused to scan the audience.
'How many uses can we find for a brick?'
Mike noted the number of heads that nodded and smiled. Around a tenth of his listeners were psychology students.
'I've got a poser about a brick.'
Mike paused for a sip of water.
'A builder had received several delivery errors. Last week was the final straw. Missing taps – they arrived two days later. He had to drag plumbers off another site to finish the job. All at extra cost that the supplier refused to bear.
'Guv, I checked the number myself, exactly one thousand red bricks as ordered,' the driver said.
'I want to see them,' the builder said.
''Ere, under this tarpaulin, all neat 'n tidy. Strapped in a pyramid and easy as pie to check for yerself.'
The driver pulled the cover off the neat pile. The base formed half the order with twenty-five by twenty bricks, and the upper layers the rest. The builder came to the top tier. Instead of the twenty-four needed to complete the thousand, he counted five by five.
'You've brought one brick too many. I warned your boss I would return any more wrong orders. You can take the lot back.'
'You're joking, guv. I'll take the extra one off.'
'No, I'm returning them all. It will teach your boss a lesson – and don't try it on.'
He scribbled on the paperwork and pushed it forward.
'I'll expect a new order number and invoice.'
        The driver replaced the cover and set the offending brick apart from the pyramid at the end of his truck and drove off in a temper. In his flustered state, he approached a humpback bridge at speed. He crossed it with an enormous thump and sent the lone

brick on a parabolic flight over the side of the bridge onto the railway cutting below. He stopped the lorry to check his load. The odd brick was no longer on board. He wandered up and down the road. No brick in sight.

What was he to do? How could he show his boss how unreasonable the customer had been? Maybe he should try again. Perhaps the builder had calmed down. He had been adamant about fresh paperwork. Could he alter it? No. Could he re-arrange the bricks? Such ridiculous ploys were even more implausible. Has anyone any bright suggestions for this hapless driver?'

Mike surveyed the hall's blank expressions. Eventually a handful of people offered some impractical advice: most tending towards petty crime.

'The builder had marked the delivery note *wrong quantity,*' Mike said. That put ideas of forgery to rest and dampened any further enthusiasm.

'Well I did say it was about a brick and creativity. But this particular conundrum has no solution. So you can *all* create!'

Bemused, they relegated Mike to some kind of weirdo. Their astonished expressions were a sight to behold. What was going on here? How could he tell such a feeble story? If it was meant to be a joke it hit the ground harder than a lead balloon laden with the thousand bricks. Mike had gone from hero to zero in a matter of minutes. He stood his ground – feeling a slight lack of confidence, as only polite silence filled the room. This was worse than catcalling, and more voluble.

'I do apologise for that – it was poor – sorry. Let me make it up to you with a genuine shaggy dog story.'

If facial expressions groaned and sighed, so did this inaudible audience. The psychology group expected much better from a man at the top of his profession. Most of the other students had come because of his recent fame. Their disappointment showed. He held his nerve. Deep breaths – *here we go again* – this time with a hint of PGW in the telling.

'Some years ago, a Bertie Wooster type gent, impeccably dressed – glossy black shoes to bowler hat – was on the morning commute from his country house to the City. Cautious, he carried an umbrella, whatever the forecast, together with a briefcase and *The Times*. As the train departed, his carriage door violently opened and a tramp clambered in, holding a shaggy dog under his arm.'

The puzzled looks from two young girls in front mellowed into fleeting smiles.

'The tramp's face was lined and worn, like it needed watering. He wore a greasy raincoat tied at the waist by a piece of old rope and leaned on a crooked stick. An old, moth-eaten, trilby sat on his head. Most offensive of all, a pipe, churning out clouds of foul-smelling smoke was clamped in his jaw. By way of apology, the matted mongrel lay on the floor, lowered his head and raised his eyes.

'Damnation – you can't stay in here,' the city gent said.

'Who's gonna stop me? I can't get off.'

'Harrumph! Well you can put that pipe out. See that notice. This is a No Smoking carriage, and First Class.'

His fellow travellers peaked over their newspapers. They unanimously deemed it a private matter.

'Shan't,'

'I warn you.'

'Yeah. What you going to do?'

The city gent got up and opened a window. He fixed the tramp with an imperious eye and moved a step closer to the malodorous pipe, grasped it from the tramp's jaws, and dispatched it out of the window.

'Right mate – you'll be sorry for that.' The tramp reached for the pristine bowler and smartly sent it spinning, Frisbee-style, through the window.

All hell let loose as in turn the city gent and the tramp jettisoned the old trilby, the umbrella and the stick. Fellow travellers held tightly to their belongings and watched in stunned silence. The tramp grabbed the briefcase and *The Times* for an unscheduled stop. The city gent was seething and, though celebrated in social circles for his love of animals, reached for the dog.'

Horror entered the eyes of the girls in the front. Mike heard an 'Oh no.'

'The tramp called his bluff. All caution was literally thrown to the wind as out went the briefcase and the newspaper. That was the detonator. The tramp's rugby tackle failed to prevent the city gent make an accurate two-handed long pass, sending the yelping dog harmlessly onto the soft grass verge.'

The young ladies in the front row smiled, their worst fears placated.

'This *did not* calm the tramp. The train slowed and made its first stop. A full-blooded fight erupted. Fellow travellers at last intervened and held the contestants apart. But they wriggled free. Both spilled out of the carriage door onto the platform, once more at each other's throat. The station guard tried to calm them down. Failed. He phoned the local police station. The train pulled out, each carriage in turn getting a ringside seat and a story to take into the office. The two combatants exhausted themselves and lay prostrate on the platform. The local bobby arrived on his bike.

'What's going on 'ere?'

The guard related what he had been told. The policeman noted the details down.

'Eight items in all, including the dog, to collect as evidence,' he concluded.

'The warring pair, reminded of the lost items, drew upon the last vestiges of energy to start the affray once more. As they pointed down the track, berating each other's offences, they saw the shaggy dog in the distance, trotting towards them.'

That relieved the girls in front.

'They noticed the dog was carrying something in its mouth.'

Mike paused and scanned the auditorium.

'What do you think it was?' he asked his audience.

Generating a rising cacophony they placed their bets on all seven items. Mike smiled, relaxed for the first time since entering the hall.

'Hold on a moment. It's impossible to make out a word in this din. Let's go through the list one by one and we'll take a show of hands.'

Mike called out each item and jotted down his rough count in round percentages.

'Have I missed any?'

He got no reply, apart from a few shaking heads.

'Most of you, about fifty per cent, have gone for the tramp's stick. The least popular choice was the briefcase. The results were much as I expected.'

Mike heard one or two people congratulating themselves. That soon stopped.

'None of you has given me the answer I was after.'

Mike kept them in suspense for a moment.

'You have all missed the right answer.'

Long pause. They glanced around at each other frowning, spreading arms and shrugging shoulders, but gave no reply.

'Anybody?'

Another pause.

Eventually one excited student raised his arm and confidently called out, 'The brick.'

'Yes, the *brick*. Thank you. Thank you.' *Thank goodness for him.*

Mike watched from his lectern as the brick's shock waves rippled through the sea of faces in the hall to shatter the windows of their minds and – after two or three seconds – *all* the glazing.

I've done it. He had restored his credibility and held them in the palm of his hands. They were primed for his core talk and the story's slow induction predicted some permanence for the lesson. 'That story is important. It gives some idea of what it's like to practise as a clinician,' he continued. Mike explained in depth, to the attentive room, how the two parts of the story compared to separate sessions with a patient. A split could delay finding solutions. Whilst different themes can dominate sessions, insights can arise from the most tenuous of connections. 'Complex cases can appear facile once resolved. Much of the input is redundant,' Mike told them. 'I search for crucial items that need attention with an open mind. It can be as daunting as trying to find three or four matching door keys from a chest of thousands.'

'Your choices for the dog to carry were governed by pre-conceptions and expectations. The easier-to-carry items and those associated with its master formed more acceptable visual images than the heavy briefcase of the stranger. You had no evidence whatsoever to form a conclusion. Your choices were, therefore, pure guesswork. You had to think laterally to find the answer. It can be like that in practice,' Mike continued. 'Obvious answers are frequently wrong. In the past GPs would often label patients with medical jargon and use pure guesswork to refer them to specialists. Some persist in solely treating symptoms, but increasingly GPs refer non-medical cases of stress and partly medical conditions like reactive depression directly to a psychologist. Headaches, stomach ulcers, diarrhoea, physical pain, or chronic backache, can be generated by depression or clinical stress and overworked adrenal systems pumping hormones throughout the body. CBT can help and is much in demand. Qualified clinicians are in short supply,' Mike said, hoping some might pick up the baton.

In full flow, preaching his gospel, Mike brought their attention to prejudiced perceptions and distortions in cognition.

He urged them, whether they went into psychology, or if their interests were elsewhere, to have respect for people. 'First appearances can be misleading,' he gently chided his listeners – primarily for treating him in awe purely because they had seen his recent exploits in the media, and then, within a few minutes, for thinking him a buffoon after the first part of his shaggy dog story.

'Try to be unbiased, listen attentively, retain details, and never reject apparent trivia without good cause.'

He told of a bedraggled woman sent to him. She tried to cope with unhappiness by blaming a neighbour, 'him next door'. She revealed a past life of glamour and a glittering stage career that contrasted with her current obscurity.

The eager questions and discussions that followed the talk went on well beyond his allotted time. The applause at the end confirmed Mike had hit his mark. These youngsters were enthused. He was delighted to have achieved his goal.

'Well done, darling,' Helen said.

'You enjoyed it, then?'

'Yes. And they certainly did.'

Mike and Helen mingled with the crowd. Three students came over. They made no mention of the talk. They were all seasoned rock climbers, keen to hear first-hand about Mike's experience on the crane.

'Do you get a bit scared up high cliffs?' Mike asked.

'Sure, that's what it's about,' one replied.

'Yeah, controlling your fear,' another said.

'Weren't *you* jittery up on that crane?' the third asked.

'Well, yes, actually I was!' Mike said.

'Come off it, Mike. Tell them the truth. You love heights,' Helen said.

'I *was* affected. I'm *scared* of heights,' Mike pleaded.

'Yeah, but you kept your nerve, like us.'

Mike latched onto that. Well, well, he thought – they also have fears – and raced into denial. *Lately, I've reacted the same. Have I freaked out or been sick? No. I'm no different from them. It must have been Helen all along.*

He was *so* glad they had spoken to him. He was afraid with Clayton. Could anyone blame him? But he had managed, eventually, to suppress his fear – as he did skiing. He wasn't – he rationalised – that afraid of heights. It had been magnified by Helen's anxiety with Lionel. Since that had dissipated he had questioned if he was clinically acrophobic. These young men had confirmed that he wasn't. In spite of his deeper doubts he judged that *he* didn't need any further treatment. *His* symptoms were simply a petty annoyance. It was an impetuous conclusion. He had a different take on patients' mild symptoms.

Another young student approached them.

'Dr. Daniels – I will always remember the brick – it was sick,' he gushed.

'*That* good?' It sounded a compliment, so Mike treated it as such.

'Yeah – you ripped it up.'

'Thank you,' Mike said, with similar speculation.

'Are you going into psychology?' Helen asked the student.

'After a gap year surfing the globe.' He wandered away to join his friends.

'You're in with the in-crowd,' Helen said.

Mike detected a hint of gentle mockery.

'I got through to them – that's what matters.'

'More important than your papers?'

'Much more – it was worth making the effort,' Mike said, ambiguously. It was a half-truth. The *much* had far more to do with his alliance with rock climbers.

The next day the clinic was calm and functioning normally. The towering crane outside the window held Mike's gaze as firmly as a conquered K2 might a mountaineer. He noted the rapid progress of the new hospital wing over the past fortnight. The jibes, –'Here comes Spiderman,' 'My hero,' 'Save me from this drudgery, Spiderman,' – had at last ceased. But at lunch colleagues were eager for details of his talk. They had heard on the grapevine it had gone down well.

'Do you think you steered anyone towards a clinical career?'

'Who knows? I gave an encouraging *aperitif.*'

'Are we going to get a taster?' the pretty trainee asked.

'It's too long to repeat and far too boring to hear,' Mike replied, dismissively.

'Come on, you said it wasn't complicated,' urged one of the Medics.

'Well. Yes and no. It's difficult to explain. It's a bit like doing crosswords. If you're familiar with the compiler they're more solvable.'

They got no further with Mike but he had stimulated their conversation. They remembered how last week both a heart surgeon and the urologist at the hospital described their jobs as plumbing.

'Yes, and remember that guy in orthopaedics who went on about being merely a mechanic?' one said.

'Amazing, isn't it, how some people go the other way? Helen had a chat with our chimney sweep yesterday. She had a good laugh with him over his trade association. They suggested their members call themselves 'flueologists.'

'So which way do you go, Mike?' a colleague asked.

'I'm an ordinary man – perhaps just a regular crossword solver.'

PART

THREE

Completing the picture

CHAPTER TWENTY-SIX

The adventures first; explanations take such a dreadful time.
LEWIS CARROLL

House lights are harsher and brighter that early in the morning. They accentuated the pitch black outside. Helen robotically resisted her body's demand for more sleep. Mike began singing from his repertoire, briefly interrupted by his cold shower. That increased her irritation with the early start. How could he? In the middle of the night! I'm married to a lunatic, she muttered to herself. She jerkily dressed as in infancy, struggling to follow the routine she had organised for herself before going to bed. Glowing, grinning and bouncy, Mike emerged from the bathroom – singing.

'You're insane. Do you realise what time it is?' Her harsh whisper failed to dampen his spirits.

'You're a grumpy old dragon,' he murmured, kissing her forehead. 'Aren't you excited? The girls are – they beat the alarm clock.'

Mike had switched off his monitoring systems for others' sanity – or his own. He would be the family man for a few weeks – a welcome break. Free from the stress of being actively intrusive in his clinic. Free from the pressure to remain silent and impartial wallpaper. He was at last as enthusiastic about their trip as Helen and the girls. She had been saying for weeks how impatient they had become. Like Helen, he had set his clothes out the previous day, but unlike her put them on effortlessly, then bounded downstairs and un-set the burglar alarm.

Amy and Claire came down humping their bags, ready to go. They were excited with no appetite for any early breakfast. Mike abandoned his kitchen routine and made Helen and himself coffee. He let his cool whilst he turned off and switched on, and locked and unplugged, the various listed items that preceeded going away.

Helen quietly sipped from her cup but the caffeine made no impact on her wan face and red eyes. When the taxi arrived she was alert enough to have Mike confirm he had the passports, visas and tickets, as he helped the driver with their luggage. After they had checked in, and had breakfast in the departure lounge, she began showing her enthusiasm again.

Soon after take-off, Helen, pillow lodged against the window frame and her headrest, made inroads on her lost sleep. Half way into the flight Mike and the girls joined Helen and Morpheus.

Helen had organised each of the fourteen days in great detail. The hotels were excellent. They had a small complaint. One had a non-smoking room reeking of cigarettes. Helen intervened and got them upgraded to a luxurious suite – no extra charge.

'Impressive. What a PA,' Mike said.

'It's the squeaky wheel what gets the oil,' Helen replied, reminding Mike of his mother's aphorisms.

The many intervals of heavy rain in the so-called dry season failed to dampen the girls' plans. In the first week they gently held baby turtles; were amazed by bird-sized butterflies; saw the splendour of Lake Arenal and its volcano; and, as promised, did whatever they fancied. On a memorable river trip through the rainforest jungle they were thrilled by Jesus Christ lizards running on the water, alligators close up, and endless exotic wildlife on the banks. And they all got drenched by one tropical downpour – even with the bright blue waterproofs provided.

Towards the end of the second week the girls chose to visit the Monte Verde reserve set high in the rain forest. A guide pointed out the nest of a Quetzal, familiar to Mike as the national bird of Guatemala. Amy and Claire's interests and idea of adventure seemed so different to Mike, from Ben's.

Coming down from the reserve Mike went off to buy an extra memory disk for his camera. The girls and Helen sauntered ahead toward the local restaurant the guide recommended for lunch. Mike joined them there.

'Where's Mummy?'

'She gone to the loo,' Claire replied.

'We want to do a Sky Trek,' Amy said.

'What's that?'

'It's flying over the cloud-forest on zip lines,' Claire replied.

'Zip lines? Where did you see that?' Mike asked.

'The office up the road; the guide said we should do it. We can get tickets now for after lunch.'

'You'll come with Mummy, won't you?' Amy called out.

Helen came in from the restaurant's charming garden, captivated by the exotic flowers that bordered its trim lawn.

'You can ask Daddy. I'm staying here,' she replied, having reflected on their plans in the Ladies.

'It sounds a bit hairy to me. Your mother doesn't even enjoy Disney rides,' Mike said, concerned for Helen – not himself.

'Mummy you'll be fine. You're attached to a safety harness,' Amy said.

'Helen,' Mike called. He drew her attention away from some hummingbirds. 'They're adamant we go…'

'You go – you love that sort of excitement,' she said – intent on excusing herself.

Mike encouraged her to join in the fun.

'Come on, it'll be as safe as houses.'

'I'm sure it's safe – they wouldn't endanger people – but I don't think I'm up to it.'

'*Up* to it?' Mike teased. 'You talked me into a family trip. Remember? Let's *all* do it together.'

'I might spoil it for them,' Helen said.

'You'll be fine.'

Mike put an encouraging arm around her shoulder. Helen's nervous shrug gave her consent.

'Girls – Mummy says yes. Go along and buy the tickets.'

After a leisurely lunch of grilled fish followed by an exotic fruit salad and ice-cream, they returned to Monte Verde. Sky Treks were organised in two daily sessions, the second after a midday siesta. The girls' eagerness placed the Daniels family the first group to go that afternoon. They were given a twenty-minute talk on safety procedures. Mike thought it deliberately excessive, designed to hype up a sense of danger and adventure. Helen cast a smile at him. Perhaps even she agreed. They were fitted with waist harnesses and given a pulley each to clip on to the cables. 'Your lives depend on them,' the guide said.

The groups of trekkers set off in turn with their guides. The first thrill was to negotiate rope bridges with the one free hand, the other gripping the vital pulley. Two of the bridges were short, but of a three-rope design. The balancing act proceeded slowly along those inverted *triangular* corridors. Each individual footstep vibrated through the entire convoy as it crossed safely, with nervous giggles, over the hazardous drop to the torrential rivers and rain forest below. Mike and Helen enjoyed every moment, as much as the girls.

'Here's our first line. It's short – to get you used to zip-lining,' the guide said.

'Short? It must be at least sixty yards,' Helen whispered.

'It's a doddle. I'll go first,' Mike said.

'My Daddy's fearless,' Amy said to the guide. 'He saved someone up a crane. He was in all the papers.'

'Eez so?' the guide asked, his question directed to Helen.

'It's true. He loves heights.'

'This is a special treat for Daddy,' Claire said.

'He'll enjoy this, senorita.'

The guide carefully attached each pulley and sent them off one by one. Mike went silently, grinning all the way. The girls and Helen squealed until they reached the other side. Their screams were louder on the next couple of lines. These had stretched to some two hundred yards, and were much higher. Everyone, Mike included, was a trifle more apprehensive.

'We begin our journey up to the longer lines,' the guide said.

'Longer? How much longer – how many?' Helen asked.

'Eight, including the ones you've done. Four more to go,' the guide replied.

'Up there, Dad. That's the last one,' Amy squealed.

It was the first time, like Ben, she had called him Dad.

'What!' Helen said.

'She's teasing,' Mike said.

'You'll see,' Amy said.

'She means it, Mike.'

Helen nervously moved towards the guide. Mike pulled her aside.

'Don't be silly. It's a telegraph wire or power line across the valley. Nobody's on it,' Mike said. The assuagement was short-lived.

'That's because we're first – you wait,' Claire said.

Helen knew that wicked grin. It was the same as Mike's when he was up to no good.

'Take no notice,' Mike said.

The next few lines were longer and higher but they gradually got used to the sensation of zip lining; even Helen.

'Are you all happy? We've come to the hard part – our long ascent,' the guide said.

The girls grinned at their parents, mischievously. Mike and Helen were unsure what to make of them. The answer gradually came into focus, as they climbed, and climbed, and climbed.

'Now do you believe us?' Amy said.

'Mike. They can't expect us to do that,' Helen said. She paused for a moment and peered at their telegraph wire high above them. 'I want to go back. Immediately.'

'Even if they're right, it's got to be safe. We'll manage somehow,' Mike said phlegmatically. Solely for her sake – he was sweating heavily. Yes, it was the humidity and the effort, but he was also suppressing a rising anxiety.

'We're half way up. Take a rest. You'll need it,' the lead guide said.

The girls sat down and soothed tired legs. Mike moved away toward the other guide.

'Does anyone ever chicken out?' he asked aside, as nonchalantly as he could.

'Everyday Mister, eez always one.'

'So what do you do?'

'Do? I not do – eeza one-way on these lines – and others behind us.'

'So what happens?'

'They scream a lot,' the guide said with an evil laugh.

'You're all good with heights – you wouldn't be here otherwise,' the leader said.

The words hit Mike in the stomach. He showed no reaction.

'But you must be careful when we get to our main attraction.'

'Is it really *that* line?' Helen asked.

'That's the one. It's over a half a mile long and 4500ft above sea level and you'll be flying about 500ft above the cloud forest canopy.'

Helen's features froze.

'I can't do it,' she whispered to Mike out of earshot of the girls.

Mike's heart thumped.

'We've got no choice. I've asked.'

'To get to the other side of the valley safely we have to use a specially raised platform. That's where you need to be extra careful; going up the ten metre ladder and standing at the take off point,' the guide warned.

A deep rumble of distant thunder stirred within Mike. *How could I be so stupid?* Where, now, was his notion that girls were less adventurous than boys? *It must be safe: would they put the girls and Helen in danger?* But increasing raw anxiety grabbed him by his parched throat. *Pull yourself together.* During the few minutes the others sat quietly bracing themselves for thrills Mike became increasingly enslaved to fear, guilt and shame.

They got to their feet to continue their journey. By then it had sunk in. This was his punishment. He was a condemned man. His suppressed history had finally caught up with him. It started to break through his defences. All through those past years he had found it too painful to revisit and had blanked out the briefest of snapshots. Unable to control those memories – the barrier breached – an entire album swamped his brain. Fear gnawed at his stomach. From nowhere, guilt flooded his head. Horrific images flashed and flickered in front of him. Veins were throbbing in his neck. The shame. *Why, why, why? Why didn't I listen to my parents?*

Mike resumed the remainder of the climb as a zombie, the memories vivid. 'Promise never to go out on that roof again.' 'I promise, Mum.'

Why didn't he keep that promise? Why did he give in to the gang? Why did Ginger beg him? *I could have stopped it happening.*

Following his initiation and its aftermath, he was a member of the Atlas House gang – a questionable honour. He kept away from them for a week. Some of the kids were rough. Others had played football and cricket with him but not as true friends. He had joined their gang for Ginger's sake.

'You have to help me. I might get captured again. I must join,'

Ginger said.

'We'll go and speak to them,' Michael said.

The gang agreed, provided Ginger passed their test.

'You're worth two of *all* of them,' Michael said.

Ginger had to undergo the same initiation as his. Having seen Michael's performance, he deemed it do-able rather than daunting.

'You gonna join us – do the walk – or are you chicken?' the leader, a big boy eleven years old, asked.

'No sweat,' Ginger said. Macho. He turned to Michael. 'Are you going to come up with me?'

'I can't. I'm sorry, I promised Mum and Dad.'

'You're in our gang. We stick together. You obey our rules,' the leader said.

'Yeah, we don't need no mummy's boys,' another said.

'Please Michael – we won't tell. You can watch from *inside* the attic,' Ginger said.

'I promised them,' Michael said in a whisper.

'They said *out on* the roof. Well you won't be. Will you?'

Michael gave in to his pleas. They made their way up the stairs. None of the others had followed yet. It was hot in the attic even with the open windows.

'Let's go outside,' Ginger said.

'I told you. I can't.'

'You're supposed to be my best friend.'

'I am.'

'They said out *on* the roof. You won't be going on it, will you?'

Michael gave in again. They lifted themselves onto the windowsill and out to the balcony. It was a lovely sunny day. They could see the green copper dome of Highgate Church and the mast of Alexandra Palace as they surveyed the northern suburbs of London.

'You don't have to do this. Aren't you a bit scared?'

'No. You weren't, were you?'

272

'I was OK. Don't peer over the edge. Keep your eyes on your feet and you'll be fine.'

The gang came charging up the stairs and clambered out to join them. 'You ready?' the leader asked. Ginger nodded. He nervously hauled himself up onto the ledge. More cautious than Michael had been, he followed his advice and made his way round the first corner. Round he went, with the gang tailing him. One boy joined him on the ledge, several yards behind, just for fun. He reached the last corner. Michael cut across the attic and got out on the other side, to be first to cheer him home. Ginger saw him smiling and beamed in triumph. He had done it – the last few paces left. Neither of them noticed it: such a small oversight. Just a slippery worn heel and a fresh bird dropping – that's all. That's all it took.

Michael witnessed the milliseconds stretch and remove Ginger's radiant smile. The frozen, blank stare that replaced it vanquished time. It was to haunt Michael's subconscious forever: put him in denial all those years. Ginger's legs and arms flailed in ultra slow motion. He seemed to hover as stationary as a kestrel. In an instant, with a sudden frenetic flurry of limbs, he was gone. All Michael heard was a faint murmur before that terrible thud.

The gang rushed downstairs. Some went to help – some to escape the scene. Michael remained; stunned. He grabbed the wall to steady his shaking hands and forced his head over.

He looked down.

CHAPTER TWENTY-SEVEN

*Secrets, silent, stony sit in the dark palaces of both our hearts:
secrets weary of their tyranny: tyrants willing to be dethroned.*
JAMES JOYCE

Nobody had got to Ginger yet. He was lying alone.
Miraculously, his head moved. He *raised* his head – its
shadow grew larger – he was still alive! A second later
the truth sunk in. The expanding umbra was *shiny and deep red*.
Michael slumped and curled up in a ball against the wall. In
shock and disbelief he strained to reverse the clock. Moments
earlier, he was happy, smiling, enjoying life with his best friend.
The contrast was grotesque and unbearable. In an attempt to
vanish from the scene he contorted his tiny frame in agony and
squeezed until his entire being had oozed away. Raw emptiness
was left in its wake. All else that remained was numbness and an
alien, hollow body – until a violent surge followed. The void
filled with searing hot guilt and fear. His external senses and
antennae were obliterated. His vision became scrambled and
piercing white noise screeched in his ears. He was deaf to the
first shrieks, the rushing feet and the squeals of windows
opening. Paralysed by the overload of sheer terror, shock and
guilt, even the ambulance's siren failed to register. Finally the
desperate screams from his mother shattered his stupor. 'Where's
Michael? Where's my Michael?' Nobody could tell her. His
body's foetal coil sprang open and he violently vomited.

Loud memories, in sharp focus, overwhelmed Mike.
Incapable of rationalising them he was desperate for help. He
needed to share the pain with someone. He had absolutely
nobody he could turn to. The girls had even bragged about him to
the guides. They said they had booked this as a *treat* for him. It

would be impossible to explain to the guides however hard he might try. Their English was limited.

Helen had her own problems – she was visibly shaking – she would be utterly distraught if he told her. She would absorb it all – fuse it with Lionel. She had delayed her last visit to the churchyard, making that decision alone – without Mike badgering her. This was a major trial for her. He could undo all that progress. If he confided in Helen it would make matters worse and prove unhelpful to both of them.

The long ascent turned single file. It was difficult for any conversation, even when they were not out of breath. The higher they went the lonelier Mike became with each step. The higher they went, the longer the silences became as they braced themselves for the test above. The higher they went, the more he recalled.

The silences with Mum and Dad – they were at a loss how to deal with or comfort him. He was convinced they blamed him, deep down, for Ginger's death. Everybody did. He could again taste the sour acid of remorse and fear that filled his mouth for weeks. The policewoman's interview had terrified him. He was overcome with guilt in the coroner's office – filled with shame at home.

He struggled, head bowed, through the weeks prior to the funeral. Michael had attended one before. That was for his grandfather. It was Jewish, quickly performed the next day, with the immediate *shiva* and people mourning without any delay. *Why couldn't they bury Ginger like that?* The long wait made it far worse on the day.

It was his first acquaintance with any church. This one was Catholic. The collective guilt was palpable. It echoed in the women's wails and the choir's sorrowful voices. It became physical, as pious people knelt and crossed themselves. The congregation's whispered responses to the Father's supplications created an eerily existential guilt. The strange rituals, the intimidating vestments, the cloying incense, people eating the bread of Christ, drinking his blood, were unbearable. He sobbed throughout the long service. He was in limbo. The Priest mentioned purgatory – a word unfamiliar to Michael. He knew precisely what it meant.

They reached the end of their long odyssey and waited below the guide's ladder. Mike surveyed the vertical metal. It was his deserved path to the gallows. He was the walking dead. He had nobody to turn to this time. No son, no suicidal patient – nobody to save him.

The girls and Helen in particular were uneasily quiet as they weighed up the long cable above the ladder. Halfway across it hid in a cloud. Mike glanced at Helen. She looked dreadful – pinched features – stressed out. Unselfish as ever, she sensed the girls' concern and played down her own.

'Daddy will show us how safe it is,' she chirped nervously. Searching questions passed across Amy's face as she scrutinised her father.

They watched him mechanically wrap his pulley-holding arm behind the ladder. He clung firmly to each rung with the other hand as he moved upwards. He had no choice. The automated motion drove him through brick walls as he lived his dreaded nightmare. His safe ascent was exemplary. It may have allayed the girls' fears, raised by the guide over this risky part, but Mike's were on what was ahead. He gained the last rung and hoisted up his leaden body onto the platform. It had a single rail, on the far side. The take-off point was unprotected. The platform swayed as Claire took the ladder.

Mike fought urgent gastric spasms and a swirling tornado inside his head to drag himself over to the rail. No chance of a reprieve. He was doomed. He awaited the others – an eternity. He used every ruse he could muster to hold himself together. He needed someone to share his horror. Plead with the guide perhaps? *No. No. I can't.* Not with Helen and the girls standing by. It would terrify them.

Visible in the distance, he could see the stable *triangle* of the placid Arenal volcano. Mike was sitting on top of a violently active one. He forced it down, stopped it erupting from second to second, minute to minute. Pressed like an orange, the last juice and flesh was wrung out of his body, until the pith of his boyhood trauma fused with this moment of reckoning. No trace of his existence between these two events remained. Like a murderer brought to justice after concealing his crime for over forty years, his entire history – his career, his family – was all gone. He no longer felt human.

Assembled, holding tightly to the rail and deeply introspective, they all gauged the daunting zip line – too nervous to notice anyone else's fear.

Mike was no longer his own master. Guilt and horror blotted out his finer points; love for his family, responsibility for their welfare, altruism. His actions were strictly instinctive – his features gothic. He was in a trance.

'So, Mister, you going to lead the way?' the guide asked. Mike moved forward.

'You're too close to the edge,' Helen shouted. 'You heard the warning…'

'Stand back a bit. It's a long way to fall,' the guide said.

'Daddy, please,' Amy said.

'*No hay problema.* Papa is *very* good with heights,' the guide said, echoing her words.

Mike had no option. Didn't even try to find one; didn't think at all. Robotic, he would go over the top, 1914-18 style, to his fate. He would place his head on the guillotine block. Wait for the trap door to open with his noose in place. It was surreal. He moved from the rail toward the unprotected edge. As he stood facing the open 500ft drop, the trap door did open.

He looked down.

He confronted his last terrifying height with steely clinical eyes, soulless, rasped and hollow inside. Inhuman. Mechanical. Finale.

Nobody witnessed the fall.

Nobody other than Mike would ever know what happened. Four decades of suppressed angst and deceit compressed into a single mass. In this final moment it became dense, heavy matter, as tangible and as physical an experience as he had ever had. Gravity pulled hard, wrenched at it. An agonising scream resounded in his ears. His head had been thrust into a furnace. His brain had swollen into a molten globe. A fiery, heavy pounding crashed against the insides of his skull. He was in excruciating pain. Something had to give. It did – and tripped an emergency breaker switch. An uncontrollable force roared into life and propelled the searing agony down from his head. The pressure within Mike's cranium immediately fell: the tortured hammering ceased. The unbearable load plummeted past his chest, his stomach, and forced its way down the length of his body. Finally, split into two red-hot pokers, it coursed through his legs, exited through the soles of his feet. His angst, his guilt, his shame – his constipated phobia – were flushed into oblivion.

A silent calm followed. A gentle breeze caressed his face. Mike was euphoric. Yes – euphoric. His legs were sturdy – his breathing even. His pulse no longer raced. For the first time since childhood he was – at an open edge, facing a sheer fall – rock solid secure. He was the one person, on that platform, *blasé* over the zip line. He patiently waited as the guide did safety checks on the harness and carefully clipped the pulley to the line.

Fleetingly, his boyhood notion that he could fly popped up. The guide pushed him away. He glided serenely, accompanied by the quiet hum of the pulley wheel as it made its way along the cable.

He looked down. Way down, at gnat-sized birds flying over the forest canopy below. He passed through a damp cloud and eagerly absorbed the distant scenery as it re-emerged. He wished he could linger much longer up there – take it all in at leisure. The platform, at the other side, soon came into view, his one-minute flight over. Joyously, at the very rim of that platform, he awaited the others.

A miracle: after all those years of self- help – all those failed attempts – he was genuinely cured. He had stubbornly persisted with his behavioural therapy for years, ignoring both overt clues and covert signs to more effective treatments. Purely by chance the one method outlawed at his clinic had cured him. If he had been subjected to flooding – without the crutch of his son or his suicidal patient to lean on – it might have done so long ago.

He watched Helen's progress as she followed over. Mike's manic grin came into view. She managed a nervous smile for the last few metres of the line and the eternity of her fifty-eight seconds. She grabbed him. He held her tight. She was shaking from head to toe, unable to speak.

Next, Claire arrived, chastened, less adventurous, but safe – that helped calm Helen. Then they heard Amy in the distance make her crossing singing at the top of her voice, '*I am flying. I am flying*' to the tune of Rod Stewart's '*Sailing*'. She came into view – ever the tomboy, suspended solely by her harness, arms and legs spread-eagled – free as a bird. Claire cheered her home. Mike roared with laughter. Helen emitted a long sigh of thankful relief.

'That was A-brilliant. Can we do it again?' Amy asked – answered by her mother and sister's stunned expressions.

'That was marvellous, incredible. Thank you,' Mike said – his arms around the girls.

'We knew you would love it,' Claire said.

Mike felt like Moses coming down the mountain. He was a changed man, with a new philosophy: a mature perspective on Ginger. The return journey was quickly made. During that descent Mike – no longer in denial – speedily came to terms with his unsuppressed guilt. What a heavy burden he had unwittingly carried. Unable to open up to Helen – the guilt had been unbearable – Ginger's death had made him feel partly responsible for Lionel's. *How could I think it was my fault? I was eight – it was an accident: they happen.* At last he was free – free to tell Helen at the earliest opportunity – and free to fully empathise with her.

The guide enjoyed their company and had finished his stint for the day.

'Do you want to get close to the quetzal nest?' he asked.

'Ooh yes please,' said Amy.

'You two go,' Mike said.

'Yes,' Helen agreed. 'We could do with a drink.'

'Meet us where we had lunch,' Mike said.

'See you later, alligator.' The girls traipsed off with the guide.

Mike ordered two G &T's and carried them through to Helen at the end of the restaurant's exotic garden. He was cautious – how was Helen feeling? How would she react? She had been shaken to the core, but had pulled herself together. Her relief phase was at an end. Since that big row and her cathartic visit to Lionel and the smaller sobbing sessions that followed Helen had been a trouper. Mike braced himself. Her anger could be re-kindled any moment after what they had been through. The experience must have set her back – she had been terrified. The upside was it had freed *him*. He could reveal his ordeal – be honest and help her.

'Thanks. I need that,' Helen said, taking her glass.

'You all right?' Mike asked taking her other hand.

'Almost. What an experience! Those girls – as crazy as you.'

'Like me?'

'Yes. Adventurous – full of beans – fearless.'
'You're not angry with them?'
'No. Why *angry*?'
'Are you angry with me?' Mike asked.
'No. Should I be?'
'For making you do it?'
'Of course not – I can't believe I coped so well. I wouldn't fancy doing it again though.'
Mike peered at Helen long and hard.
'What?' Helen asked, puzzled.
Mike remained silent. Studied her.
'What?' Helen asked, defensively.
The sun came out from behind a cloud. A golden corona backlit Helen's hair – a softer light adorned her face. Mike had never seen her look lovelier. His serious expression changed into a broad smile, beaming in the bright sunlight.
'What?' Helen asked again, with the hint of a giggle.
'Lionel – the fears, the anger – they've gone.'
'I suppose they have,' Helen said, jutting her chin forward.
They sat quietly facing each other. Mike recognised, loved, Helen's dreamy gaze. She radiated it after childbirth, after they had made love, after Ben got into Uni. It was as serene and as beautiful as at any of those moments.
'You've finally accepted Lionel's accident. You're over it,' Mike said.
'Do you know what, I think I am,' Helen said calmly.
Mike's moment had finally come.
'Yes, and I'm better.'
'You? Why you?'
'You remember a few months ago I told you I wasn't a drunk driver?'
'Mike, don't start me on that again. You said I was over it.'
Mike put a finger to her lips and spoke slowly – deliberately and quietly – no longer feeling any guilt or responsibility for Lionel's

death.

'Please darling, listen to me. I was not a drunken driver.'

'Why do you say that – what do you mean?'

'Somebody else did die. I was partly to blame.'

'Mike you're frightening me. What are you talking about?'

'I was eight years old…'

Immediately mollified by the childhood setting, Helen listened intently. Soon her eyes started to sting. Mike and his narrative moved in and out of focus. She gently stroked his hand – gripping it at times – as he related his saga. She sobbed uncontrollably at the end of his story.

'I'm *so* sorry, Mike. How could I?'

'Could you what? It's my fault. I should have told you long, long ago.'

'I can't believe you kept it from me all those years.'

'I missed chances to tell you. I desperately yearned to.'

'Why on earth didn't you?' Helen asked.

'I can't say. It was partly the guilt. I couldn't take the risk.'

'That isn't like you. What was the other part?'

'I tried to protect you *too much*, I imagine.'

'You were never joking – you were always afraid of heights? On Striding Edge, at Grand Canyon, that black ski-run?'

'Yes, Yes. All of them.'

'At Tikal with Ben – what was that all about?'

'I tried to explain. I didn't force Ben up to the top.'

'Ben couldn't look me in the eye. He was evasive – hiding the truth.'

'No Helen, he did tell you the truth. And *I* told you the truth.'

'But that wasn't the whole truth, was it?'

'The truth – the whole – nothing but? It's nonsense Helen – that notion is pure fantasy.'

'What actually happened?'

'Ben challenged me to the top. I…'

'You couldn't resist,' Helen interjected.

'I didn't give it a second thought.'
'What about that photo? You enjoyed it!'
'Below that smile I was anxious. I panicked at the start of the descent.'
'And frightened Ben?'
'Possibly, but he didn't show it. He helped me down, inch by inch.'
'*The crane!* What about that crane?'
'Terrified. I *had* to do it. That young man's life was at stake.'
'Mike. I love you. I'm so sorry.'
'No. It's my fault. I hid Ginger. I could have helped you with Lionel long ago.'
'And I could have helped you.'
'Well, we're both sorted at last.'

Mike held her; stroked her forehead, kissed her full on the lips, and vaguely hummed, close to her ear. The subconscious hum changed into a tune and *Send in the Clowns* emerged. In his low, bass voice, he softly sang the opening line.
'*Isn't it rich? Are we a pair?*'
'Aren't we just? I clung to my memories – your past filled you with fear,' Helen said.
'That's so right!'
'I'm glad you agree.'
'I do; but I meant that line – it scans perfectly.'
'Does it?' Helen asked, puzzled, searching for the equation.
'Yes it does,' Mike said with his funny clown face. He sang again – light-heartedly.
'*Isn't it rich? Now everything's clear.*
You were ruled by your memories – mine chained me to fear.
You see?'
Helen shrugged her shoulders, jutted out her chin, and laughed.
'You fool. Not exactly what I said – not quite Sondheim either.'
'Close enough.'
'Are *we* close enough, Mike?'

'As we'll ever be.'

'No more secrets?'

'No more secrets.'

Mike held each of her hands and gently squeezed her slender fingers. Helen pressed their hands together. They gazed at each other.

'They're on the bench outside,' Amy called into Claire. The girls ran up the length of the garden full of excitement. Mike and Helen stayed huddled together.

'You missed an extra special surprise,' Claire said.

'Guess what – we saw a quetzal hatching,' Amy said.

'You can watch the nest on the web-cam at home,' Claire said.

'That zip-lining was great,' Amy said. 'Can we do it again?'

'Once is enough,' was Helen's firm reply.

'You were scared, Mummy, weren't you? – I certainly was,' Claire said.

'*So* was Daddy,' Amy said.

'No I wasn't,' Mike said, catching Helen's eye.

'Yes you were!' Amy said.

'Your father scared? What gave you that idea?' Helen asked, returning Mike's service.

'Well: his eyes went all funny at the bottom of the ladder.'

'Maybe *you* were scared,' Helen said.

'No way – and it wasn't my imagination, I saw…'

'Remember what grandpa used to say… believe only half what you see.'

'Yeah *Dad* – what about the other half?' Amy asked.

'There is no other half,' Mike said and nuzzled up to Helen to whisper in her ear 'not any more'.

THE END

Printed in Great Britain
by Amazon.co.uk, Ltd.,
Marston Gate.